AMERICAN LITERATURE READINGS IN THE 21ST CENTURY

Series Editor: Linda Wagner-Martin

American Literature Readings in the 21st Century publishes works by contemporary critics that help shape critical opinion regarding literature of the nineteenth and twentieth century in the United States.

Published by Palgrave Macmillan:

The Anti-Hero in the American Novel: From Joseph Heller to Kurt Vonnegut
  By David Simmons

*Indians, Environment, and Identity on the Borders of American Literature:
From Faulkner and Morrison to Walker and Silko*
  By Lindsey Claire Smith

*The American Landscape in the Poetry of Frost, Bishop, and Ashbery:
The House Abandoned*
  By Marit J. MacArthur

Cormac McCarthy: American Canticles
  By Kenneth Lincoln

CORMAC MCCARTHY

American Canticles

Kenneth Lincoln

palgrave
macmillan

CORMAC MCCARTHY

First published in 2009 by
PALGRAVE MACMILLAN®
in the United States—a division of St. Martin's Press LLC,
175 Fifth Avenue, New York, NY 10010.

Where this book is distributed in the UK, Europe and the rest of the world,
this is by Palgrave Macmillan, a division of Macmillan Publishers Limited,
registered in England, company number 785998, of Houndmills,
Basingstoke, Hampshire RG21 6XS.

Palgrave Macmillan is the global academic imprint of the above companies
and has companies and representatives throughout the world.

Palgrave® and Macmillan® are registered trademarks in the United States,
the United Kingdom, Europe and other countries.

ISBN-13: 978–0–230–61226–6
ISBN-10: 0–230–61226–1

Library of Congress Cataloging-in-Publication Data is available from the
Library of Congress.

A catalogue record of the book is available from the British Library.

Design by Newgen Imaging Systems (P) Ltd., Chennai, India.

First edition: January 2009

10 9 8 7 6 5 4 3 2 1

Transferred to digital printing in 2009.

for Barbara
who let me do it

And I took the little book out of the angel's hand, and ate it up; and it was in my mouth sweet as honey; and as soon as I had eaten it, my belly was bitter.

And he said unto me, Thou must prophesy again before many peoples and nations, and tongues, and kinds.
                    —St. John the Divine, *Revelation* 10:10–11

Morituri te salutant.
                    —Joseph Conrad, *Heart of Darkness*

CONTENTS

Acknowledgments

Heartfelt thanks to Cal Bedient, Don Lamm, Mike Fonash, Peter Nabokov, Mike Rose, Sam Scott, Page Stegner, Linda Tolly, and John Warnock for supporting the work. My loyal doctorates Kathleen Washburn and John "Kimo" Reeder gave fine-tuning resistance to sharpen the discussions. It's a pleasure to work with colleagues who understand true literature, an honor to have such good friends.

Penetrant and Simple:
The Common Reader

I wrote a Cormac McCarthy guide for the common reader with classic masters and current cultural debates in mind. W. B. Yeats in an essay on Homer's *Odyssey* notes "the swift and natural observation of a man as he is shaped by life." Some still read the Greek epics as cultural benchmarks and codes of behavior. Odysseus is an alert man on-the-go, wily, passionate, quick-witted, and strong-hearted, a man among men admired by women. More statesman than warrior, more storyteller than soldier, the Ithacan king questions war and empire, serves country and clan when required, saves the day at Troy, and traverses the unknown seas returning home. He loses many good men along the way. Where are the valiant of honor, action, and grace in our own time—the fathers, sons, husbands, and brothers beside us through peace and war? Western canticles keen elegies for assassinated leaders and lament fallen comrades back through the whale-road Seafarer's *ubi sunt* to Virgil's *sunt lacrimae rerum,* "these are the tears of things" destroyed by war in Carthage.

Many-minded Odysseus faces the world's trials head-on and wastes no will or words. If only those who critique literature would do the same. The good doctor-poet William Carlos Williams declares of American writing, "Such must be the future: penetrant and simple—minus the scaffolding of the academic." Many literary critics, particularly the bricoleurs of postmodernist theory, have fallen from their scaffolds on blunt swords. Beyond some fine scholars and perceptive readers, I've come to hedge writers on writers over the literary pundits, to avoid academic in-groups, to take the characters and stories clean, to trust my own hunches.

Distinctly removed from literati, Cormac McCarthy is a college dropout and autodidact spanning popular border cultures and the high broad arts of American letters. He blends adventure tales and excruciating tragedies, mixes high jinks and low spirits, fuses the lyric sublime and revulsive grotesque. This self-made writer cobbles his own hybrid genres from history, literature, and science. The novels and scripts cross tall tales with gritty truth, fuse adult westerns with futurist apocalypse, pair raw innocence with mesmerizing debauchery, etch pure love of land and natural life-forms into Southern Gothic, city wasteland, and Southwest naturalism. McCarthy would never condone the violence and depravity unearthed, but the novelist's role is to chronicle, not to correct. Like the magician or historian, a writer is and is not what he portrays. The novelist knows his subject complete to present it convincingly; he knows its comparative shortcomings and need not apologize, if the story is true to its makings and the implications speak for themselves. A reader can regard this author's fictional horrors as lamentational canticles of warning, not directives.

McCarthy's epic lineage traces through Faulkner, Hemingway, Joyce, and Shakespeare to Dante, Sophocles, Ecclesiastes, and Homer, among others. Popular writer Richard Preston in the 2007 *The Best Science and Nature Writing* speaks of weaving scientific exposition through narrative as naturalist literacy, going back 2,600 years to the Greek hexameter chant: "the Homeric poems stand among the earliest surviving, and still the best, examples of storytelling." Inheritor of ancient epic, McCarthy is carving out classical American letters as Ezra Pound hectored his modernist cadre to "make it new"—bring the catalytic classics forward into our own writing, the selected best of language and cultural histories as touchstones for present letters and thought.

The Iliad tells us something terrible and courageous about conflict in our own time, just as millennia later Hemingway writes "hard and clear" about modern violence and wounded masculinity. *The Odyssey* is a timeless journey home from war, and Greek tragedians stake the field of human suffering, city-state hubris, and fallen heroism. The Bible gathers an encyclopedic compendium of poetry, ethics, history, and prophesy, no less than Faulkner plumbs the depths of character, circumstance, and fate in the postbellum South. McCarthy's Appalachian Gothic novels, his Southwest *Border Trilogy*, his class, kin, and culture theater pieces, his Western noir thriller and futurist threnody infuse classic gravitas and regional genius into contemporary letters. The writer's world is idiosyncratic, his view apocalyptic, his values clearly masculine in an older tradition of honor, courage, pity, and due reckoning.

History is cultural literacy in action, and truth does not come embossed. Consider our Greco-Roman legacy of imperial cataclysms from the fall of Troy and sack of Rome to Hiroshima and 9/11, the Dark Ages of mass poverty and religious persecution, Renaissance greed thrusting into the New World, Puritan purges and Revolutionary bloodshed, nineteenth-century racial jingoism and twentieth-century fall from agrarian grace—crises today of global pollution and viral pandemics, political chicanery and faux fundamentalism, ethnic terrorism and "great" world slaughters followed by countless dirty wars. The U.S. government preemptively wages shock-and-awe strikes without borders or endings. To chronicle these upheavals invokes the names of St. John the Divine, Virgil, Dante, Shakespeare, Voltaire, Bradford, Jefferson, Twain, Gibbon, Steinbeck, Rachel Carson, Noam Chomsky, Al Gore, and Jared Diamond, to name a few.

No less than the classic masters, cultural historians, or modern prophets and eco-scientists, McCarthy alerts us to the disasters of history, the monstrosities of moral deviance, the absurdities of human fate, the sublime ranges of will and courage, the depths of suffering, pain, and psychopathology. He writes about old-time, frontier, and futurist America from the bottom up, portraying men from the decent and conflicted, to the raw and grimy, to the deformed and malign. He lyricizes landscape, climate, and animals with native reverence. He chronicles the search for justice and redemption with tragic sorrow and heroic stoicism. In lineage with Hemingway's homosocial focus on male agonies, McCarthy writes unapologetic canticles of masculinity about the challenges, dreams, betrayals, and defeats of men, as Adrienne Rich or Alice Walker focus on women.

It's fair to note what a writer is not. McCarthy's portraits of men are less than politically correct, though honest bedrock to western history and engrained in American myth. His writings are not domestic or psychological dramas, never novels of manners or morals. He draws western epics of the land and people, full-scale heroic and tragic conflicts of mountain, frontier, and border cultures gone feral, rancid, or lawlessly violent and always precipitously dangerous. In some respects these are cautionary tales, antimodels of culture and personality, and the storytelling craft is everything. Above all, McCarthy's skill, accuracy, pitch, texture, range, and play with language constellate his greatest gift.

Cormac McCarthy: American Canticles is a roadmap to the author's artistic life and work written for the generally literate public—a grounded, minimally scaffolded, book-by-book engagement with ten novels, two plays, and a screenplay over some fifty years. No post modern theory, no theme park, no identity politics, no rhetorical haze. What do we make of the words and the stories in our own time?

Kenneth Lincoln
Santa Fe, New Mexico

Western Storykeeper:
Life and Times

Charles Joseph McCarthy Jr. was born third of six siblings, July 20, 1933, in Rhode Island during the Depression. His Irish Catholic family with two older daughters Barbara and Helen moved to Knoxville in 1937 where the four-year-old's father litigated for the Tennessee Valley Authority. They first lived on Cherokee Drive, then along Sherrod Road, finally in a white-clapboard house on Martin Mill Pike in the wooded hills, as two more sons William and Dennis and a third daughter Mary Ellen were born. In 1967 the family moved to Washington DC where Charles Senior worked as a principal TVA firm attorney. The McCarthys were relatively well off. Charles Junior eventually revised his name to "Cormac" for the ancient Gaelic king of Blarney Castle, "son of Charles" Joseph McCarthy Sr. and Gladys Christina McGrail.

Curious to distraction, the writer says that he had more hobbies than any kid around and hated the classroom from the day he set foot there. Charles Jr. attended Roman Catholic high school in Knoxville, then the University of Tennessee as a liberal arts major in 1951–52. He dropped out and drifted, joined the Air Force where he acted and hosted a radio show for two years in Alaska, and started reading in the barracks for his own edification, becoming an autodidact with thousands of books in storage over a lifetime. The young man returned to college on the G. I. bill and majored in engineering, then business administration, and published two short pieces of fiction, "Wake for Susan" and "A Drowning Incident," in a University of Tennessee student literary magazine. "C. J. McCarthy, Jr." won the 1959–60 Ingram-Merrill creative writing award with these stories. The writer again left school for Chicago, worked part time as an auto mechanic, drafted his first novel, and in 1961 married former

Tennessee collegiate poet Lee Holleman. The marriage lasted four years, and Lee McCarthy keens these threadbare years in *Desire's Door* (1991): "I feel the hard facts gnarl in every joint /—wooden crone, crippled saint, woman alone / in a mirror, out a window, in a room." They had one son Cullen and settled south of Knoxville in Sevier County, Tennessee, the novelist's childhood home grounds on Martin Pike Hill and locus for his early writing. Looking back, the ex-wife sifts marital debris: "It is snowing in El Paso where his father lives whose teeth / are healthy but everything else has hit the rocks, gone on the / skids. I hope it's a regular blizzard, that his teeth chatter."

McCarthy published *The Orchard Keeper* in 1965 with Random House editor Albert Erskine, William Faulkner's former editor, who sponsored Malcolm Lowry's *Under the Volcano* and Ralph Ellison's *Invisible Man*. Erskine speaks of "a father-son feeling" with the shadowy novelist, though Random House made no money on his books. *The Orchard Keeper* received favorable reviews from Orville Prescott in the *New York Times,* Granville Hicks in the *Saturday Review,* and Walter Sullivan in the *Sewanee Review* and won the first-novel William Faulkner Foundation, now PEN-Faulkner Award. Still, printings of a few thousand never sold out.

That year Cormac and his wife Lee divorced, and he sailed for Ireland with a $5,000 traveling fellowship from the Academy of Arts and Letters. The first night on the boat to his ancestral homeland he met entertainer Anne DeLisle, fell into a whirlwind romance, and married the British pop singer-dancer the next year. A Rockefeller grant financed the newlywed Mediterranean tour, and they settled in an artist-colony of Ibiza Island where McCarthy revised and finished *Outer Dark.* These were years of leaving and coming back home.

The couple returned to Rockford, Tennessee and lived in a rented pig farmhouse, eating beans and bathing in the lake. *Outer Dark* was published in 1968. Two decades later, Anne DeLisle told a reporter for the *Knoxville News-Sentinel,* Don Williams, her Gaelic-American husband "was such a rebel that he didn't live the same kind of life anybody on earth lived. He knew everything that there was to do in life." She recalls they chronically had no money. "We were always scrimping and scraping. He couldn't have had children, it would have driven him crazy." The author turned thirty-four, times were hard. McCarthy says when they were down to nothing and out of toothpaste, a mail sample would show up by blind luck. His daily concerns were hardscratch literary. A Guggenheim fellowship allowed them to move into a barn near Louisville, Tennessee. Renovating the farm for eight years, Cormac gathered stones, cut and kiln-dried wood, and salvaged bricks from James Agee's boyhood house nearby. The hermitic novelist declined thousand-dollar university invitations to discuss his work, nor would he entertain literary questions about his writing process, though quietly becoming a legend among Southern Gothic novelists.

McCarthy always disdained the teaching of writing as a hustle. Since his aborted college days he seldom published piecemeal in magazines except for 1965 early outtakes from *The Orchard Keeper* in *Sewanee Review* and the *Yale Review*, a 1979 excerpt from *Suttree* in *Antaeus*, and a 1993 section from *The Crossing* in *Esquire*. One of his scarce literary friends was the desert maverick Edward Abbey. He has known more than a few "gracious" drug dealers, the reclusive writer says, passionate equestrians, ladies of the night, and alley pool sharks as well as Nobel prize scientists and cardsharps.

Drawn from local newspaper accounts of a Sevier County serial murderer, *Child of God* was published in 1973 to mixed reviews, both astonished and horrified. Over the next two years McCarthy wrote a PBS screenplay *The Gardener's Son* airing January 1977, a documentary script about a South Carolina milltown murder published two decades later by Ecco Press. He typically researched his writing from the road.

McCarthy separated from his second wife in 1976 and moved to El Paso behind a shopping center in a Coffin Street stone cottage where he quit alcohol. He considers drinking an "occupational hazard" to writing, allowing that all his early booze buddies are dead. He and Anne DeLisle divorced in 1978. Random House published *Suttree* in 1979, a two-decades-old first manuscript that Anne recalls typing twice in full, all eight hundred pages. Jerome Charyn in the *New York Times Book Review* marveled at the story's "horrifying flood" of words, and Edward Rothstein in the *Washington Post* called the author "some latter-day Virgil with an unabridged dictionary."

By now Cormac McCarthy had proven an eclectic witness of Western cultural tradition back to Homer, interested in the way details look and sound, feel and smell—a realist observing not so much how things seem, as what they are surface-to-substance, including the heft and tare of polysemous words that sing and curse and call the world to consciousness. "His people are so vivid they seem exotic," says Anatole Broyard in the *New York Times*, 30 January 1979, "but this is just another way of saying that we tend to forget the range of human differences." He adds in praise, "McCarthy's hyperbole is not Southern rhetoric, but flesh and blood. Every tale is tall, if you look at it closely enough." In *The Practice of Reading* Denis Donoghue says teaching McCarthy brings into service the *American Heritage Dictionary* over the *Oxford English* counterpart, given the border vernacular and regional frontier range of his diction, "muleshoe" white whiskey, say, or "wampus cat" for a critter. Donoghue argues that the novelist uses hard or peculiar words carefully to pace attention to the narrative, requiring careful, sometimes slower and deeper reading. This legato measure would seem a leavening strategy not unrelated to Pound sprinkling his *Cantos* with Greek, Latin, or Chinese seeds and Eliot tossing German, French, Italian, or Hindu shards into *The Waste Land*.

Like Joyce or Dickens, Twain or Faulkner, McCarthy works off Scripture, the classics, and Shakespeare down to hillbilly riff, street rap, and soon-to-be-mastered southwest Spanish beside border ranching dialect. In the 1970s Carlos Castaneda was fictionalizing the cryptic teachings of Yaqui *brujos* across the Mexican border to new-age global audiences, as the United States rediscovered several million lost Indians, bedrock for an eco-native groundswell against postmodernist carbon, steel, glass, and microchip. McCarthy had his own rebel take on native cultural resistance and never failed to notice ancient aboriginal campfires, cliff pictographs, and stone petroglyphs pocking his American landscapes. Native ruins backdrop his border tragedies.

In 1981 the now middle-aged writer lived alone in a friend's Knoxville motel room, when he received a $236,000 MacArthur "genius grant," recommended by Saul Bellow, Robert Penn Warren, and Shelby Foote, among others. He bought the Coffin Street stone cottage in El Paso and went on to write *Blood Meridian,* a gore-drenched 1840s history of U.S.-Mexico border wars. Yale's Harold Bloom in *How to Read and Why* deems it one of the century's greatest apocalyptic novels, a "prose epic" worthy of comparison with Melville, Shakespeare, and Homer.

Here in his Southwest plains tales McCarthy remains as painstakingly curious about language, literacy, and life-forms as about violence, history, and mortality. He considers dying the major human concern, finding it strange that few talk about an inevitable end. The novelist has read existentialists like Camus and Sartre, pondered the philosophic words of Kierkegaard and Buber, watched struggling organisms all around him, and concluded that death is the axis from which a man begins to live attentively. Heidegger's adaptation of Freud's *unheimlich* or dread of the unfamiliar, literally "un-home-like" anxiety, posits that all authentic existence is "being-toward-death" in

Being and Time. "For you, for me, for all of us," the novelist told *Vanity Fair* journalist Richard Woodward.

McCarthy privileges a hardheaded naturalism over personal impressions. At MacArthur Fellow reunions the writer prefers the company of scientists like whale biologist Roger Payne or nuclear physicist Murray Gell-Mann, now his colleague at the Santa Fe Institute scientific think tank. He views twentieth-century physics among the universal human flowerings, men practically "kids" who changed the nature of reality (Woodward 2005). In a 1992 *New York Times Magazine* first of two evasive interviews published to date, the novelist holds there's no life without bloodshed, an indigenous "regeneration through violence," as W. C. Williams coined the national penchant. Richard Slotkin documents that blood-soaked epithet in revolutionary times and more recent follow-ups, *The Fatal Environment* and *Gunfighter Nation.* Tooth-and-claw blood realism, to be sure, permeates McCarthy's writings, and he regards notions like species betterment or universal harmony as dangerous. To think so is to give up the sincerity of soul and freedom, he argues, a naïve fantasy enslaving a person and rendering life vacuous. Survey human history and consider the probabilities of cruelty and violence.

During the 1980s, McCarthy says he wrote in the mornings, road-researched the Southwest, collected rare books, and played golf and pool. In the *Southern Quarterly* Garry Wallace recollects meeting the recessive novelist in El Paso during March 1989 with World Series poker legend Betty Carey to talk about writing stories. McCarthy was diffident toward Wallace the stranger, advising his friend Betty Carey to scavenge Stephen King, Hemingway, Melville, Salinger, McFee, Chatwin, McMurtry, Faulkner, and William James for models of strategy and craft. He said to educate yourself, since school can get in the way of learning to write; trust your reader, tell the truth. Don't hit and be fair, as everyone knows by kindergarten, the rest is personal test and experience. "All great writers read all other great writers." McCarthy said he could write in a train station if people didn't ask for directions, adding that Faulkner wrote *As I Lay Dying* at a power plant custodial night job, sometimes using an overturned wheelbarrow for a desk.

In 1990 at the age of fifty-seven McCarthy was inducted into the Southwest Writers Hall of Fame, but did not attend the ceremony or allow his photo taken. With Erskine retiring from Random House and McCarthy's attention leaning west, the author shifted to editor Gary Fisketjon at Alfred Knopf and in 1992 published the first of *The Border Trilogy,* a more callow, less horrific tale than the preceding,

All the Pretty Horses. Luck seemed to turn, talent paid off. Written like everything else over fifty years on a blue Olivetti manual typewriter, his Southwest cowboy novel won the National Book Award and the National Book Critics Circle Award for fiction. Though again McCarthy did not attend the awards ceremonies, over two years *All the Pretty Horses* sold out its publication run of 180,000 hardcover and 300,000 softcover books. Director Mike Nichols gave him a six-figure advance for movie rights.

The off-stage writer granted his first interview, as noted, to Richard B. Woodward of *New York Times Magazine,* 19 April, 1992, "Cormac McCarthy's Venomous Fiction." According to the interviewer, the earliest of the best-selling *Border Trilogy* gave McCarthy cash to buy a new pickup to roam ranchland Texas into old Mexico. "I've always been interested in the Southwest," he says. "There isn't a place in the world you can go where they don't know about cowboys and Indians and the myth of the West."

The native stones speak. McCarthy's hands-on, rock-deep survivalism tracks back to Paleolithic caves and petroglyphs, forward to quarries, cliffs, masonry, gravestones, and cobbled road life. His first published story fifty years ago appeared in the 1959 literary supplement *Orange and White* to the University of Tennessee student newspaper. "Wake for Susan" portrays a boy Wes fantasizing a beloved through an abandoned cemetery headstone: "From a simple carved stone, the marble turned to a monument; from a gravestone, to the surviving integral tie to a once warm-blooded, live person." Thirty-five years later, Ecco Press published *The Stonemason* after a stillborn 1992 attempt with Washington DC's Arena Stage to produce the real-life theater about three generations of a Kentucky Black stone mason family. In 1993 scholars and devotees held the first McCarthy conference sponsored by Bellarmine College in Louisville, Kentucky. Then Knopf released *The Crossing* as a second best seller in the trilogy, and Billy Bob Thornton directed the film *All the Pretty Horses* starring Matt Damon and Penelope Cruz.

In 1998 *Cities of the Plain* completed *The Border Trilogy* and the author married a Texas college alumna, Jennifer Winkley, the next year bore a son John Francis with his third wife, and moved to Tesuque, New Mexico where he keeps an office at the interdisciplinary Santa Fe Institute. *No Country for Old Men* was published in summer 2005 and *The Road* in spring 2007. Magazine pundits like James Wood in *The New Yorker* carped about rhetorical theatrics, male clans, rigged plots, and *The Road*'s "metaphysical cheapness with a slickness unto death all its own," but dedicated readers ignored the urban sniping ("Red Planet," 25 July 2005). As Mae West said of aging, McCarthy's books are "not for sissies," and there's no fairy dust on the characters. Not a fan of magazine critics, he's also indifferent to political correction, gender wars, parlor book talk, and literary fads. The writer is country genteel, no offense or apology needed.

Judging from the few extant photos the man is hazel-eyed, handsome, and middle-statured, now with some miles on him. He dresses Western in boots, jeans, and a freshly pressed shirt. Acquaintances say he speaks in a softly lilting Tennessee accent and is wildly curious about everything, including Mojave desert rattlesnakes. "It's very interesting to see an animal out in the wild that can kill you graveyard dead," he told Woodward in the 1992 *New York Times Magazine* interview. "The only thing I had seen that answered that description was a grizzly bear in Alaska." Fifteen years ago, the Manhattan journalist rode shotgun with McCarthy across the Texas-Mexican desert in a Ford pickup, slumming through El Paso pool halls and stopping in local diners. "For such an obstinate loner, McCarthy is an engaging figure, a world-class talker, funny, opinionated, quick to laugh." Except the 1992 interview is not so much McCarthy commenting on himself or about his work, as it is Woodward's redacted overview. "He cuts his own hair, eats his meals off a hot plate or in cafeterias, and does his wash at the Laundromat." The author does not gloss himself.

Thirteen years later in August 2005, McCarthy granted Woodward a second interview for *Vanity Fair*, "Cormac Country." Again, the journalist observes details about the writer's red Ford-350 diesel 300 hp pickup; his interdisciplinary presence as a translator among scientists at the Santa Fe Institute; his punctilious sense of meetings; his disinclination toward fellow writers, artists, and contemporary architecture; his Tesuque backyard of SUVs, old trucks, and son's toys; his love of talking about horses, hawks, physics, game systems and string theory, biological evolution and poker—but quotes little of McCarthy himself or his work in his own words. Foreground the writing, not the writer. Wallace Stevens said everything was in his poetry, not his personal life. "I have spoken too long for a writer," Hemingway ended his 1954 Nobel acceptance. "A writer should write what he has to say and not speak it." Locals recount occasional McCarthy sightings in Santa Fe bookstores and restaurants, but the novelist keeps to himself at the Santa Fe Institute near his Tesuque home. The less readers know about Shakespeare or Homer as individuals, some say, the more they focus on their texts. Woodward does note that McCarthy keeps four to five novels in-process, researching and rewriting drafts of coming work. In 2004 the novelist flew alone to Ireland for six weeks to write *The Road.* "It's amazing what you can get done," he told the journalist, "when there's nothing else to do but write."

In June 2007, at age seventy-three, the camera-shy author astonished his following with an appearance on daytime television for Oprah's Book Club. Knopf printed 950,000 additional paperbacks of *The Road* and a few weeks later McCarthy signed another two-book contract. Feature film production of the novel starring Viggo Mortensen was scheduled to begin in January 2008 with Australian director John Hillcote, as Hollywood rumored that Scott Ridley's next film would be adapted from *Blood Meridian.* In January 2008, the *New York Times* reported, the author sold his archived correspondence, notes, drafts, and proofs of eleven books for 2 million dollars to the Southwestern Writers Collection of Texas State University-San Marcos.

McCarthy appeared to be surfacing from recalcitrant shadows with a 2007 Pulitzer Fiction Prize for *The Road* and a movie of *No Country for Old Men* directed by Joel and Ethan Coen and produced by Scott Rudin. Garnering raves at the spring 2007 Cannes Festival, the picture starred Tommy Lee Jones, Josh Brolin, Woody Harrelson, and Javier Bardem. On Internet coverage, 8 November 2007, the national film critic Roger Ebert reviewed the work as "startlingly beautiful, stark and lonely," indeed a four-star "miracle"—"a masterful evocation of time, place, character, moral choices, immoral certainties, human nature and fate." By January 2008 in the prestigious Critics' Choice Awards the film had won best picture of the year, best directing by the Coen brothers, and best supporting actor for Javier Bardem. A week later *No Country for Old Men* received two Golden Globe awards for best screenplay and supporting actor, and the film was headed with eight nominations for a totebag of Oscars, winning four.

The "Book Club" daytime television show featuring Cormac McCarthy on *The Road,* available in Internet outtakes, begins with Oprah Winfrey asking why this is the author's first live interview. McCarthy says such things are "not good for your head." A writer should be doing a book, not talking about it. "I'll work my side of the street," he says with a twinkle, "you work yours." They sit in large leather chairs by a fireplace with flowers and leafy branches in a barrel vase and walls of shelved books—a fireside chat at the Santa Fe Institute with no fire. A Pueblo Indian pot stands on the mantle and basketry hangs on the wall. The SFI scientific community is "full of bright, interesting people," McCarthy says, so he comes there daily.

You've "always been fiercely private," Oprah pries, the author admittedly more comfortable in front of his portable Olivetti type-writer than before television cameras. Considered by most "a man's man writer," she squares off, there's not a lot of engagement with women in your work. He smiles and says after all these years and three marriages that "women are still mysterious," and he doesn't know enough to write about them well. He seems honestly flum-moxed, a bit bemused. She asks what it's like being a father at this time of life. "Oh, I don't know," he pauses and drawls softly, "you 'preciate it more."

This is our one flesh-and-blood look at the inscrutably elusive author shunning public exposure for over five decades. McCarthy wears a blue denim workshirt, tan chino slacks, and brown-leather, snub-toed boots. He clasps his fingers before a receding hairline and leans sideways into a pillow, shoulders sloped, a figure spilling down the overstuffed chair. The man seems inordinately shy, kindly and soft-spoken, a bit willowy or even elder fragile in a back-porch coun-try manner. Understated and thoughtful, he uses his tongue to pause and punctuate his carefully chosen words. McCarthy's chestnut brown eyes are lambent in an older man's way, deeply set and deep with understanding of what he's doing. He does not want to talk much about writing, rather just do it and keep quiet. The writer lets Oprah come to him with the framed questions, going along with her suggested responses, revealing little that isn't apparent, remaining courteous and yet circumspect. Game-faced, quietly wry, country recessive, he's ever respectful and careful, as the "Old Man" of Taoist China, Lao Tsu, advised men crossing a winter stream.

Oprah asks whether Cormac writes from passion, and the novelist says that's "a pretty fancy word." He prefers to say, "I like what I do." McCarthy offers that he starts a book from some "perfect image" as a "signpost," but the novelist is not so much conscious of direction as hoping "today I'll do something better than ever before." Do you write every day, she asks, or just when you're inspired? He says Faulkner was asked that question and replied he was inspired to write every day. "I take the work seriously." McCarthy admits he "can't plot things. You just trust in...wherever it comes to."

Twenty-five years ago, Oprah ventures, *The Road* would have seemed "futuristic," but now it feels "ominous and real." Yes, he agrees, heading off her apocalyptic tack, graciously stoic about com-ing years. Times are perilous, but admits "we've lived pretty good."

Looking quizzical and raising up a bit, Oprah pushes for the nub of the book. "What do you want us to get?" She pauses. "You haven't worked up to the God thing, have you?" Well, he responds wryly, it "depends on what day you ask me. Who or what to pray…doesn't really matter. You can be quite dumb about the whole business and still ask for help." As for success, he'd rather not think about millions reading the book and doesn't concern himself with the numbers. "It's okay," he fesses up diffidently. Oprah says with astonishment, "You are a different kind of author, that's for sure."

Regarding technique, she asks about the lack of punctuation. "No semi-colons," he says, "you don't need punctuation if you write properly." So you're "not all comma'd up," Oprah redacts the style. He answers that you write well and reduce punctuation, so the reader can follow the speech in "simple declarative sentences—period, capital, age-old comma, and that's it." Use the colon, if need be, or even the semicolon, if it comes to that, but no needless punctuation, including quote marks. There were none in the old slave narratives, none in people speaking. "No pretension," he adds. Oprah likes that.

"So you've never been interested in money?" she asks again with lifted eyebrow. Through the "poor years" it wasn't a concern, he says, something would always turn up. You're really a "different kind of man," she repeats and hurries to note that most people would have "a lot of anxiety, a lack of self-worth" if they couldn't earn money to live. He laughs. "I don' know, I was pretty naïve and always assured I'd be taken care of." When things were most "bleak," something "totally unforeseen would occur." For example, he was house-sitting in Lexington, Kentucky with no money. It wasn't "not much, I didn't have any." Oh, there were a few groceries left in the house. A knock came at the door and the man asked if he was Cormac McCarthy. "There were no warrants out for me, I thought, so I said yes I was," and he signed the courier's document and took the envelope. Inside was a $20,000 check from a foundation with Coca Cola money for fellowships.

"Lucky?" she laughs, "or was something else going on?" Oh don't get "superstitious," he counters, the "laws of probability" will put all of us in the lucky and unlucky charts equally like a poker player in Las Vegas or the stock market analyst. "I've been lucky and blessed, one of the luckiest people I've ever known, but not picked out for special…What would pick me out? I haven't done anything to deserve it."

A man does what he loves, McCarthy says, "that's the blessing," or perhaps the curse, another might add, or both. He is rumored to love billiards along with golf. "I always knew I didn't wanta work," he admits. "You have to be dedicated, really."

No 9:00–5:00 job, Oprah says, "so you have worked at not working." He underscores with no hesitation, "absolutely," the critical issues are "food and shoes." She says he seems "happy with very few things," and there's a reflective pause. "Yeah," he repeats, "but you've got to have food and shoes."

So much for the author glimpsed by the public. He tells us to focus on the work itself and the traditions of the trade.

CHAPTER 1

Canticles Down West: Hyperrealism

Down west,
Down west we dance,
We spirits dance,
We spirits weeping dance.

—Modoc

Canticle means to sing in praise, as in Latin *cantare*—elsewhere to lament, to prophesy, to warn. McCarthy's self-styled elegies surface as authorial "threnody" in the texts, an archaic blues lament for the wounded, suffering, and dead. The praise-chant or grief-song contains terrible personal tare; the prophetic story or vatic warning carries shocking public texture. Both are colored with rich lyric rhythms, living regional diction, and idiosyncratic native imagery, as well as keenly edged with original narrative arc, strange character development, and disruptive historical context. There's a dark vein of scripture beneath it all. The biblical prophet eats his little book from the mighty angel's hand, John the Divine says, honey-sweet to taste, bitter in his belly. And the angel commands him, "Thou must prophesy again before many peoples and nations, and tongues, and kinds" (Revelation 10: 10–11).

Something bawdy and irreverent, strangely spiritual and ghastly medieval lies at the old soul depth of McCarthy's work, not far from Chaucer's Summoner and Wife of Bath, lamenting a fallen Green Knight and epileptic Prioress, grieving a poisoned dream of the rood martyr and lost crusaders. There's also a wildly merry dance of death with the seven deadly sins around the Maypole of hell, no renaissance hope of redemption, and only a glimmer of the search for God eclipsed by terrible darkness.

The ancients through the Middle Ages held tragedy to be the fall of great men. No real great ones in McCarthy, certainly a passel of misshapen monsters, villagers gone wrong, and pathological deviants—a miscellany of loners brought down mercilessly by time, circumstance, character, and fate, not far from the barren heathscapes and tormented victims of Thomas Hardy or the rocky woodland paths and abused Puritans of Nathaniel Hawthorne. The angry God sermons of Jonathan Edwards would slide seamlessly into the fictions.

Guy Davenport in the *National Review*, March 16, 1979, argues that McCarthy "must summon his world before our eyes, in all its richness and exactness of shape, because that is all he is summoning"— what the critic calls "irrational intrepidity" in textual tempo with mannered diction and baroque speech rhythms. Marion Sylder pushes the margins of the law and serves time in *The Orchard Keeper*, never knowing the boy he befriends is the son of a man he killed and dumped into an abandoned insecticide pit. In *Outer Dark* bleeding Culla Holme sweats lifelong for sibling incest and wanders the roads of Appalachia finally to witness the cannibalizing of his inbred son. Lester Ballard in *Child of God* blasts social ostracism and lonely lust with the serial violation of young lovers whose bodies he necrophilically caches in a mountain cave. *The Gardener's Son* documents on film the postbellum murder of a mill owner's son James Gregg by a one-legged worker Robert McEvoy avenging his sister's honor and family's social station. In the novel bearing his surname, Cornelius Suttree descends into the riotous debauchery of the lower rings of urban hell and squalor and never finds his way back home. The Tennessee kid in *Blood Meridian* scalp-hunts the Southwest with the demonic towering Judge and wades through bloody massacre and the ruthless desecration of Mexican border communities. Gothic horror gets no gorier than in these early fictions.

Lacey Rawlins and John Grady Cole lose their teenage American innocence south of the border in *All the Pretty Horses*. Billy in *The Crossing* is spiritually martyred with his wild she-wolf, as John Grady in *Cities of the Plain* dies avenging the prostituted body of his epileptic young love. The black mason Ben Telfair in the five-act play *The Stonemason* cannot save his age-old trade, family, or centenarian grandfather Papaw from mortality and the sociological ravages of history. Sheriff Ed Tom Bell walks away from the unadulterated evil of a Texas homicidal rampage taking the lives of Vietnam veteran Llewelyn Moss and his young wife Carla Jean and a dozen others. The black born-again in the one-act *The Sunset Limited* fails to rescue the white academic suicide. A good nameless father in *The Road* lives long enough to walk his son through nuclear winter to oceanic origins for one look before it's all over.

McCarthy's slope toward oracular "deep song," as Lorca spoke of the flamenco *duenda* from beneath gypsy tongues, draws the novelist into lyric meditation and strange reflection. It is a dark place where André Breton argues *surreal* art to be the "real" real down inside things. What may be called McCarthy's *hyperrealism* pushes the natural credence of things to lurid depths, giddy heights, and ironic abruptions. Such startling philosophical realism is stony kin to a "natural supernaturalism" torqued by Thomas Carlyle through the weird compendium of muse, fiction, and humanist science in *Sartor Resartus*. Across the migrant water Emily Dickinson saw her New England supernatural in the natural "disclosed," a visionary hyperrealism backlighting "Zero at the Bone—." Ghostly holograms trace across millennia. Classic Greek muses were said to visit mortals as *daemons* of inspirational "genius," intermediary spirits later demonized by Christian pontiffs. This surcharged vocabulary is shared by dreamers, visionaries, poets, mad and holy men, not generally associated with Southern Gothic or country-western novelists.

In postmodern theory the term "hyperreal," lately cribbed from classical mathematics and twisted synthetically by cultural theorists, has become synonymous with fake—Jean Baurillard's simulacra of real culture in Disneyland and Las Vegas, for example—or "going virtual" as students say of computer blogs and video games. Who can tell the difference between fantasy and fact anymore? In reality television shows, cyberspace, or media advertising, illusion skews objectivity to the point where the perceiver cannot distinguish between fabricated or fixed things, faux objets d'art or terra firma. "The authentic fake," Umberto Eco calls this deracinated "hyperreality." Jean Baudrillard goes further, "The simulation of something which never really existed."

Notwithstanding the definitional forays of Marshall McLuhan through Ferdinand Saussure and Guilles Delueze, Baudrillard and Eco through Frederic Jameson and semiotic phenomenology, consider the original scientific definitions of *hyperreality*: the unlimited existence of "hyperreal" numbers or "nonstandard reals," infinite and infinitesimal, that cluster about assumedly fixed or "real" numbers and factor through transference differentials. Even though a person can't conventionally see or count these endless black hole numericals, they're there, mathematicians say. The term "hyper" implies dimensions of radical data beyond the supposed or given consensus, and hyperspace posits a physics of time/space beyond three dimensions. Perceived distortion may reveal hidden depths, and after a second look, suspected illusion may conjure holographic truths. In Cormac McCarthy's hyperreal novels a reader may assume the story fabricates reality, but on further reflection the fiction stands truer-to-life than flat dimensional "reality," that is, art real to the point of abruptive disbelief and breakthrough discovery.

Start over with hyperreal definitions. Given his literary self-learning and the scientific humanism around McCarthy's residence at the Santa Fe Institute, allow the argument to ground in some working terms of hyperreality. In *The Achievement of Cormac McCarthy* Vereen Bell speaks of the novelist's "photorealistic style" that stays naturalistically precise and "charismatically rich." Anatole Broyard in the *New York Times* notes "a hypnosis of detail" in *Suttree* making the reader feel that place and event ring "palpably real." Critics write of Ray Carver's "dirty realism" as suburban spill from Hemingway, but McCarthy is never tediously median or small-time ragged, always stretching the margins of human behavior toward epic fall and philosophic muse. This novelist is no minimalist or fallen middleclass modernist. Unlike any other contemporary novelist, he writes within a severe tradition of radical realism and surcharged subject, crossing Greek drama and medieval morality play, consonant with classical texts and the natural sciences. Here artists and researchers experiment, read, talk, think, and write hard toward tandem mastery of nature's radicals; their fusional experiments shatter prior assumptions of human character, moral truth, and real matter into truer understandings of the world we live in. Hyperrealistic fiction and drama prove no exception.

Etymology helps to clarifiy terms. *Hyper* comes from the Greek meaning "over" or "above," evolving into the Latin "super." The early Greek singers of tales spoke of Hyperion, later identified with Apollo, a Titan who sired Helios the sun father, Selene the earth mother, and Eros their union. These gods bred superheroes and monsters, projections of natural forces and human extremes exceeding common norms. Hence, the hero was the best of humanity, the villain the worst, and early Greeks claimed that the hero's fall through *hubris* or excessive pride constituted tragedy.

Classical heroic models run thin today. "Where's the all-american cowboy at?" Billy opens *Cities of the Plain,* and back in *The Orchard Keeper* patriarch-killer Sylder tells the boy, "they ain't no more heroes." Officer Gifford nails the coffin of the boy's father, "he wand't no war hero." Given the New World fall from agrarian pastoral,

McCarthy's hyperrealism focuses on a violent frontier—unheroic American history purportedly hyperbolized, but really "disclosed," a lethal reality terrible, unknowable, but everywhere ironically present in shattered human affairs today or yesterday. Stoic endurance may be the most of this struggle.

By an earlier century analogy, a natural disclosure of the supernatural is purported to be reality unnaturally exaggerated, termed "Gothic" after John Ruskin's Victorian lectures on arts of the wilderness, wolves, grottoes, and hyperextended architecture in *The Stones of Venice*. Still the virtues of the Gothic, back to the Stone Age, ground a primitivist counterthrust against faux progress, moral decay, and technological superficiality. Exposing medieval decadence of his day in *The Divine Comedy*, Dante Alighieri hyperbolizes personal corruption in lust, gluttony, greed, sloth, wrath, envy, and pride, or any other denied deadly vice that undermines human history, cardinal sins translated from *Luxuria, Gula, Avaritia, Acedia, Ira, Invidia,* and *Superbia*. Young Cormac surely heard Latin aplenty in his Irish Catholic schooling, and satanic gargoyles, polyglottal speech, and barbarous reprobate forces fill his stories where crimes fester. Add to these hit-listed failings hypernatural disasters like flood, drought, famine, fire, typhoon, earthquake, scourge, or other natural tragedy categorized an act of God. Consider hyperextensions of everyday norms like wrecks, cancer, rape, larceny, murder, or war. Think of medieval painters Hieronymus Bosch, Pieter Breughel, Lucas Cranach, or Tommaso Masaccio crossed with Mathew Brady, Francis Bacon, Walker Evans, and Jackson Pollock.

For better or worse, humans have always been fascinated with tragic mishaps and Gothic distortion, any perversion of so-called normalcy—a curiosity about outlaws and deviants, sexual aberrants and freaks, killers and sadists, grotesques and malformed beings at large. These miscreants are rogues of the hyperreal, cousins of the grotesque where Wolfgang Kayser finds estranged, absurd, and demonic characters at dark play in *The Grotesque in Art and Literature*. Dante's *Inferno* bubbles with a desert of burning sand and a river of boiling blood, vipers and vile insect demons, sinners crammed headfirst into holes and reverse-headed walking in circles, a father gnawing on his son's skull and men violating each other. Western culture has long been roiling with scalawags. Reflect on the ancient human history of murder mysteries, lewd pornography, science fiction, carnival sideshows, crime stories, cautionary tales, medical dramas, ghost fables, royal betrayals, political coups, and horror extravaganzas.

McCarthy's Gothic is never voyeuristic prurience. In an ancient classic tradition, his fiction would expose evil for what it is, face up to God's wrath, speak honest truth to corrupt power, and witness atrocity without moralizing. His telling turns on one true sentence after another and an eye-level vision of survival in a world threatened by violence, greed, denial, destruction, and abuses of power, expressly in the screenplay *The Gardener's Son* and the theater piece *The Stonemason*. Hyperrealism on a human plane engages the reality that few dare to face, not the oddball or distorted variations from the norm, but a familiar weirdness at the heart of things: death as a mortal touchstone, for all who live must die sooner or later, and how one dies defines a life, particularly in *The Crossing* and *Cities of the Plain*. Risks are legion. War marks a constant in Western history, along with lawlessness, racism, sexism, slavery, injustice, fundamentalist terrorism, and variations of inhuman intolerance, the deadly sins plus a few in *Outer Dark* and *Child of God*, everywhere in *Suttree* or *Blood Meridian*.

Conditions seem relatively better in some places, but comfort zones from mass crime and displaced populations may be an affluent illusion, especially in coastal cities everywhere when the oceans rise and the skies dim and the lowlands flood, as Hurricane Katrina demonstrated. Just so, chilling recent novels *No Country for Old Men* and *The Road* serve as nightmarish wake-up predocumentaries. Nuclear holocaust is a probable apocalypse, biblical Revelation and the Rapture notwithstanding. The unanswered question is to be how life-forms will continue, or whether any beyond cockroaches, rats, and flies would want to survive a nuclear winter. Professor White in *Sunset Limited* has had enough and wants out. Dedicating *The Road* to his eight-year-old son John Francis gives McCarthy cause to warn the public of imminent threat, to prepare for the worst personally, and to continue voicing his canticles of praise lament and prophetic warning.

The father novelist writes of these threats from no safe haven. An American metastasis of the frontier cowboy myth, from Marlboro lung cancer to *Bring-'em-on* presidential manifestos, could wipe out continents. Global pandemics threaten to butcher entire populations. Terrorism is no fiction, and still the homeland security devil may be more within than without, as ancient warnings portray inbred evil. Environmental instability, speeded by abusive technology like carbon or nuclear fuel debris, threatens to do humanity in—global warming, poisonous waste, weaponry fallout, polluted air and water, chemically altered foods, industrialist and lobbyist cover-ups. This is neither new nor comforting information, but the novelist holds to historical fact, scientific odds, stoic courage, and true consequences, if the world wants to reduce the probability of catastrophic end-times. The hyperrealist weighs lethal odds against the numbers. Witness Jeremiah or John the Divine, someone must speak up with insight and conviction about "unpleasant truths," as Nobel-winner Al Gore has written of global warming and governmental denial.

Western literary history shows no immunity to hyperreal catastrophe and terror. The Homeric epics are full of armed violence and personal suffering, especially *The Iliad*, a city-state founding war story, and Odysseus spares no suitor at the end of *The Odyssey*. *The Aeneid* is even gorier. Beowulf rips off Grendel's arm and tacks it to the mead hall rafters, and *The Battle of Maldon* floods with blood. When the Gothic hordes sacked Rome, they nailed Italian heads to trees, and the Black Death eradicated a quarter of Europe in the Middle Ages. As cited, Dante's *Inferno* overflows with human suffering and hellish grotesquerie, lyric highs and narrative lows that are sublimely ghastly. Even Chaucer's "gentil Knicht" in *The Canterbury Tales* has been on the bloody Crusades and fought as a mercenary, and the dour Prioress tells an anti-Semitic tale of slitting a child's throat. Shakespeare's tragedies and histories "incarnadine" with guts at a time when London Bridge was bedecked with heads on stakes. Edmund stomps out Gloucester's eyes with his boot heel in *King Lear*. So literary terrors offset the "sweetness and light" of the best ever thought or understood, and the cultural history of violence around the world casts a dark shadow over celestial grace, no point discussing the history of warfare itself. Twentieth-century holocausts slaughtered over a hundred million people. Theodor Adorno said that after this carnage, art was barbarous.

From a McCarthy perspective in an interdisciplinary office at the Santa Fe Institute, historically or scientifically, the unimaginable may be the sine qua non and futurist challenge (see the Oprah.com Web site "Themes in *The Road:* Where Fiction and Science Meet" with six cross-disciplinary SFI global scientists commenting on the novel). Humanity either confronts the hyperreal immanence of death and its demonically armed retinue, the testaments imply, or ignores it on the road to secular devastation and hell. From the sublime to the grim, deviations from the norm *are* the norm in human history because there is no controlling norm, only assumptions about middles based on denials of extremes all around us, death no exception. Citizens bide time until upheavals in their lives. Fortunately, the extremes are neither constant nor imminent, more a fractal gathering of forces that grow to critical mass before they erupt.

So thankfully life is not a cataclysmic gush in most populations, but a riparian flow where flashfloods, droughts, earthquakes, or human interference unexpectedly rupture the balance of restraints. Most people live their lives humbly, try to get along each day, and warily circle the roadkill. Many deny or distract from negatives that threaten their world, finding comfort in illusion or repression of unsettling facts—the history of warfare, nuclear holocaust, greenhouse gasses, or actuarial statistics on mortality. As in the relentless arc of McCarthy's dramatic plots, the crashes are either brewing or breaking out in flash points, immanent like global warming or human death, waiting like nuclear winter or viral pandemic. Witnessing readers face these catastrophes hysterical or horrified, mute or depressed, aghast or enraged, or simply deny the unthinkable. No one can confront these natural facts or read McCarthy's fictions with indifference. Generally speaking and perhaps an understatement, men seem more accepting of his hands-on diction and working detail, tendoned syntax and unfettered visions, hard edges and cataclysmic events, human courage and historical slaughter.

Heroes are said to seize the perilous day down through the classics, match the moment when challenged, live nobly and die with courage—but in the modern world let's reflect whether "they aint no more heroes." Perhaps the prophetic stoic is our global village crier. The virtue of the heroic moment is choosing how to meet deadly struggle, when to live or die with fortitude, where to accept destiny, and great writers from Homer to Hemingway have always chronicled these stories, not without hope. And still, aside from shock-and-awe slaughter and stewing ecological storms, the hyperreal novelist considers everyday miracles that evoke awe and wonder—western sunset and eastern sunrise astonish creatures in his Appalachian stories and border chronicles, the mystery of darkness and promise of returning light as core cultural myths worldwide. The dramas of birth and death serve as wake-up catalysts for humans caring and loving each other generation to generation, from the stained patriarchy of *The Orchard Keeper* and twisted incest in *Outer Dark,* through family legacies of *The Stonemason,* to orphaned cowboys in *The Border Trilogy,* to the sheriff's wedded sense in *No Country for Old Men,* to father-son loyalty and love in *The Road.* Courage and honesty raise moral high bars in the ranchland west, as passion and humor ground allegiances in McCarthy's desert bunkhouses. Justice and compassion nurture social ideals in his poor villages. Humility, forgiveness, and grace rise as ultimate virtues crossing cultures, Southwest Native, Hispanic, and American émigré, rooted in spiritual and stoic legacies, however backgrounded.

Bear with the argument. The term hyperrealism, contrary to Eco's authentic fakery or Baudrillard's postmodernist American tiff, does not override everyday givens or the particulars of a cited text, but helps to establish the author's instinctual through-line to a calculus of culture, unsettling or no. His threnodies are lament-songs of narrative warning and prophetic vision. His canticles crescendo to disquisitions, rants, musings, dreams, illusions, and philosophical prophesies that mystify more than a few readers at key moments in the fictions. As Longinus wrote classically on the sublime long ago, the novels take a witness to the ecstatic heights of visionary perception and plunge him to the ghastly depths of grim realization. Reviewing *Child of God* in *The New Yorker*, August 26, 1974, Robert Coles argued that McCarthy *sui generis* is a novelist "of religious feeling" who defers judging idiosyncratic deviants to God: "His characters are by explicit designation children of whoever or whatever it is that we fall back upon when we want to evoke the vastness or mystery of this universe, and our comparative ignorance and uncertainty."

Return to the linguistic base. Real comes from Latin *res,* that is, objective "things." What we *think about* things constitutes the subjective world read daily. Dreams, deeper feelings, and words-as-signs of things make up the experiential subjectivity of human consciousness, or how we *feel* about what we sense and think of reading everyday things. With cognitive sense, art may be a revelation or "disclosure" in a world of things appearing unreal to skeptics. Despite McCarthy's dark mask for some readers, true art dis-covers the awe-ful hyperreal in the novelist's West.

Words are what various language cultures, some six thousand extant today, call things variously, or what people locally *say* about what they consider real. The writer knows his native lingual limitations. Dreams funnel free associative musings *around* things, McCarthy senses throughout his stories, and hyperreal visions see *into* things. History is the narrative inquiry, literally *histo-* or "tissue," that we believe about things temporally, and fiction constructs the story we *make up* about timed things. Historical fiction would fall somewhere between honest belief and candid fabrication, the imagined "tissue" of things strung together truthfully, as in most of McCarthy's writing. Finally, the ancient word *art* comes from the Proto-Indo-European language root *ar-* meaning to "connect" or tie things together in credibly moving stories and songs, commanding portrayals and kinetic art forms of dance or film, usefully beautiful structures like architecture or applied sciences. If the artist does not connect with an audience, as in the oral traditions of tribal camp and town village, his art dies.

A hyperrealistic language is the accented speech of "men speaking to men," as Wordsworth asked poetry to come down to the lives of British-Gaelic border people through their own lyrical ballads. Hardly fake, seldom academic, and by no means virtual, the common diction would be what it says it is, semiotics notwithstanding. Confucius told humans to look into their own hearts and not tell lies, and Hemingway wanted to write one true sentence about real things. McCarthy's words have the credibility of knowable working objects. Tap them and they ring true. The novelist hears the hill country folk speak their dialects of Old World English and New World slang, "Appalachian phrases as plain and as functional as an ax," Guy Davenport reviewed *Outer Dark* in the *New York Times Book Review,* September 29, 1968. McCarthy captures the various ethnic idioms across rural and reconstruction border states. He knows how cowboys talk in bunkhouses and the joking repartee of riding fences. He riffs in barfly banter and captures the advice of older men trying to help younger ones through hard times. He knows all the registers of storytelling, from truncated pain talk to unpunctuated ruminative rap, nighthawk cattle songs to country-western ballads to Mexican folk *corridos,* inventive cursing to low poker humor, sexual come-ons to scatological broken lyrics. He can sweet-talk minims between lovers or murmur soft-spoken laconic fatalisms of men risking their lives. His is not parlor, academic, or clerical diction, but a working register of common idioms.

The author knows at certain times the less said the better, when to hold and when to fold his cards, how to press things close to the chest, or where to keep your trench topknot tight and utensils clean. He knows actions over words and he trusts active words that act well, forcefully, accurately. He knows the language of witticisms, parables, tales, jokes, advice, and warnings: *no pockets in a shroud, honey catches more flies, you can't squeeze blood from a stone, a penny for your thoughts, all over you like a cheap suit, no more brains than God gave a pissant,* and *up the long ladder, down the short rope.*

From the South and Southwest McCarthy gathers hill country sayings and biblical prophesies, worn saws and old bromides made new, cowboy barbs and black blues and western ballads. *What did I do to be so black and blue?* He knows inventive speech, true stories, telling songs, worn proverbs, kindnesses and courtesies and manners of the day. *He's got a way with women and he just got away with mine.* He knows how to get down among the people. *Drier'n a cow pissin' on a flat rock.* So bear in mind these working tools and definitions of art, history, semantics, speech, culture, and philosophy as we trace McCarthy's fiction and drama from the populist history of Appalachia, including slavery and Civil War aftershock, to southwest cowboy border history, to present drug crime and war vets and postwar culture, to the postnuclear future of the world.

McCarthy has studied as well the ways and words of old biblical prophets, Ezekiel, Daniel, Leviticus, Isaiah, or apocalyptic Saint John the Divine, who warned the people of their transgressions, shortcomings, manifold sins, and pilgrim exodus—lamentations in the desert, cries from the mountaintops, dire predictions over cursed cities like Sodom and Gomorrah, signs from the heavens down through Revelation. Apocalypse means to "reveal," as in Dickinson's natural disclosures of supernatural visitations, but the poet's revelations are "slant." It is significant that Moses stuttered and had to talk through his brother Aaron to the Pharaoh. When the burning bush spoke and the prophet came down off the mountain with the stone commandments, his people were naked and worshipping the golden image of a calf, so the speech-defective savant broke the graven tablets on the ground. "If there is a prophet among you," Yahweh says, "I the Lord make myself known to him in a vision, I speak with him in a dream. Not so with my servant Moses; he is entrusted with all my house. With him I speak mouth to mouth clearly and not in dark speech; and he beholds the form of the Lord" (Numbers 126: 6–8).

And remember, too, all this prophetic "dark speech" is admittedly conjecture and hypothetical tale-spinning with no real proof or scientific certainty, only imaginative witness, logical probability, and literary faith—an unwilling suspension of awed disbelief toward hyperreality—for McCarthy's reader a series of revelations in fictions, songs of lamentations, threnodies of the wounded soul cleansing itself singing the southwest blues and making up tales of sorrow and painful expiation. And so it is with the Western history of speech, language, literacy, and art from oral cultures to print, the book in our hands. These are past and present voices in the wilderness out west, heeded or not. Like Tiresias with Oedipus or Odysseus, the blind prophet can't change anything, only forewarn in sorrow and decry stone-faced. The burning bush consumes its words, and the stuttering savant receives engraved stone commandments that cannot be obeyed, the wordless, futile Word sacred, not to be spoken, shattered on the ground.

McCarthy's "dark speech" fictions are full of crazed street priests and born-again baptizers, hermit seers and blind visionaries, from the blind maestro in *Cities of the Plain* to the novel's final Nietzschean stranger under the Arizona overpass, from the guardian aunt Dueña Alfonsa in *All the Pretty Horses* to the black-bearded "minister" of the unholy trio in *Outer Dark* and the quirky hermit who takes in Culla for a sup. The satanic albino judge in *Blood Meridian* may be the red-eyed anti-Christ, as the crazed Mennonite warns at the outset. The dream narratives in *Suttree* show the gutter poet as grievous angel fallen from Southern worldly grace. All along *The Road* father and son cross with derelict pilgrims and shuffling soothsayers. There are, as well and thank God, a few kindly elders: the centenarian grand-father Papaw in *The Stonemason,* the local commonsense judge who frees Rawlins's horse to Billy in *All the Pretty Horses,* sheriff Bell's forgiving solo uncle in *No Country for Old Men,* the compassionate ex-con "Black" come-to-Jesus in *Sunset Limited,* and the shotgun father who adopts the boy at the end of *The Road*.

As with Gárcia Lorca's discussions of gypsy "deep song" or *canto jondo*—crying through the starless dark, weeping "tears of narcissus and ice"—hyperrealism's terrors are fathomless, its arts shattering, its heights breathless and depths suffocating. The ancients called this *mysterium tremendum,* an astonishing mystery that makes one tremble, as in the tremoring word "tremendous." Jorge Luis Borges searched for an arresting *asombro* and *sagrada horror* or "holy dread" in literature. Picasso said he didn't want his audience to marvel at a work like *Guernica,* but to froth at the mouth and scream. The real is truly startling, a sometimes violent revelation, and the gods don't birth gently. During the Irish Civil War, W. B. Yeats spoke of disinterring "a rich, dark nothing" where love "has pitched its mansion in the place of excrement." Nobel poet of the Irish Troubles, Seamus Heaney claims that he rhymes in boyhood wells "to set the darkness echoing." Aboriginals of the Gaelic Isles, McCarthy's ancestors have a penchant for dark, aged, gnarled, and mystic things—ancient recipes for stewing morbid concoctions, like Dublin's Poldy Bloom frying the inner organs of beasts and fowls for breakfast, or an Irish-American cowboy putting broken egg shells in bitter camp-boiled coffee, or a Mason-Dixon Line stonemason receiving shattered dreams as visions. Yeats spent his adult life tracking spirit guides and alchemical teachers cached in the supernatural poetic compendium *A Vision.*

In an unpublished McCarthy screenplay, "Whales and Men," the marine biologist Peter Gregory addresses the Irish Parliament to question whether dreams carry an ancient life-form dialogic lost to conscious naming. Down under, speech alienates humans trying to speak for or over the life or thing pointed at, Gregory says, a decentering nod toward so-called hyperreal semiotics. Words fail to express the experience gestured, the way humans futilely witness the genocide of beaching whales or the extermination of wolves as killing an unknown mute God. "Everything that is named is set at one remove from itself," the character fears. "Nomenclature is the very soul of secondhandness." So prelingual dreams or visions may intimate a lost interspecies connection of all things, say among horses, birds, and dogs for starters, wistfully intuiting a peace that would reconnect humans with ancient knowing and belonging. "A thing named becomes that named thing. It is under surveillance," Peter Gregory speaks for his author. "We were put into a garden and we turned it into a detention center."

Not the thing named statically at cognitive remove, tribal storytellers say—revere the lyric spirit that moves *through* the names of things sung and spoken. My homeland Lakota call this kinetic life-force *Takuskanskan,* the spirit-that-moves-all-that-moves; not one god, but many primal spirits move through all places and things. A living syntactic energy flows through Homeric song-stories in performance, Parry and Lord demonstrated in *Singer of Tales.* Kinetic *chi* animates the wisdom of the Confucian Odes, as translated to the West through 2,600 years of cultural continuity. D. H. Lawrence spoke of "free" verse in his American Southwest *New Poems* (1919) as the "running flame" of the red rose.

Cormac McCarthy mixes classic, biblical, ballad, and literary genres to write in an old-style song-tale crossing lyric with narrative. His work traces a redline back to Homer, the Bible, Chaucer, and Shakespeare, forward to Melville, Welty, O'Connor, and Faulkner, excluding *artistes* not his kin such as Henry James or Marcel Proust. Neither psychological novelist nor literary aesthete, the Tennessee expatriate is an olden-time epic storyteller, literate of late. "The ugly fact is books are made out of books," the writer in the *New York Times Magazine* insists of oral traditions grown literate. "The novel depends for its life on the novels that have been written."

Richard Pearce, his script-writing partner and director of *The Gardener's Son,* a twice Emmy-nominated 1976 PBS film, writes in the foreword to the screenplay that chronologically follows the first three McCarthy novels: "By never presuming an author's license to enter the mind of his protagonist, McCarthy had been able to insure the almost complete inscrutability of his subject and subject matter, while at the same time thoroughly investigating it. Here was 'Negative Capability' of a very high order." Indeed, a willing reader suspends disbelief toward hyperreality, knowing all the while that the mystery, glory, candor, and horror of true events and tactile characters lead the witness forward through strange seas of unknowing.

McCarthy takes his hard-won place in a Western tradition of honest storytellers and lyric thinkers and hyperreal seers. The novelist "writes hybrids of mytho-poetic saga and red-dirt realism for our age," Peter Nabokov notes in reviewing this manuscript, "with a wise, dubious, existential edge that makes readers reflect on the deepest American themes of regeneration through violence, the roles of men in the creation of our inescapable national identity, and whether a country so created out of blood and greed can ever redeem itself." This fierce iconoclast may well be our most seasoned fiction writer today—a Dostoyevsky prophet of exile and darkness, a Hemingway scribe of courage and truth, a Faulkner raconteur of local color and global fascination. For better or worse, Cormac McCarthy is one of us, by God, canticling a man's truth down West.

CHAPTER 2

Back to Appalachia:
The Orchard Keeper

Like nothing else in Tennessee.

—"Anecdote of a Jar," Wallace Stevens

Hyperrealism starts locally and rises from the ground up. Something of a Smokey Mountain apprentice piece, *The Orchard Keeper* opens in italics with three men cross-cutting an old elm twisted round a wrought-iron fence. They cease sawing and the Negro testifies. *"Yessa, he said. It most sholy has. Growd all up in that tree."*

The story proper then drops back fourteen years from the frame that will close the novel in a graveyard. The tale begins with an unnamed hitchhiker walking a white scorching road under a reddening western sky, archetypal warning in McCarthy's fiction. By store talk reckoning it's 1934, seventeen miles from Atlanta. Some 197 miles from Knoxville, Kenneth Rattner is headed home where "the red dust of the orchard road is like powder from a brick kiln," and the timber stands flush with possum grapes, muscadine, toadstools, ferns and creepers piled in primordial heaps. And so Cormac McCarthy begins as Appalachian Western storykeeper.

The narrative gathers disparate mountain hillbillies and Knoxville carousers to the Green Fly Inn, swaying precariously as a listing skiff in the Red Mountain gap. Marion Sylder has gone away for five years and come back in gabardines and driving a late-model Ford coupe. He picks up young walkers on their way to Knoxville and his car supposedly vapor-locks in front of the Olive Brand Negro Baptist Church. "Not him," his male companion June says. "Not the other one," and the scene again shifts to an old makeshift druid Arthur Ownby asleep on his porch. Between scenes, as June later tells Marion, he has screwed the backseat girl "in a nigger shithouse sittin on the…" No model of male behavior either, Marion has his own way with the other girl in the black church.

Back to Rattner drinking beer at the Green Fly Inn: the porch breaks away and plummets into the mountain hollow, all in italics, taking family thieves and local drunks down with it. The narrative lurches in sweats and jerks from one country porch to another, young slatterns and good old boys and hopeless boozers and nameless barflies all swarming about Red Mountain like misshapen villagers in a medieval painting. The vignettes recall Joyce's debut with *The Dubliners*, this young Irish-American clawing his way through sorry caricatures and out of the Great Smokeys of dear, dirty Appalachia. Indeed, the novel's beginning invokes the end of "The Dead": "Some time after midnight on the twenty-first of December it began to snow. By morning in the gray spectral light of a brief and obscure winter sun the fields lay dead-white…and the snow was still wisping down thickly, veiling the trees beyond the creek and the mountain itself, falling softly, and softly, faintly sounding in the immense white silence." Roman-lettered current scenes, set against memoried italics, skeeze along indiscriminately, often a running interior monologue. Like a mountain tracker, the reader must stay alert to narrative switchbacks and voice shifts, trusting the storyline to draw it all together eventually, which it does, more or less.

Sylder loses his job at the fertilizer plant over a fight and drives all night to Atlanta. On his way back to Maryville, he thumb-strangles an odious drifter who has broken his shoulder with a car jack. "Kin we hep ye?" a voice calls from a passing truck. Not if Sylder can help it, the dead man lying under his coupe. Marion dumps the body in a deserted insecticide spray pit on the mountain top. Some two years later, the winter solstice of 1936, the Green Fly Inn finally burns down and drops into the hollow for good. Falling alcoholic debris has little to do with advancing plot or character.

The second section opens in past-reflective italics. The old man of the peach orchard is led to the deserted insecticide pit by a terrified berry-picking boy and girl to witness a stinking corpse that rots there for seven years. All this is told in the humid mood and languid geographical context of Appalachia during the Depression, hard times for people hard-pressed under any times. Narrative consciousness comes in fractals and fissures with no lost feeling for the low-life, more static portraits frozen in mountain timelessness, as though the author were writing his way away from his roots.

John Wesley Rattner grows up fatherless in a squatter's cabin trying to trap muskrats (young McCarthy's sport) and goes through a
mandatory sexual awakening without consequences. "In the slow
bleeding month of October" he sees "her" by the stream. "The tips
of her breasts were printed in the cloth like coins. She was watching
him watch." She flirts shamelessly about her name and his needs.
"Wanita, she said. If you jest got to know," knowing that he wants to
know but doesn't know how or dare to ask. Wanita Tipton gets a
leech on her bare white leg wading in the creek and screams at John
Wesley to pull it off, and they end up tumbling in the stream, and the
scene is dropped. Back in the cabin with "her high nasal hum" John
Wesley's mother makes him swear he'll find the man who took away
his father. The plot twists are set. "That was how winter came that
year."

Storylines skitter all over McCarthy's Red Mountain. Ef Hobie
was the last of a whiskey-making family during Prohibition, and his
widow and son Garland live a hardpan existence in the shale and
limestone mountains where "hard luck dogged them." Jack the
Runner is arrested and sent up three years after leaving moonshine in
the honeysuckle brush for Marion Sylder to run whiskey around
Knoxville in a 1933 Plymouth coupe. With pocketknife "circum-
cised" shotgun shells, the old orchard keeper Ownby blasts an X in
the deserted insecticide tank, marking the spot below which the
nameless hitchhiker's corpse lies rotting in a pit. "Low in the east and
beyond the town a gray soulless dawn gnawed the horizon into
shape." The sleepy story settles in predawn silence and tendriled
mountain space, dialogue little advancing character or action, all
events in a slow-motion haze of memories and seemingly fragmented
scenes.

Sylder the bootlegger has a blowout barreling down the mountain
and wrecks sixty gallons of white lightning in John Wesley's muskrat
stream. Like the "last survivors of Armageddon," the man and boy
trudge up the mountain to the cabin of the old carousing buddy June
Tipton and his missus. "Godamighty" is all anyone can say, and Sylder
gives the boy one of Lady's pups, ironically befriending and surrogate
fathering him. Neither knows John Wesley is the son of the murdered
man in the pit.

A man named Jefferson Gifford, or just plain "Gif," all-weather
sheriff cum alcohol control officer, inspects the wreck in the Red
Branch creek and takes four gallons of unspilled moonshine. The
locals in John Shell's country store gather to discuss this and sundry
mountain matters. "It ain't so much that as it is one thing'n another,"

Shell says in oblique reference to this narrative skipping along the Appalachian hills. John Wesley goes coon-hunting with Sylder and saves Lady from drowning in the creek and his mother makes him take back the pup.

The tale wends dangerously close to Tom Sawyer's river escapades when John Wesley and two others start a cave fire that burns out of control under the mountain. The boys carry a "polecat skunk" to ancient Uncle Ather's cabin and drink "muskydine wine" with the old hermit who tells mountain stories of the "wampus cat" or "painter" varmint that stole his hogs, interspersed with italic memories of his wife leaving and his own leaving the homestead for Sevierville, all meandering to the smoke-filled sinkhole cave that lays something to rest for Ownby. Is the stinking corpse of John Wesley's father here smoked and cremated?

The narrative switches to first person John Wesley telling Sylder that the half-wit deputy Earl Legwater took his muskrat traps for hunting without a license. Sheriff Gifford threatened to send the boy up for three to five years if he didn't help them find the runner of the bootleg wreck in the creek. "He couldn't catch cowshit in a warshtub," Sylder says.

Marion Sylder, ever resourceful whiskey runner, has a new auction car to spirit hooch to the city, remembering italicized Florida smuggling days on a naval cutter when his toe was shot off, while driving at night through the ice and snow to Jefferson Gifford's cabin bedroom to smash him in the face. Where does this take the story? Marion goes home to sleep beside his wife wondering, *"Why was that old man shooting holes in the government tank on the mountain?"*

Throughout McCarthy's early Appalachian fiction, thickening tone, regional texture, and local tale-telling cadence the story and tendon the action. Section four opens in a rain and hail storm as Uncle Ather is struck by lightning on the mountaintop. The storm floods Red Mountain down into the sinkholes, creeks, fields, hollows, and red-muddied gullies. "In Tipton's field four crows sat in a black locust, ranged upon the barren limbs with heads low between their wingblades, surveying the silvergray desolation, the silent rain in the country." A wild cat finds a dead mink. "She squalled once, hugging the ground with her belly, eyes turned upward at the colorless sky, the endless pelting rain." It pours for three nights and days, and on the fourth morning John Wesley goes to his traps on Red Branch creek. The story pokily gathers momentum in lowly local detail and motley characters. Two days later Marion Sylder finally leaves his house on another bootleg mission.

The sheriff and his men come three times for old man Ownby, by now the titled and Adamic orchard keeper atop the mountain. Arthur holds them off with a shotgun in his kitchen, taking out three Prohibition deputies, then escapes. Harnessed to a sledge, Uncle Ather and his dog Scout set out south along the road in the rain. They descend to the rail tracks, climb the south slope of Chilhowee Mountain and on toward Sevierville, catching a ride with a driver who takes them home for a mason jar drink of "right nice little whiskey." These sidebar peregrinations weave in local color and ballast McCarthy's stories to come.

Meanwhile, Marion Paris Sylder of Red Mountain, Tennessee is answering a police blotter check-in and later warns fourteen-year-old John Wesley come to visit him in jail, "And I didn't jest break the law, I made a livin at it." Just so the boy's dead father, only worse. Marion adds to punctuate the moral, "they ain't no more heroes." So the man who unbeknownst to everyone killed the boy's fugitive pap and threw him in the insecticide spray pit is abetted by the boy and jailed for three years. It's an ironic kind of justice without tragic, let alone heroic overtones. McCarthy rests firm in these Sophoclean fatalisms, a grim American determinism back through Frank Norris and Theodore Dreiser to Honoré de Balzac and Emile Zola's nerves-and-blood naturalism. The hard truth of character, place, and history is the story's whetstone.

The Knox County Welfare Bureau visits old man Ownby in jail over the mountain. Trying futilely to answer their forms, he says he's either eighty-three or four, depending on when he was born, and where's still in question, which places his birth in Appalachia somewhere before the Civil War. For residence, he says vaguely, just put down Twin Fork Road. "Well, I'm a old man and I've seen some hard times, so I don't reckon Brushy Mountain'll be the worst place I was ever in." John Wesley brings him some Beech-Nut "tobacca," and Uncle Ather predicts from jail, "They's a good warm spell comin on. Won't nothing make, won't nothing keep. A seventh year is what it is." The old man knows about the sinkhole corpse, incinerated in the mountain cave fire started by the boys. He tells John Wesley that he just knows things about weather and happenings and mountain folks and other matters. "Get older, he said, you don't need to count. You can read the signs." Marion seems to have told the boy the whole story.

Seven years now after the corpse's cremation and burial, presumably by Ownby, the half-wit animal "humane officer" Legwater camps on the mountain and scavenges for the skull and teeth of one Kenneth

Rattner, wanted in three states as a shoplifter, pickpocket, and probable murderer. Legwater excavates bones from the urn-pit, looking for a war-wound plate in the alleged veteran's head and loose teeth fillings to get rich. "By nightfall he was a feathery gray effigy—face, hair and clothing a single color. He spat gobs of streaky gray phlegm. Even the trees near the pit had begun to take on a pale and weathered look." Officer Gifford shows up to say "he wand't no war hero," and Legwater growls of John Wesley's confession, "The little bastard was lying, he said. He got it his ownself, the lying little son of a bitch." Gifford simply says, "Let's go, Earl." On their way down the mountain "humane officer" Legwater shoots Uncle Ather's old coon dog Scout, leaving him dead in the road ruts.

The novel grinds to a close, the narrator pronouncing the dead now "at one with Tut and Agamemnon, with the seed and the unborn." John Wesley's mother Mildred dies in 1945, and her tombstone quotes from Exodus: "If thou afflict them in any wise, / And they cry at all unto me, / I will surely hear their cry." Three years later John Wesley, now a young man returning to Red Mountain, touches "a carved stone less real than the smell of woodsmoke or the taste of an old man's wine. And he no longer cared to tell which were things done and which dreamt." The line serves as the story's epitaph.

A car outside the cemetery stops at a city streetlight. "The sun broke through the final shelf of clouds and bathed for a moment the dripping trees with blood, tinted the stones a diaphanous wash of color, as if the very air had gone to wine." It's a signature tag, often an opening to a McCarthy novel, here a sunset closing and soft ending. "They are gone now. Fled, banished in death or exile, lost, undone. Over the land sun and wind still move to burn and sway the trees, the grasses. No avatar, no scion, no vestige of that people remains. On the lips of the strange race that now dwells there their names are myth, legend, dust."

And so the old stories pass, a gentle settling of times gone, hill folk receded, the quieted tales of little people dwarfed by mountains and time, their own insignificance in the scheme of things and eternal cycles of temporality. A no-good pap, a kindly bootlegger, a cantankerous old mountain man known as the orchard keeper, a fatherless boy, a village of local dullards, dwarfs, cretins, nits, and run-of-the-mill "idjits," hillbilly fools all. The elm tree grown round the iron graveyard rail in the opening is felled and the workers leave. The fallow green Edenic apples are lost in the hills, the countryside eclipsed by valley traffic lights and passing cars and the postwar bustle of the 1950s.

The Orchard Keeper is a dark carnival of Breughel antiparables tinged with the satiric surrealism of Bosch's tryptichs, early marks of more terrible and crafted McCarthy works to come—a dank, furtive, ricocheting piece of first fiction, the young writer crossing the age of thirty and finding his path through the Appalachian debris of his past, working his way out of the dark undergrowth. In these hillbilly scary tales, he clearly has original materials, a lexicon from heaven to hell, an inventive sense of craft and high regard for the masters of storytelling. Many loose threads and questions are left hanging: Who knows why in the end? What has been learned or resolved around the unsolved murder? Where are the ruminations that later chronicle and play metaphysically around McCarthy's tale-telling? What of justice, honor, courage, or truth in the face of universal cupidity, hard times, dirty deeds, wanton violence, and inexplicable bloodletting? The grave stones lie mute. There are no more heroes, the story leaves it at that, they are all gone, if ever a part of the scheme of things. So be it.

CHAPTER 3

Dark Is a Way: *Outer Dark*

In a dark time, the eye begins to see.

—Theodore Roethke, "The Waking"

A hyperreal marker, the italicized opening of *Outer Dark* lets the reader know the writing will pitch to lyric, despite the story's hellish descent. *"They crested out,"* the narrative begins, *"their shadows long on the sawgrass and burnt sedge"* moving in single file slowly above the river's *"implacability."* The nameless figures walk *"strung out in silhouette against the sun,"* then drop with blue light touching their heads *"in spurious sanctity"* until the day sets, *"and they moved in shadow altogether which suited them very well."* The assiduous musical rhythms augur shadowy fable around an eclipse to come—masterfully cadenced, patiently crafted, perhaps to the end of the world, Adam and Eve done in.

The nameless figures sprawl fully clothed in the mud with *"mouths gaped to the stars,"* rise at first light and eat wordlessly with belt knives, until the bearded one stands *"spraddlelegged before the fire"* and precipitously attacks the other two, and just as suddenly they cease fighting and slouch west along the river again. The nightmarish page reads as minor-keyed overture. *They* are dark figures from hell, the scourge of earthly revelations—a satanic trinity to harass and to judge and to execute the innocent and the guilty, the witless quick and the wandering dead. Western good and evil comes in threes, mostly macabre in McCarthy's world of darknesses visible, the three preternatural figures perhaps an antimagi outtake from Joseph Conrad's late, languidly dark allegory *Victory.*

The dreamlike rhythms shift domestically to a man nightmaring in bed with a pregnant woman. "SHE SHOOK HIM awake into the quiet darkness. Hush, she said. Quit hollerin." As with the French custom adopted by Joyce, no quotation breaks between dialogue and narrative, dialect straight from the streets and country roads—the lines move effortlessly one to another in simple declarative sentences and breathless conjunctive compounds. The man dreams of a prophet among the detritus of mankind, "blind eyes upturned and puckered stumps and leprous sores," and under an eclipse the dreamer cries out, "Me, he cried. Can I be cured?" The prophet says perhaps, but of what, the reader wonders, and "then the sun buckled and dark fell like a shout." And the troubled man wakes to his sister's on-coming labor.

The brother shoos away an itinerant tinker, since the former "ain't got no money" and his sister's got an "old fevery chill of some kind," and anyway he can't "cipher" very well. "Naw. Not good." No, the man of the cabin doesn't want to trade for a dirty little book of "pitchers" graphically sketching "a grotesquely coital couple." The plot is set. Culla, for that is the brother's name, harbors a dark sibling secret and ignores his sister asking for a fire against the cool night. "Maybe, he said, not listening, never listening." In this rural setting women call for warmth and comfort, and their men folk look away whittling. "Is it it?" he asks of her pains, refusing to call for the midnight midwife, "a old geechee nigger witch noway," and his sister wishes the varmints would hush. They wait for the cursed birth, time standing still around their sibling fall from grace, and when the baby comes, Culla delivers it among the "bloodslimed covers, a beetcolored creature that looked to him like a skinned squirrel."

"I'm done ain't I? she said. Ain't I done?" and she wants to know "what is it" and he mutters "a chap." He tells her to sleep some. "I wisht I could, she said. I ain't never been no tireder." The dialogue of "he" and "she," incestually cross-gendered, trades on minims of speech from a barely literate, blooded couple who should not be sleeping together—the lost, neglected, and sullied underbelly of backwoods America. The "immiscible stain" of mud in the river betrays inbred sin in fearless diction, a writer pushing on his reader's literacy, taking chances from backwoods unlettered dialect to scripture and classic metrics.

The tale seems allegorically Gothic, a terrifying morality play from medieval imagining. The logic of the plot lies tangled in Christian mythology as an apocryphal antiparable of inbred sin. If Adam and Eve were God's earliest human creations, and she came into Eden from his rib, as the Bible says, they're bodily related, likely brother to sister. Their begotten issue, indeed all of us biologically to follow, are by definition bastard born of evolutionary incest. Wandering and witless, "he" and "she" portray first man and first woman east of Eden in hardscratch times—he damned to labor by the sweat of his brow, Genesis warns, she cursed to suffer childbirth pains and bruise her barefoot heel on the crawling snake. The brother will work at anything but has no trade, the sister conceives in sibling lust and births an inbred urchin of sorrow, all cursed three wandering over God's green earth for all time. Brother, sister, and ungodly issue frame our American bastard legacy from Old World exodus to rootless New Eden. God's homeless chosen prove Satan's fodder of dubious promise and uncertain end.

The man veers through the woods with the newborn "it," the novel's blank verse compacting in hard double accents: "The *country* was *low* and *swampy*, *sawgrass* and *tule*, / *tuft*ed *humm*ocks *among* the *scrub trees*." And the infant cries out in metric spasms: "It *howled redgummed* at the *pend*ing *night*," a squamous verbal heap of spondees abandoned in the woods, "the *shapeless white plasm strugg*ling *upon* the *rich* / and *incunabular moss* like a *lank swamp hare*." Reckon the richness of rhythm and variably edged diction, the poetic tare and lift of the writing, for this fiction will be rifted with masterpieces of the past, including Shakespeare and the Testaments where the passage about "outer darkness" appears, literary cadenzas like no other in much contemporary writing (see Arnold). Jesus says in parable that a man came to a wedding without proper garment, where the king told his servants: "Bind him hand and foot, and take him away, and cast *him* into outer darkness; there shall be weeping and gnashing of teeth." McCarthy's teeth-grinding adaptations of scriptural texture may not be for the timid. "For many are called," Jesus adds, "but few *are* chosen" (Matthew 22: 13–14).

The man leaves his incested burden in the black haw clearing and withdraws to the river and spits. His saliva slides "inexplicably upstream," and he runs back to the infant in the moss clearing trying to reverse things downhill, to turn time and journey back to some point of expiation. "It *howled execra*tion u*pon* the *dim cam*arine *world* of its na*tiv*ity / *wail* on *wail* while he *lay* there *gib*bering with *pals*ied *gawhasps*, / his *hands put*ting *back* the *night* like *some wit*less *paraclete* / be*leag*uered with *all limbo's clam*or." The reverse metric hexameters, end pentameter and trimeter churning with spondees, saw the dark in the fury of Homeric cadences, a dankly sonorous canto that frames the opening third of three structural movements.

Tracking the man's path through deep pineys, a spooky tinker finds the abandoned love child. "Well well, he said, kneeling, you a mouthy chap if ye are a poor'n." He scoops up the babe and carts it off to a lone woman in a dark farmhouse, and the two set out to find a wet nurse. The rich prosaic images, syntactic music, languid rhythms, and Faulknerian shadows whisper the couple's dark night journey onward with the unwanted incest child of the woods.

The brother named Culla creeps back to the cabin under a "small hot moon" and takes an axe and hacks madly at the earth. "Where's it at?" the sister-mother stirs to ask, and he says "it" died. She's bleeding again and they need provisions, so he heads to the store, the rural scene turning surreal. "A horsefly followed behind his head as if towed there on a string." The Christian storekeeper won't open on Sunday, so Culla goes back to his sister's fouled bed empty-handed and stomps outside to draw outlandish images in the dirt. He cannot get free of the babe's birth-stunned face and black blood seeping from the navel. "Mend, woman," he says, but refuses her plea to peer outdoors through a darkened pane. "I ain't warshin no winders, he said."

She wants to pretty "where it was you put him," and he refuses again. "Flowers, he said. It ain't even got a name." The brother mutters prophetically that people "don't name things dead." She begs to know the grave site and he finally gives in. She goes to find the lie of undisturbed ground, and he follows her furiously shouting, "Now you done it." The final image rivals the miscreant shame and sorrow of Massaccio's *Expulsione* in the Florentine Carmine Chapel. "And her own face still bland and impervious in such wonder he mistook for accusation, silent and inarguable female invective, until he rose and fled, bearing his clenched hands above him threatful, supplicant, to the mute and windy heavens."

The second movement returns to the italicized shadowy trio. They seem demented wise men who parody unholy trinity, raiding a barn of spade and brushhook, *"advancing against the twilight, the droning bees and windtilted clover."* The story lightens and picks up pace with small-town caricatures in a country store. Awkwardly homey and surely homeless, as Ellis documents, Culla's surname Holme surfaces as down-home boy from Chicken River. He looks for work in the boggy streets and meets a beady-eyed squire who swears by hard work, "Daybreak to backbreak for a Godgiven dollar." Someone in the night steals the squire's new veal boots. Earlier the three bad kings of the night swiped his brushhook. The furious squire follows with a shotgun in a wagon, as the italicized figures accost him on the road and break his spine with the brushhook.

Meanwhile, cousin to Faulkner's Lena Grove in *Light in August* (see Guillemin), "she" with a flower in her brushed dead yellow hair sets out blithely with her bundle to find the tinker abducting her child. "I'm a-huntin that tinker is what it is," she tells a storekeeper. Fifty-nine pages into the story she offers her name, Rinthy Holme. Guest at a farm dinner table, she says she was raised hard. After supper that night, Rinthy is bedded with the farmer and his wife in the hot dark silence, the man "mounting awkwardly bedward like a wounded ghost." Next day they give her a mule wagon ride to town, setting out drolly and offering, "Do you ever pass this way again just stay with us." The five women on chairs, farmer, and son etch the horizon with a wagonload of fools. The author clearly relishes the down-home country humor of Southern burlesque, the oval simplicity of stock comic caricatures out of hyperreal Dickens, O'Connor, or Faulkner. There's no overload of thematic or structural scaffolding beyond regional detail and texture.

Rinthy tells the farm-boy that she's a "wider" when he invites her to a town show. "You ain't got ary beau have ye?" he asks witlessly. A tinker's name, Deitch, crops up in another store, and Rinthy wants to know if he has a little chap with him, but no one knows. The section ends with images carved into time and frozen against the landscape, as Keats would burn them into an urn or Dickens ink them against the sky. "On their chairs in such black immobility these travelers could have been stone figures quarried from the architecture of an older time."

The third movement initiates the italicized manhunt for those who killed old man Salter, "stobbed and murdered," and soon two itinerant millhands hang like drifting chimes from a blackhaw tree in a field on the edge of Well's Station. Seemingly charmed, if pathetic in her innocence, lactating Rinthy trails the tinker who took her babe. "Emaciate and blinding and with the wind among her rags she looked like something replevied by grim miracle from the ground and sent with tattered windings and halt corporeality into the agony of sunlight." Butterflies trail her and birds in the road sit still as she passes, humming to herself a child's song from an old dead time. Fairy tale blessed or scripturally fated, this child of dark love floats like a fey sylph through the butterfly sunlight.

Rinthy tells a truculent farmer who asks where she's from, "I ain't even got nowhere to run off from." His butter-churning shrew says they don't need no sorry in their house of hard times. "Sorry laid the hearth here." Rinthy allows that she's nineteen years old, the time the couple have lived in the house. Her birth marked their home. "You flaptongued old bat," the farmer snaps at his wife, "don't call me sorry," and the two ensue slinging butter, as Rinthy slips away from the kitchen down the road to the deep woods. She finds an old witchy woman in a moss-and-lichen rotted cabin who probably weaned Hansel and Gretel. "I don't ast nobody's sayso for what all I do but I'd not have ye to think I'd been a-hoein," the old snuff-dipper says by way of greeting. Guileless Rinthy admits she's always scared alone on the road, "even when they wasn't nobody bein murdered nowheres."

Elsewhere by blooded parallax, Culla meets a cabin hermit in the sunless wood and asks for a sup of springwater. The recluse says he wouldn't turn Satan away for a drink. "They's lots of meanness in these parts and I ain't the least of it," the bearded cuss with two hounds and a ten-gauge double-barrel shotgun allows. He used to hunt ducks by the dozen with a four-gauge scatter punt-gun. He also hunted rattlesnakes and moccasins, though they don't pay much and spell trouble. The geezer thinks snakes carry medicine, but doesn't give them no mind. "Study long and ye study wrong." Stay on, the old-timer implores, but Culla has to track down his barefooted sister wearing a blue dress.

> She got ary kin she might of went to?
> No. She ain't got no kin but me.
> Kin ain't nothing but trouble noway.
> Yes, Holme said. Trouble when you got em and trouble when you ain't. I thank ye kindly.

Come back "when ye can stay longer," the old man says again, a sorry adieu echoed throughout McCarthy's stories.

Shortly after, the two hounds rise from the geezer's porch and descend into the outer dark, underlining the novel's title. The italicized trio taps at the door, one of them looking like the tattered minister in a dusty black suit who spoke over three disinterred coffins in Well's Station. The long bright wink of a knife blade sinks into the man's belly and expertly disembowels him. Does death track Holme, or is this just bad luck?

Culla walks on to Preston Flats and out into the shadow country to sleep in a fescue field with his hands between his knees, looking up at bird motes crossing the moon. He eats old shelled field corn for breakfast and meets a lunching turpentine crew of negroes and asks the foreman how he is. "I ain't worth a shit. You?" Culla says he's tolerable, thank you, taking the man to be the boss. "No, I work for these niggers," the man snorts. The laconic foreman says he doesn't need a day worker and tells Culla to ask a man named Clark in town.

Motley village characters meet and cuss him variously, "Hidy" and "Howdy Bud" and "He don't know shit from applebutter," as the latter lunges wildly at passing wasps. There's no end to local dirty color. "Yonder comes the son of a bitch," the foul-mouthed cracker-eater says of the bossman.

An irate farmer wants the hanged men out of his field tree, but boss Clark says the law takes time while they're "good advertisin for the public peace just now." He hires Holme for a dollar to spade the hanged men's holes behind the church while two negroes dig Mr. Salter's grave out front. Culla sleeps in the lee of a hayrick sensing something fearful. In the morning he watches two buzzards circle three more lynched men in a dead tree. Back in town he discovers Clark's hanged silhouette on the floor, and Culla runs away down the road again.

In yet another squalid village Rinthy asks a somewhat smiling man whether he's a doctor, and he says no he's a lawyer. "I get the winners, he gets the losers." She and her brother, the wretched innocents of the earth, are clearly among the latter. Rinthy waits in the lawyer's office while he smokes a cigar, then the doctor arrives in a rain squall, and she tells of birthing the missing child six months ago in Johnson County and now her paps bleeding. "They just run by their own selves." If she's not dry, she deduces, the baby's not dead, now is he? Pump and salve those breasts, doc says, go home and come back in a couple of days. "I don't live nowhere no more, she said. I never did much. I just go around huntin my chap. That's about all I do any more." It's her tawdry, if sorry, and wretchedly homeless condition as a teenage sister-mother out of wedlock.

Culla crosses a flooding night river by ferry, a stormy torrent of night-sea myth, as the ferryman is swept overboard with a stamped-ing horse and rider. He shores near the silhouetted trio incinerating blackened chunks of doubtful campfire meat—a rifleman picking his teeth, a slavering nitwit, and the black-bearded minister in a shapeless suit with a rag knotted at his neck. With "predacious curiosity" they quiz Holm over the mummified meat that cannot be chewed, the black-bearded leader with red mouth and dead eyes like "shadowed lunettes with nothing there at all," perhaps the devil in the flesh. "I don't believe I ever et no meat of this kind," brother Holme says. The char has "the consistency of whang, was dusted with ash, tasted of sulphur," presumably human flesh from hell's fires.

The bearded man talks cryptically of not naming things that can't be claimed and forces Holme out of his dead man's veal boots. The ragged crew, "filthy, threatful," and most unnamable, except for one with the rifle called Harmon, they needle their campfire guest in "malign imbecility" and vanish into the night. Culla stands lucky to be alive.

By the road with a flower in her hair, Rinthy waits for the tump-harnessed tinker and naively asks for her chap back. "I wouldn't want it if it wasn't mine." They start back down the way she has come and reach an empty cabin for night rest, Rinthy repeating, "Is it far to where he's at?" The goat-faced tinker gulps his whiskey and sops beans with cornbread, as Rinthy pleads to work for her child since she "ain't never had nothing."

> Nor never will.
> Times is hard.
> Hard people makes hard times. I've seen the meanness of humans till I don't know why God ain't put out the sun and gone away.

Eclipsed by her own innocence among foul events, she'll give anything to get back what's "mine." The tinker says personal misery and societal rejection can't be bought, his sorry existence truly among the lost of God's creation. He's given a lifetime wandering despised in a country where he was strapped to a cart "like a mule till I couldn't stand straight to be hanged." Under his prodding, Rinthy confesses the "chap" is her brother's spawn, "hisn." The goatish tinker recoils at incest talk from the "goddamn lyin bitch" and swears prophetically that she'll see him dead before she sees the child again. The goat man stomps into the night, haunted by the ancient keening of mother Eve: "lost as the cry of seabirds in the vast and salt black solitudes they keep."

Her brother fares little better. Culla finds a maggoty cabin with a dead cat and wakes to a double-barrel shotgun framing a bright china eye. The local squire summarily convicts him of trespassing, and Culla says he can't spell his own name, so he signs the admission with an "X beside the X" and is fined five dollars, or ten days work. Adamically penniless, day-work is Culla's earthly lot. Elsewhere, Rinthy is again "she" caring for another nameless "he" until the girl leaves on impulse at dawn, "poised between the maw of the dead and loveless house and the outer dark like a frail thief." A monstrous silhouette horse and rider passes her down the road, a roving figure of death.

Culla is on the road again, watching a porcine flood below him, a "howling polychrome tide of hogs." The drover speaks of mute-foot boars and jews not eating pork, "one of them old-timey people from in the bible," he explains. They discuss hogs and scripture, coming to no understanding of either as the cleft-toed flood surges on. Stampeding hogs and harried drovers swell to scriptural scourge, tumbling into the river below, the faces of the drovers taking on the grizzled medieval roughage of a Pieter Breughel canvas.

Recalling the bearded "minister" in caricature, a parson in a dusty frockcoat and carrying a walking stick checks the mounting drover anger toward Holme for spooking the herd and not stopping brother Vernon from going over the edge. "He wore a pair of octagonal glasses on the one pane of which the late sun shone while a watery eye peered from the naked wire aperture of the other." And the roving parson prates against judgment curried inversely. "Ah don't hang him, he said. Oh Lord don't hang him." There follows idiotic gabble about hanging over pushing Holme off the bluff. "Let's hang him if he don't care," says one of the churls. "I ain't never seen nobody hung." But they have no rope.

The parson pauses to sermonize the virtues of blindness. "In a world darksome as this'n I believe a blind man ort to be better sighted than most." Jesus loved the lame, the halt, and the blind, he admonishes, those scarred with heavenly mercy and stricken by God's love. "Ever legless fool and old blind mess like you is a flower in the garden of God. Amen." Without a word Holme leaps into the river.

Nearing the end, the tinker wanders into the italicized campfire of the three wise guys. A little while along, Holme arrives to behold his unrecognizable bastard son all furred with dust and fire-scarred up a side with "one eyeless and angry red socket like a stokehole to a brain in flames." The dark trio defers questions of the child to the tinker hanged in yonder tree. The bearded one preternaturally figures out Holme's incestuous kinship and toys satanically with him. Summer water and winter fire are all the needs he has, the dark one says cryptically, then spits in the fire where sparks fly up. He lifts the ravaged babe over the flames to judge and slits its throat with a blade wink.

> The child made no sound. It hung there with its one eye glazing over like a wet stone and the black blood pumping down its naked belly. The mute one knelt forward. He was drooling and making little whimpering noises in his throat. He knelt with his hands outstretched and his nostrils rimpled delicately. The man handed him the child and he seized it up, looked once at Holme with witless eyes, and buried his moaning face in its throat.

Vampires, cannibals, or deranged devils, these three scourges infest the bottom of "outer dark" scavenging its foul edges. The satanic silhouettes disappear wordlessly as they came in the beginning.

Some time later, so the tinker prophesied, Rinthy "delicate as any fallow doe" circles the deserted campfire of "chalk bones, the little calcined ribcage," and blackened pots—not knowing what to make of the charnal ruins and tinker's "bone birdcage" twisting in yonder tree. She remains searching to the end.

In later years uncounted, homeless Holme meets up with a blind man on the road who says he doesn't need to survey God's creation.

> What needs a man to see his way when he's sent there anyhow?
> I got to get on, Holme said.

Like all of McCarthy's primary characters in homeless lineage, Thomas Hardy to John Bunyan, the barefooted pilgrim has to keep moving from disquisitions on darkness: "his shadow be-wandered in a dark parody of his progress. The road went on through a shadeless burn and for miles there were only the charred shapes of trees in a dead land where nothing moved save windy rifts of ash that rose dolorous and died again down the blackened corridors."

Holme wades through hell's wake to reach a post-Hemingway swamp draining all two-hearted rivers out of Eden. "And that was all." The blackened trees stand "dimly hominoid like figures in a landscape of the damned. A faintly smoking garden of the dead that tended away to the earth's curve." His foot sticks erotically in the mire, "a vulvate welt claggy and sucking." Culla vacantly wonders why any road should come to such a place. The blind ending is no end, only a horrific story that quits with no way to make it right or to tie things up or to draw characters together. Forget fictive denouement.

Rinthy meanders witlessly alone. Her brother Culla wanders the earth from day-work to work. Their incested issue lies cremated in the campfire. This pilgrim way nears the road's swamp-end where a blind man heads to hell, no conclusive naming of the nameless dark or the cast-off damned. Regardless of how far or wide McCarthy's fictions take readers, all the way to nuclear winter in *The Road*, pilgrim scriptural warnings of "outer dark" were planted in the beginnings some forty years back. The cultural scaffolding is our own Western heritage.

CHAPTER 4

Child of Whose God?
Child of God

Hath the rain a father? or who hath begotten the drops of dew?

—Job 38: 28–30

If we are all God's children, as some hold, what kind of god made
liars, thieves, rapists, sadists, murderers, cannibals, and necrophiles?
"A child of God much like yourself perhaps," a local witness describes
the gnomish Lester watching from the barn door as a mountain folk
melee comes to the forced county auction of his farm, "a caravan of
carnival folk up through the swales of broomstraw." Always a trol-
lish outsider and not quite right in the head, as "child of god"
implies among country people, Lester Ballard is of warring Saxon
and Celtic blood beyond the flowering apple trees of Appalachian
America. The unshaven, dirty, little figure stands "straddlelegged"
after pissing in the straw humus. "Buttoning his jeans he moves
along the barn wall, himself fiddlebacked with light, a petty annoy-
ance flickering across the wallward eye." Something is not quite
right here, a strange and unsteady feel about the story winding
tenebrously under a pastoral sunlit setting. The hyperreal may be
getting uncomfortably real.

The sale auctioneer torques up the microphone blather, "but looky
here," CB says, good young timber is growing overhead while "you"
lie sleeping. "I'd buy it myself if I had any more money." The pitch is
kinfolk addressed to you-the-reader, as the narrative will later bring
us personally into questions of good and evil, punishment and pity
around social pariah Lester. How and why such trolls dollop the
Appalachian mountains like fetid mushrooms is a morbid curiosity of
McCarthy's early fiction. The small grizzled figure interrupts the

bidding with a childhood rifle in hand. The gun never leaves him the rest of the story.

> What do you want, Lester?
> I done told ye. I want you to get your goddamn ass off my property.
> And take these fools with ye.
> Watch your mouth, Lester. They's ladies present.
> I don't give a fuck who's present.

The auctioneer slows his voice to explain that the land is no longer Lester's, and the high sheriff of the county stands yonder there to enforce the state sale. "I don't give a good goddamn where the high sheriff is at," Lester bellows. "I want you sons of bitches off of my goddamned property. You hear?"

Low comic humor, folk vulgarity, squalid genetics, perhaps a comedy of fools, or worse the violence of nitwits and deviants. How does everyone count as God's children among these? The story abrupts to an unnumbered chapter break, a jumpcut jerk to one of many local witnesses. "Lester Ballard never could hold his head right after that. It must of throwed his neck out someway or another. I didn't see Buster hit him but I seen him layin on the ground." Buster stands over the troll with an axe, and the sheriff hauls rifle-toting Lester off to the pokey.

The narrative line fractures again to Fred Kirby the bootlegger. "Kirby turned his head to one side and gripped his nose between his thumb and forefinger and sneezed a gout of yellow snot into the grass and wiped his fingers on the knee of his jeans. He looked out over the fields. I cain't do it, Lester, he said." The gnome swaps his pocket knife for promise of some white lightning, but Kirby can't find where he hid it. "Well shit fire," Ballard fumes. "Well goddamn." This is a little man of limited vocabulary and lower intelligence, a notch below most animate beings outside of paradise. "Ballard passed by and went behind the barn where he trod a clearing in the clumps of jimson and nightshade and squatted and shat. A bird sang among the hot and dusty bracken. Bird flew. He wiped himself with a stick and rose and pulled his trousers up from the ground."

Lester partially clears a littered cabin to resettle in the mountains above the valley, as the story drops level by level to his substratum. "In the night he dreamt streams of ice black mountain water, lying there on his back with his mouth open like a dead man." The narrative promises less and less light, more and more shadowy Gothic degradations.

The staccato chapters or scene breaks slant with sharp cuts, the story coming in broken cherts and shards of witness, strewn with local mannerisms of defecation and nose-blowing and ruminating under the distant blue hills. It's a mountain valley tale in voices of the common people, realistic audience to the foul residue among good folks. "I never liked Lester Ballard from that day," a local says of him busting the Finney boy's nose for nothing at all. "I never liked him much before that. He never done nothin to me." But he will, to us all, at least in our dreams of monsters and the aftershock of monstrosities.

"Ballard lay in the night-damp with his heart hammering against the earth," the next fragment opens. A voyeuristic night predator from the "weeds that rimmed the Frog Mountain turnaround" watches a parked car with panting lovers in "slaverous lust." Lester peers through the back window at the naked couple and masturbates on the fender as the girl climaxes, "O Bobby, o god, she said." The radio stops and a car door creaks. "Ballard, a misplaced and loveless simian shape scuttling across the turnaround as he had come, over the clay and thin gravel and the flattened beercans and papers and rotting condoms. You better run, you son of a bitch." The night honeysuckle blooms darkly and the car rolls down the mountain.

Vignettes of Lester Ballard's strangeness get stranger, way beyond mountain road coupling in the steamy backseat of a parked car. "I don't know. They say he never was right after his daddy killed hisself," says a witness who chopped down Lester's daddy "like cutting down meat." The father's wife left him and he hung himself. Nine or ten-year-old Lester just stood there watching. "The old man's eyes was run out on stems like a crawfish and his tongue blacker'n a chow dog's. I wisht if a man wanted to hang hisself he'd do it with poison or something so folks wouldn't have to see such a thing as that." Since Lester witnessed the horror of his father's suicide among other as yet undetailed atrocities, at twenty-six and now alone he goes barbarous mad in his cabin nightly.

Cut to the dumpkeeper Ruebel with nine feral daughters named from an abandoned medical dictionary, Urethra, Cerebella, Hernia Sue. They fuck any "old lanky country boys with long cocks and big feet" and spawn litters of half-wit children, only to be incested by their ursine father. Lester has been shooting frogs and stealing field-corn to stay alive, foraging the valley gardens like a rutting hog. "I'll tell ye another thing he done one time," a villager unloads more gossip. Under a "rimshard of bonecolored moon" in early winter, Lester found a whisky drunk woman in her nightdress at the Frog Mountain turnaround and slapped her around and tore off a handful of her nightgrown. "I knowed you'd do me thisaway," she snarled. Sheriff Fate confers with Darfuzzle, a man with his lower jaw shot away who speaks "with a mouthful of marbles," that the drunk mountain girl reported Ballard as an attempted rapist. "Let's go get the little fucker, said the sheriff."

The story builds in fits and starts, by sorry and soiled rags and pieces here and there, Lester Ballard getting crazier, the rumoring mountain folk not far behind. The narrative jerks in slang clots and sentence particles, the overview seemingly none too fond of its subjects, exposing them in twisted pointillist sketches at some distance through sordid comic riffs. Low dark satire and soiled medieval caricature, *Child of God* is a ragged mutt of a fiction, nothing to please readers of Jane Austen or George Eliot. Whiskey and women prove Lester Ballard's nemeses, and he sneers at the taunting sheriff who lets him go, "I ain't ast nothin from nobody in this chickenshit town."

Back to the rifle he's had since a child. "He could by god shoot it," a local says. At a county fair of carnie roustabouts, trick marksmen, and boxing apes, crack-shot Lester bags two stuffed bears and a tiger taken home to the squatter's cabin, "their plastic eyes shining the firelight and their red flannel tongues out." He has just watched the fireworks display and "a young girl with candyapple on her lips and her eyes wide," much as Poldy Bloom surreptitiously pleasures himself watching Gerty McDowell on the beach in *Ulysses*. The undertones here are more unsettling. "Her pale hair smelled of soap, womanchild from beyond the years, rapt below the sulphur glow and pitchlight of some medieval fun fair."

The monster's pulse beats faster as the narrative heat rises in this circumscribed, mountain-shadowed, incestuous place of narrow minds, tight fists, little worlds of squalid choices. Lester Ballard's grotesque humanity, if indeed he is a child of some Feral God, is compelled to split this world open violently and lawlessly. His virile monstrosity will not be contained by small people, though he himself is smallest of all. The nearest fictive kin to such a tale of little folk is Faulkner's *As I Lay Dying* where an ill-formed family of Mississippi sharecroppers carries the corpse of their mother home to a shallow grave. These are weird Southern border tales of weirder people, hill folk dementia and genetic grotesquerie as Southern Gothic humor. Eudora Welty in a dark mood, William Faulkner gone nasty, Carson McCullers randy. The stunting mountains loom over scrub humanity, inbred and gene shallow, a derelict migrant-pooled, low-imploding

America that can't escape its belittling history and towering escarpments and jagged ridges hanging darkly above.

McCarthy is childhood-fettered to these smoky hills and caricatures of humankind. None of the big skies, open ranges, and footloose cowboys of *The Border Trilogy* to come a decade later when the author lets loose his rhythmic imagination and vertiginous lexicon. There's a strange and unsteady feel about the story, as though it were some farewell to the writer's hill country origins, pay-back to mean-spirited village trash talk and small-time self-righteousness, dropping down to the hyperreal base of his fated roots. Or maybe it's all a sour joke gone rancid in a late century, millennial America rotten from migrant-reject origins.

From a characteristic distance on the mountain, Ballard scans the vicious balletic hunt of snarling hounds tearing apart a wild boar: "watched the lovely blood welter there in its holograph of battle, spray burst from a ruptured lung, the dark heart's blood, pinwheel and pirouette, until shots rang and all was done." He absently observes a meticulous blacksmith fire, hammer, and sharpen his axehead. "Soft water, hard steel." And he finds a robin in the snow, a portent of spring, gifted to the idiot-child Billy of the dumpkeeper's daughter. "I brung him a playpretty," he slavers. To keep the robin close by, the child tears off the bird's legs and eats them.

"There wasn't none of em any account that I ever heard of," a local says of the Ballard clan lineage. War-dodgers and pension-connivers, he dubs the White Cap vigilantes that continued to lynch blacks, steal from the commons, and snipe the hills of the Mason-Dixon Line after the Civil War was long over. The first of three sections ends with tawdry village snipe.

> I'll say one thing about Lester though. You can trace em back to Adam if you want and goddamn if he didn't outstrip em all.
> That's the god's truth.
> Talkin about Lester...
> You all talk about him. I got supper waitin on me at the house.

Can Lester outstrip everyone in horrific scandal? Read on, citizen.

The vignettes continue in short attention spans and kinky sidebars and tight-lipped sketches, flinty bits of story scavenged from the bone pile of a rag-end America where few visit their mountain folk cousins or get to know their sorry kin ways. Is it too close to home for a hillbilly boy, too island-narrow for an immigrant Irishman? Back to Adam's fall, Lester tops them all, the man-monster to chatter about when there's nothing else to do, and that's much of the time. Village talk, folk tale, ghost story, horror legend, dark rumor, nasty stink—the voices of common doings among crackers and trailer trash and cabin hermits, low-life all around.

The second section goes where we sense the story will inevitably go. Hunting squirrels with his omnipresent rifle, "as if it were a thing he could not get shut of," Lester comes on naked lovers asphyxiated *in flagrante* as consummating corpses in a car backseat at the Frog Mountain road turnaround. "Them sons of bitches is deader'n hell, he said." Rolling the man off his mount, Lester discovers the dead man's wet-yellow, condom-sheathed penis pointing at him. "They godamighty, said Ballard," near speechless over his good fortune. After rubbing the woman's nipples and sniffing her underwear, he lowers his trousers and fucks the corpse, her one-eyed, dead lover staring from the backseat floorboard. Lester leaves and comes back four times, robbing the sorry man's wallet and pilfering the lifeless girl's purse, then carries her body off to his cabin.

He shops in Sevierville for girl's clothes with the dead couple's cash and dresses her body in red for necrophilic consummation in six-below weather. "You been wantin it," he says hoarsely to her rotting corpse after building a raging fire. The body ascends and descends by attic rope until he burns down the cabin in a roof shingle blaze and saves the stuffed carnival bears and tiger, but not the decomposing girl. "He'd long been given to talking to himself but he didn't say a word," crouching on the smoking hearth like a scorched owl.

This "crazy winter gnome" clambers up the snow-filled, wooded mountain to a cave refuge without his cremated bride. Scenes shift from over to under. Down below, the dumpkeeper Ruebel lectures Ballard on the folly of wedlock. "You ort to be proud, Lester, that you ain't never married. It is a grief and a heartache and they ain't no reward in it atall. You just raise enemies in ye own house to grow up and cuss ye." Things go bad to worse. The bootlegger Kirby has been snitched by "niggers," and the dumpkeeper-daughter with the idiot-child says to a pathetically aroused Ballard, "You ain't even a man. You're just a crazy thing." So once outside, he shoots her through the window and watches the girl bleed from the neck. "Die, goddam you, he said. She did." He takes the dead mother and leaves the idiot-child to burn up in the dumpkeeper's house, "berryeyed filthy and frightless among the painted flames."

The man behind the sheriff's desk accuses Lester of torching Mr. Waldrop's place, disregarding the second fire and mother-child killings. "Mr Ballard, he said. You are either going to have to find

some other way to live or some other place in the world to do it in."
And he does, only worse. Lester forages the mountain countryside
like a primordial caveman—Faulkner's Boone Hogganbeck gone
homicidal, Ted Hughes' Wodwo eviscerating small animals. "Ballard
among gothic treeboles, almost jaunty in the outsized clothing he
wore, fording drifts of kneedeep snow, going along the south face of
a limestone bluff beneath which birds scratching in the bare earth
paused to watch." All the natural world stops to stare at this paleolithic freak and human-animal gargoyle.

By winter Lester shows up trading three watches at a country store
on the other side of the mountain. "It's a sight in the world of snow,
ain't it?" the storekeeper humors the misshapen stranger. Ballard
drags provisions back to his caveman grotto high above the valley in
a bloodred cavern "like the innards of some great beast" a mile deep
in the mountain where "dead people lay like saints." Lester is collect-
ing naked rotting bodies as his own intimates, friends, and family
the way a sadistic child would gather dead mice, slowly becoming a
monstrous god of darkness and depravity and death, a great awful Dis
of primeval disorder and mis-made things.

Wearing female underclothes, then the outer clothes of women
victims, he paints his lips red and stalks Greer the man who bought
his homestead at auction. "A gothic doll in illfit clothes, its carmine
mouth floating detached and bright in the white landscape." The
cross-dressing caricature shatters the rules of political correctness and
gender decency. A false spring comes and the bats stir in his cavern
"fluttering wildly in the ash and smoke like souls rising from hades."
The keeper of the dead wonders "what stuff they were made of, or
himself," and the second section closes around him.

The descending structural trinity of horrific thirds finds another
couple necking at the Frog Mountain turnaround where the "crazed
mountain troll" summarily shoots the lovers and carries off the naked
girl. "Scuttling down the mountain with the thing on his back he
looked like a man beset by some ghast succubus, the dead girl riding
him with legs bowed akimbo like a monstrous frog." By now and
come this far, the reader is personally dragged into a flooding river of
grotesquerie with the troll. "He could not swim, but how would you
drown him? His wrath seemed to buoy him up. Some halt in the way
of things seems to work here. See him. You could say that he's sus-
tained by his fellow men, like you. Has peopled the shore with them
calling to him. A race that gives suck to the maimed and the crazed,
that wants their wrong blood in its history and will have it. But they
want this man's life."

What is the newly omniscient participant-narrator saying to us here? Gospel singers at the six-mile congregation in Sevier County would testify that good Christians are called to save the wretched and poorly served sinners of the family of man. This does not happen in *Child of God*. Humanitarians say we should pity the deranged instincts of the monstrous among us. Charity stops with Lester Ballard. Realists say we are drawn despicably to abnormal bloodlust, and some slaver over the bad blood of our subhuman ancestry. Is violent prurience a motive? Witnesses get high on hangings and lustful at executions, the dark voices whisper. Are we voyeurs of misery and suffering? Rotting guts and defilements and sado-masochistic sex draw crowds for entertainment. The historical list is written in blood. Do we want this man's defiled visage and entrails among us? The novel says he is one of us, like it or not.

In a roiling flood, the Appalachian Caliban curses a river of life that bore him and the master who taught him speech. His mudstained mattress floats downstream with the stuffed carnival animals. Dragging what he can salvage of the sodden bed, he does not stop swearing all the way back to the "stygian mist" of his grotto with "the last rancid mold-crept corpse" lugged into his final sinkhole. "He sat there soaking his feet and gibbering, a sound not quite crying that echoes from the walls of the grotto like the mutterings of a band of sympathetic apes." McCarthy's hyperrealism runs over-the-top.

The Little Pigeon river floods the town, and a reference to Knoxville informs the reader that this is indeed Tennessee, a border state split by the Civil War, a hill country half-settled by Celtic and Saxon rejects, runaways, outlaws, and derelicts of Puritan New England. The sheriff is now fully named Fate Turner, and the hill country clan wars still define the local history and hardscrabble terrain and stunted thinking. "No, those were sorry people all the way around, ever man jack a three hundred and sixty degree son of a bitch, which my daddy said meant they was a son of a bitch any way you looked at em," says old man Wade to the sheriff and deputy rowing him to the courthouse.

You think people was meaner then than they are now? the deputy said.

The old man was looking out at the flooded town. No, he said. I don't. I think people are the same from the day god first made one.

And Lester Ballard is running out of caves to hide and couples to ravage and locals interested in his folktale depravity. Dimly remembering his childhood and ghastly dream of his father, he looks down in a startling moment of self-pity on the diminutive dark-greening valley from his hermit signal post on the mountain. "Squatting there he led his head drop between his knees and he began to cry."

Wearing a dried human scalp frightwig and skirts, Lester shoots homestead-usurper Greer three times, who in turn blasts Ballard out the door with a shotgun retort that takes off one of his arms. The guns in the plot are all firing at once. Later the hospital nurse asks Lester if he even bothers to know whether Greer lived.

> You really don't care one way or the other do you? she said.
> Yes I do, said Ballard. I wish the son of a bitch was dead.

A lynching party comes wanting to know where his "fuckin" dead bodies are at. Bareshank in his nightshift, Ballard avoids hanging by leading the posse to his mountain catacombs and disappears through a fissure so small they can't follow. "He's by god gone." For three days Lester feels his way along the caves, spelunking in the wet dark, and finds another cavern home where "you might have said he was half right who thought himself so grievous a case against the gods." So this tale descends into the Stygian pit where blind men curse the gods who misshaped and misdirected them.

> He scrabbled like a rat up a long slick mudslide and entered a long room filled with bones. Ballard circled this ancient ossuary kicking at the ruins. The brown and pitted armatures of bison, elk. A jaguar's skull whose one remaining eyetooth he pried out and secured in the bib pocket of his overalls. That same day he came to a sheer drop and when he tried his failing beam it fell down a damp wall to terminate in nothingness and night.

From the bottom of the ancient ossuary, the miraculous dwarf is selfborn by way of a fist-scraped hole that opens through rocks into a cow pasture. He goes right back to the county hospital, a one-armed ogre swaddled in red-mud-caked overalls. "His eyes were caved and smoking. I'm supposed to be here, he said."

The story wraps up Gothically. Ballard is never charged with any crime, but put away in a cage for demented maniacs. His cell neighbor is a cannibal who ate the brains of his victims with a spoon. Lester dies on the floor and his body is shipped to a medical school in Memphis where he is preserved in formalin, flayed on a slab, carefully eviscerated and dissected by students. "His head was sawed open and the brains removed." After three months of vivisecting prurience, "Ballard was scraped from the table into a plastic bag and taken with others of his kind to a cemetery outside the city and there interred. A minister from the school read a simple service."

What about the caverned corpses? A farmer, Arthur Ogle, was plowing in April of that same year, folks say, when his rig fell into an endless darkness below. Two neighbor boys descended the sinkhole on ropes to find "seven bodies bound in muslin like enormous hams," a mausoleum of corpses cocooned by Lester. "The bodies were covered with adipocere, a pale gray cheesy mold common to corpses in damp places, and scallops of light fungus grew along them as they do on logs rotting in the forest. The chamber was filled with a sour smell, a faint reek of ammonia." And so *Child of God* finishes with passionate gore and garish reality and Gothic witness—the novelist as mortician and grave digger and dirge raconteur. At the story's end nighthawks rise from the dust in the mountain road "with wild wings and eyes red as jewels in the headlights."

If Lester Ballard is a "child of god" among us, and we must claim him kin, the story raises questions of human and animal nature, sexual drive and essential provisions, depravity at large and God the unholy mis-maker. The seven deadlies are crowned by lust and gluttony. Is this a grotesque ruse, a horror story gone rancid, a hill tale of crazies, or lascivious murder mystery seen several times a week on public television as *CSI* or *The Sopranos* or *Miami Vice*? Recall an old American Gothic tradition—Edgar Allan Poe with the beating heart under the floorboards and pitiless raven croaking "Nevermore," the writer bloody tongue-in-cheek; Aubry Beardsley laughing maniacally over atrocious carnage, outrageous erotics, and human misery; Frank Norris watching monstrous machines desecrate the virgin earth; Jack London running with wolves and Bram Stoker swooping with vampires; Jekyll and Hyde taking turns entertaining their victims at the turn of the century, one Anglo-Gaelic empire handing off its dirty work, soiled power, and blood-sodden greed to another younger brother across the Big Water.

It's not clear why McCarthy would want to write *Child of God* or what he thinks about the early story. A tour de force among horror thrillers, a Gothic novel to top all the others, or hillbilly hyperreality best written out and left behind? This from a young artist flexing his dark imagination in conflicted times and writing in furious lyric about the terrible disfigurations among us. The revolutionary 1960s have something to do with hyperbolic realism. Recall that the twelve-year-long Vietnam Conflict was ending in 1973 when the novel was published; social unrest and change and revolution tearing up the streets of the country; alternative cultures roiling around drugs, sex, rock 'n roll; the American use of atomic annihilation staggering everyone's circumscribed imagination toward a Third World War and silent spring; cigarettes and cancer wedded; biological and chemical warfare reinstituted in laboratories at home and sold abroad; hate crimes and mob lynchings and racial discriminations and civil rights movements verging on another internecine war across America.

Ted Hughes wrote the anti-Christ *Crow* in 1970 after his wife Sylvia Plath gassed herself and nearly took her infants with her. Jerzy Kosinski documented the young horrors of the Jewish German Holocaust in *The Painted Bird,* and Joseph Heller chronicled the grotesque battle absurdities in *Catch 22.* Kurt Vonnegut wrote of his prisoner-of-war experiences in the fire-bombing of Dresden and the stalag cells in *Slaughterhouse Five* and the darkly comic "ice-nine" end of the world in *Cat's Cradle.* William Styron fictionally documented Nat Turner's slave rebellion and mutilated assassination and lying down in Southern darkness, while James Dickey wrote poetry of the bottled sheep-child in the Atlanta museum, Gothic fictive issue of man and animal.

Dee Brown scoured the country's history for Native dispossession and genocide in *Bury My Heart at Wounded Knee.* John Hawkes and Thomas Pynchon were thickening the literary plain with novel after novel of human despair, artistic disdain, and depraved chicanery. Faulkner's freaks and Welty's serial murderers were all the Southern literary rage, a character like Percy Grimm in *Light in August* standing in for fate. Some think these were tales told by disillusioned idiots full of sound and fury and dark misshapen things. The times they were mighty dark and a-changing, family values shattered by divorce rates and free-love communes and drug addictions and runaway hustlers and kids who said they don't need no education.

The truncated sentences, stumped narrative lines, choked lyric rhythms, low-life characters, and unspeakable crimes of Appalachian pastures serve up McCarthy's genius in miniscule reverse, a kind of stunted primeval pygmy forest that a god-defying author mis-matched and left aside in the junkheap of backwoods Edenic America. The incested, stillborn, or partial-birth distorted characters shuffle and stare and lurch toward the dark overhead perimeter of brooding mountains with bottomless caverns that surround their valley of death and deformity. If these too are God's children, what kind of a God made us all?

The misbegotten child among us is not necessarily outside our religious family circle in a brave New World. Genesis and Leviticus and Ezekiel and Job and the terrible book of Revelation have their share of sodomites and incestuous fathers, drunken boatswains and hands-and-knees crawling old men, sword-wielding justices and ravaging monsters and many-headed avengers of the last days, revealing mass slaughter and individual suffering and apocalyptic judgment and divine retribution for God's plan gone wrong. "And when the dragon saw that he was cast unto the earth, he persecuted the woman which brought forth the man *child*," Saint John the Divine says of his reeking apocalyptic vision (Revelation 12: 13). "And I stood upon the sand of the sea, and saw a beast rise up out of the sea, having seven heads and ten horns, and upon his horns ten crowns, and upon his heads the name of blasphemy" (13: 1). God's children may not fare all that well in end-times. "And it was given to him to make war with the saints, and to overcome them: and power was given him over all kindreds, and tongues, and nations" (13: 7). God forbid that the born-again Rapturists know rightly about the Second Coming. The carnage will not be pretty or fictional. "If any man have an ear, let him hear" (13: 9).

CHAPTER 5

Southern Milltown Script:
The Gardener's Son

Among the turtles and the lilies he turned to me
The white ignorant hollow of his face.

—Stanley Kunitz, "Father and Son"

A screenplay in film production obviously turns on considerably more than words—acting, directing, sets, stills, camera angles, score, close-ups and fade-outs, and all manner of stage directions indoors and out. And yet, if the dialogue is not right, nothing turns out very well. So in 1975 documentary filmmaker Richard Pearce set out to find "Not just any screenwriter. A great screenwriter." Coming to no terms with Eudora Welty, he consulted the estranged wife and literary editor of Cormac McCarthy for an El Paso post office box, assured that the roving Tennessean would check his mail about every six weeks.

To his surprise, Pearce heard back that the novelist was interested and would meet to discuss a postbellum milltown story. The script treatment came from a few paragraphs in the footnotes to a 1928 biography of a pre–Civil War Southern industrialist. The filmmaker and writer met in Texas and reconvened in Tennessee, then drove through the Carolinas to Graniteville scratching around textile mills on a summer research trip. McCarthy alchemized the hyperreal data into "a strange and haunting tale of impotence, rage, and ultimately violence among two generations of owners and workers, fathers and sons," Pearce writes in the Foreword to *The Gardener's Son* screenplay. The story takes place soon after the Civil War when carpetbaggers were industrializing the South, slaves were emancipated with nowhere to go, and class struggle between rich and poor ground on through hard times. The two-hour film, made in 16mm for $200,000 and broadcast on PBS during the country's 1976 Bicentennial, was shown at the Berlin and Edinburgh Film Festivals and nominated for two Emmy Awards. Pearce named McCarthy his daughter's godfather and considers the novelist a padrone to all his films since.

A good screenplay is built carefully with structural tightness, solid characterization, rich context, and explicit detail. The plot points, story arc, act sequences, scene cuts, and narrative transitions are crafted to warrant the budget and hundreds of people involved in making the film. If it's a bust, the money, people, and production time are wasted. Coming a decade into the author's career and following his trilogy of Gothic southern fictions, *The Gardener's Son* shows McCarthy deepening, tightening, and honing his craft through dramatic dialogue and narrative pace. There is crossover literary precedent. Recall for twenty years from 1890 on, W. B. Yeats wrote a play annually for Dublin's Irish National Theater. Lady Gregory remade the dramatic house from the city morgue, a public forum for John Synge, G. B. Shaw, John Gogarty, Maude Gonne, Willy Yeats, and others. Theater is not film, but both turn on dialogue, character, set, and plot, and compact speed is all. The Irish national poet planed, edged, and thickened his old-fashioned verse from late nineteenth-century balladry to twentieth-century dramatic lyric—harder than breaking stones in a roadway, he admitted. Yeats's 1890 Innisfree chant, "I hear it in the deep heart's core," grounded him in Gaelic realities, heroic courage, and the true heart's passions, no less than McCarthy's Appalachian and border cultures are postholed in the stones, caliche, and mesquite of local homestead knowledge.

The screenwriter theatrically edges his literary tools, scours and expands his diction, focuses his plots, and deepens his sense of true character, dramatic action, and human fate. In *The Gardener's Son* he crafts living dialogue on a filmic grid, the working text as dramatic speech, telling character, and cultural history. McCarthy's only screenplay has forty-five actors and moves across South Carolina like a tectonic earthquake, gathering speed and weight as it spreads over two hours.

The script opens with a present Timekeeper off-stage (not in the edited film) saying he doesn't know what all remains in the vacant cotton mill office. "Old paper and stuff. What aint eat up." He mutters things off-stage to an inquisitor and suddenly remembers the millowner's funeral in Augusta years back when the wind blew away his brother Earl's hat in the street and a horse stepped on it. The voice fades and the credits roll. A young questioner enters the room, and the old-timer recalls sulphur burning in the streets against summer malaria. Then he recounts that the McEvoy boy broke his leg falling off the gravel train, not run over by the owner's less reputable son. Old man Gregg was a pistol, but his son James was a different cut and blood runs thin. The Timekeeper tells the boy rummaging through boxes of papers that you can't cache history in old papers or pictures. Once copied, you don't have it any more, just have the record. "Times past are fugitive. They caint be kept in no box." *Caveat lector.*

The screenplay credits end, and a series of historical sepia stills (again not in the final film) roll a so-called "overture" sketching the story in visual miniature to the final shot of an old wooden coffin loaded on a mule-team wagon. *The Gardener's Son* animates with James Gregg showing the quaint village to a wagonload of frock-coated Graniteville Mill Company stockholders. They pass a young girl, James winks at a stockholder, and the girl runs home seeing the doctor on the way.

Martha McEvoy tells her mother that the doctor "might could be here any time," and the household is a-fluster. The doctor's carriage first stops at the millowner house where he tells Mrs. Gregg that her husband is beyond his or any man's practice. Cadaverous Dr. Perceval allows that the old man despised idleness, and that it's a bad night out there, and he leaves.

The scene cuts to the McEvoy kitchen where the Missus says, "Lord Mrs Gregg you ort not to of come." It's an old stand-off between the Anglo-Scottish Greggs and Irish McEvoys of the British Isles, now transferred to upper and lower class houses in South Carolina. The industrialist Greggs hail from Charleston, the largest Southern slave port, and the cracker McEvoys have come down from the mountain village of Pickens. The McEvoy boy has a leg infested with rot that must be amputated, the doctor says, but young Robert resists heatedly that if God put rot in his leg, then let it rot off. Over the boy's protestations Mrs. Gregg insists on taking a look and recoils from the blackened stink and promises to stay nearby through the surgery. The doctor and his stout black assistant lay out the surgical tools and don butcher's aprons. The set directions read, "Mrs. Gregg's face is a curious expression of concern touched with a morbid if not salacious curiosity." Such the voyeuristic compassion of the ruling class.

The black assistant leaves the room with the leg wrapped in a sheet, and the story cuts to the burial of the millowner William Gregg. No stranger to hard work, a eulogizing stockholder says, he's brought a massive factory with "its beautiful and perfect machinery" to this hardscrabble town as if by magic. All this "shall continue to bear fruit for generations after the first laborer himself has passed away." Right kind words in hard times, but the mill grinds on and future toiling generations may not be so kindly grateful. Country manners and common civilities, *Mam* and *Sir* and *May I please,* are being replaced by a harder dialogue, less muling workers, and meaner plot.

"Did they not learn you to sir at your home?" the backstory Timekeeper asks the one-legged Robert, now an office boy sweep. The scene shifts to James Gregg the new boss turning away two dozen hillbillies come to the mill for work. He then makes a lewd pass at Martha, Robert's fourteen-year-old sister who works in the spinning room. She may be too feisty for the boys, the cocky boss sweet-talks her, indeed a handful, and Martha asks innocently, "A handful of what?" He suggestively offers her a cigar, then a ten-dollar gold piece, and she runs away. The plot is sprung.

Back in the McEvoy home, Bobby has "gone to run crazy in the woods like an Indian." The family doesn't know what to do with their one-legged heathen child and his "kindly infidel ways." The father Patrick says, "He's just got a troubled heart and they dont nobody know why." Back at the factory with Mr. McEvoy, the foreman Giles says of his boy not showing up for work, "But them that choose to toil not neither do they spin has got to berth elsewhere." Bobby's gone.

Two years later, chewing tobacco and spitting off a boxcar, Bobby rides the rails home to Graniteville with his crutch and tattered carpetbag, only to find two black gravediggers at work on his mother's grave in the company cemetery. He throws the men off the hill, and one says looking back, "I knowed when I seen you you was trouble." The troubles, indeed, toll across the Big Water to northern Ireland.

Three witchy ladies serve as hired weepers at the mother's coffin, and Robert throws them out too. Martha discusses burying their mother at the old Pickens homestead, but Robert says with tragic underbite, "When trouble once finds a house it stays on. You caint get shed of it." Martha says he's still her brother, and Robert counters, "The good book says all men are brothers but it dont seem to cut no ice, does it?" Generational brotherly love has worn thin in the milltown.

Robert goes to the family's deserted greenhouse looking for his father. "Ye'll not find him here," an old man says. Patrilineal troubles ring ominous bells. "Just cause a thing aint used is no need to beat it to death with rocks," the old man says of the run-down greenhouse.

Father Patrick is no longer the gardener, "Not no more he aint." Robert mouths the boiler-plate McCarthy line of an uneasy character, "I got to get on." The old man taps the trouble-bell ironically for the fourth time, "You want wrong to of come here. Trouble sends folks back to places where they knowed better times."

Bobby goes "huntin my old man" down the Gregg lane and meets a dignified black servant with a lantern who seems to know him. Where would you be if you were my pap? Bobby asks. The old man tells a story of lying in his own drunken vomit the night his wife Ella died. "Aint proud of it, but I give up lyin same as I done drinkin." Robert wants to know what quitting booze and lying got him. "It aint what it got me. It's what it got me from," the grandfatherly black says, and Bobby asks what that was. "Death. I seen his face. I know where he uses. How he loves the unready." Bobby says prophetically that death loves us all. The old man calls after the crippled boy hobbling into the night. "I know your heart is full. Dont spend your grief amongst fools. You listen to this old nigger. You hear?"

Bobby goes to a barn where Pinky and half a dozen crackers are drinking from a jar of muleshoe white whiskey, passing a chaser raw potato around as they play cards. Pinky says of Bobby's father, "A finer son of a bitch never wore shoe leather," and the boys proceed to get drunk through the night. "It's kindly slack times here," Pinky adds and asks if Bobby wants to work at the mill and he says no way. "I hear ye. Only way to get ahead down there is to get your wife knocked up by the boss. Give ye a little leverage." The good old boys get drunker talking about the millowner patriarch not drinking, "I guarangoddamntee ye." He adds that "niggers runnin crazy killin folks" in their county. It's Centennial 1876 and things haven't much changed since the Confederate war, though that changed most everything.

Robert shows up at James Gregg's office still looking for his father, and the new owner tries to throw the impudent commoner out saying they don't need his kind there. One insult leads to another, the two sons losing no love between them. Gregg offers McEvoy the ten-dollar gold piece he tossed at his sister and reaches for a drawer gun and the latter shoots him twice. "You raggedyassed crippled son of a bitch," the wounded owner groans, and the foreman rushes in as Confederate Captain Gregg says, "Mr Giles, he's murdered me." McEvoy runs into the street and Gregg tries to shoot him from the balcony, and the former shoots him a third time, as his father Patrick comes up and takes away the pistol. Mrs. Gregg rides by the mill office begging God not to take her son.

The scene cuts to the Aiken County courthouse and a jury of nine black and three white jurors reversing light and dark-colored clothes. Wiggins the black prosecutor for the defense reads the indictment tonelessly. The white defense attorney OC Jordan assures Patrick McEvoy that his son will go free, but all the witnesses concur that Robert shot James. The black Yankee lawyer WJ Whipper later lectures the father, "A lawyer aint a priest. Nor a doctor. Law's more vagrant than sickness or sin." They make their case and say they would be fools to surmise what a dozen other fools might think. Whipper adds that if men were no more just than God, there would be no peace in the world. "Everwhere I look I see men trying to set right the inequities that God's left them with." Tempered shades of the judge orating in *Blood Meridian*. The jury finds Robert guilty of murder and sentences him to be hung Friday the thirteenth of June, 1876.

Patrick McEvoy lights a backyard funeral pyre and drags a coffin toward it, as Mrs. Gregg in widow's black is visited by Martha. The Graniteville Mill stockholders run the company now, and the lady will return to Charleston. The Bible tells her not to heed gossip or envy or ingratitude. She pontificates that purity of blood is a trust to those possessed of it and recalls giants in the earth at one time. Martha tries to offer her sympathy, but Mrs. Gregg speaks over the girl. The Gregg family bond to Graniteville was of the spirit, not the flesh, ignoring company profits, family social inequality, and work conditions. The good lady resents the ingratitude of the poor worst. "I suppose I never understood that to an ingrate a generous person is a fool." Martha still cannot put in her consolation, but finally says she's sorry about all this so Mrs. Gregg invites her to stay for tea. Martha awkwardly tries to explain that James meant nothing by offering her the gold piece, and Mrs. Gregg turns indignant, saying her son was right "about you people" in making "fun of my husband's idealism and I wouldnt listen to it." She mocks false sympathy toward poor and downtrodden masses and has the maid show Martha out of the house. "God bless you Mam" are Martha's last words.

Cut to a photographer shooting Robert for death row pictures that might bring a little cash to the shadow catcher as well as the family. "I dont give a big rat's ass," Robert snarls and in the next scene tells his little sister Martha to go have the best life "that anybody ever had in this damned world." Standing on one leg with a black hood over his head, he is hung with no last words. Below the hanging trapdoor, an old doorman carves a piece of wood with his jack-knife as the black wooden coffin is prepared for burial. The Gregg family disinters its dead from the Graniteville cemetery along with the monument to millowner William Gregg.

Many years later, the somewhat truculent young man in the beginning of the screenplay brings flowers to Martha in the state hospital at Columbia. He's well-spoken William Chaffee from Charleston, grandson of Mrs. Gregg. Martha says she always was a fool over flowers, since her father gardened by "a touch with anything growin," but he had no luck with people. She has no kin and will die alone in state care. The young man offers that his mother has the Gregg Bible. A family story that got lost, the murder is the last thing in it. Martha mentions that Bobby is buried somewhere in a nameless grave because her daddy was afraid the doctors would dig him up for the skull. She says her daddy promised that God would know where to hunt him. Martha wonders if God has names for people, since people give names on earth. She wonders if people are not all the same to God. "Just souls up there and no names. Or if he cares what all they done. I dont know why Bobby done what he done. Once people are dead they're not good nor bad. They're just dead." This naif could be shirttail cousin to winsome Rinthy in *Outer Dark*.

Martha often wishes she never had Bobby's picture. "I ort not even to of kept it." She thinks memory serves a person better. "Sometimes I can almost talk to him. I caint see him no more. In my mind. I just see this old pitcher." *Ubi sunt*, the old sagas cry out, where are the dead brothers?

CHAPTER 6

Awakening Frontier Muses:
Suttree

Abandon All Hope Ye Who Enter Here.
—Gates of Hell, Dante's *Inferno*

Suttree and *Blood Meridian* clear the Appalachian way for *The Border Trilogy* and move into the Southwest with historical vengeance. The reader enters the suckhole density of these thick fictions at his own literary risk and nightmarish peril. They are male narratives in the best and worst of that frontier American tradition, men without women or children, homes or towns, conscience or grace. With no condescension or apology, McCarthy sketches a hellish descent into cul-de-sac decadence and male violence, negative moral paradigms at best. In these mid-career, emetic novels the author is draining Appalachian run-off and scouting southwest brush for his most focused writing to come, mining hyperreal history crossing into literary tradition. The dense narrative of a drunken ne'er-do-well and the blood-sodden redundancies in nineteenth-century chronicle of southwest border vigilantes hone McCarthy's fiction toward a hyperreal "threnody," to borrow one of the author's favorite words, literally a holographic, lyricnarrative lament for the dead.

A twenty-year work-in-progress, *Suttree* is a very big novel, an expansive urban departure from country backroads. No longer "carne-vale" goodbye to homebred flesh and blood, *Suttree* wades hip-deep through sodden things of a Southern border city, lost souls, rancid garbage, dreams gone sour, hardcore drunks, small-time thieves come to town—you name it, as with its prototype Joyce's *Ulysses,* this novel's got it, experimental modernist fiction in a decreative tradition going back through Dickens and Smollett to Balzac and Rabelais.

"Dear friend" ring the novel's first words, dropping the reader into the chambered cutting-rooms of the damned, no less than Dante's *Inferno.* The narrative details lower Knoxville by the river, storefront for an inner dark kerneled in philosophical rant and end-times prophesy, the author one of God's barkers on the street corner of bankrupt bookstores, liquor dives, butcher markets, pawn shops, brothels and bars and ill-begotten goodwill stores. Here crawl ancient survivors of ageless deadly sins, cockroach, fly, coyote, and inhuman kind. *"A fine rain of soot, dead beetles, anonymous small bones."*

A prolix opening serves as rambling italicized prelude on primordial survival, *"no soul shall walk save you."* The novel drops to an encampment of damned souls fossilized with limestone scarabs, stinking garbage, and itinerant cast-offs. *"Illshapen or black or deranged, fugitive of all order, strangers in everyland."* Countrymen from all corners of Appalachia sink through cloacal sediment to the bottom of the city by the river. And worse, the true darkness lies among shadows within: *"but lo the thing's inside and can you guess his shape?"* This venomous streaming of consciousness portends the writer's most fecund, fecal rumination on dark and homeless things yet, *"vendors and beggars and wild street preachers haranguing a lost world with a vigor unknown to the sane."*

The opening narrative shadows the beginning of Dickens's last great novel *Our Mutual Friend* with Gaffer Hexam trolling for corpses below London Bridge on the Thames. Sewage gouts gyre around a skiff adrift under the Knoxville bridge, as bottom feeders are hauled in on set lines, "cupreous and dacebright carp." The scribe loads his lexicon like a sawed-off shotgun. The river has "a granular lubricity like graphite." The novel's diction seems a sinkhole of multilingual literacy sluicing into American English—Greek and Latin, Anglo-Saxon and Norman, Scandinavian and American Indian on down to street tribal, literary academic, and gutter stink talk. The cyclonic slush moans and sings in a lyric cesspool, a narrative threnody and archaic lament-song for the damned. A reader doesn't just sit down and read this book, but lives and wrestles with it beyond the long arm of the thought police. There's no holding back. Either you jump in and wade the murky waters for days, or back away.

A bloated, crazed-grin suicide in seersucker and yellow socks is dredged with a grapel hook through his skull. "Hey Suttree," someone sings out to the main man. "Git ye a tater," an old ragpicker invites at his river campfire, a voice of the hillcountry past. This is the Tennessee River near Knoxville, more open water surface and concrete landscape than the earlier fictions, less mountain hollow and inbred constriction—varied voices, literary ranges, lyric highs and prosaic lows, culture down through subculture.

Suttree lives alone without resources in a shantyboat and trolls for finny trash feeders to make a living. In the Daedalean voice of a modernist ruminating the opening of *Ulysses,* Sut regards the "tumid river" as Roman "Cloaca Maxima," considers wasteland death by drowning the worst fate, references Christian martyr "odor of box-wood" and "fisher of men." His mother's drunken brother John pays an unannounced visit as personal details begin to layer the story, a first family portrait in McCarthy's fiction, soon aborted, since families don't go very far in this writer's schema. Stated earlier in screen-play, the novelist gives precious few biographical or personal details to read character or action. The reader sees and considers everything firsthand, figures it out for himself, and draws individual conclusions from the primary data.

Suttree is not a country cracker, but a literate black sheep of the family, some argue a fictive persona for the author. He has sisters, an off-stage brother Carl, and a stillborn unnamed twin, and he's been estranged from kin since getting out of the "goddamned" peniten-tiary back in January. Workhouse, he corrects his uncle on the mater-nal distaff side of his lineage, his father having married down. "Blood will tell," Suttree defends his fallen familial condition and rebuffs the avuncular sot come calling. God help you, Uncle John says leaving abruptly in a huff.

The action turns to Jimmy Smith's joint. "What'll you have, Sut." A Redtop beer doesn't do it, and he's soon engaged in poker back-room chatter, drinking Early Times homebrew with J-Bone and Nig who "aint almost too sorry to drink." Hazelwood raps of stinking inside out on that bathtub shit, his "liver quiver" and burned clothes the residue. There follow clotted narrative descriptions of the town and richly inebriate tone shifts, a present-tense speaker "I" entering on page twenty-eight with mention of a dark-dream father figure. The narrative teeters past to present, omniscient to firstperson per-sonal on a city walk through dear, dirty Knoxville. Suttree thus seems Irish-American kin to Stephen Dedalus in Night-Town, an interior literate gone slumming to forget his artistic or worldly callings. "A brimstone light. Are there dragons in the wings of the world?" his voice asks. "I will be hard and hard. My face will turn rain like stones."

At this point the scene shifts radically. "Somebody has been fuckin my watermelons," a farmer's voice says in unregenerate country humor. "It aint funny. A thing like that. To me it aint." Backstory

Gene Harrogate, the eighteen-year-old "moonlight melon mounter," gets a sideways load of buckshot and a stint in the workhouse upper-bunk above Suttree who regards him as an "adenoidal leptosome," but looks out for the callow young man of pure heart and pulsing gonads through the unseemly reality of raw prison life. This is no novel for the naive or innocent reader. Suttree's mother visits her Buddy at Christmas and springs him, as Harrogate runs away.

The book grounds itself 1951 in Market Street, Knoxville, Tennessee. Suttree strolls the city selling river catch, much as Poldy Bloom walks Dublin at mid-day. Sut is right away back in the Sanitary Lunch with Boneyard and Hoghead nipping from a sacked bottle of homebrew. J-Bone's fart clears the diner. They bag their party to the Huddle Tavern with whores, transsexuals, and fellow sots whose names tell all, Worm, Cabbage, Bearhunter, Blind Richard, Red, Trippin Through the Dew. Sut vomits bile into the toilet, a hazy scene parsed in evocative, spondaic blank verse: "A *beard* of *dried black shit hung* from the *por*celain and a *clot* / of *stained pa*pers *rose* and *fell* with a *kind* of ob*scene brea*thing." It may be a low literary talking point for scholars. Sut's interior monologue again invokes a poet manqué haunted by the dead: "Sinister abscission, did I see with my seed eyes his thin blue shape lifeless in the world before me?" He asks who "mansized" visits him in dreams and whether shades nurture. "As I have seen my image twinned and blown in the smoked glass of a blind man's spectacles I am, I am." The puke-caked derelict is dumped in the weeds outside town, a black shanty hole called McNally Flats where he notices trilobites in a retaining wall. "Cornelius Suttree" gives his full name to a woman porch-sitting on Grand Avenue and hears the "lyrical shitbird" thrush singing "Mavis. Turdus Musicus." His school Latin fungos the lyric delirium tremens of stinking gutters and septic pools, a too-smart drunk now gut-wrenching sick to the bone.

Country mouse Gene Harrogate walks the city, too, bringing another detailed plethora of low-life into focus, along with kudzu and pokeweed and a botanical jungle of Tennessee shrub life. A viperous evangelist leans out the window and calls him a child of darkness, back-noting a prior fiction, and screams Die! "Perish a terrible death with thy bowels blown open and black blood boiling from thy nether eye, God save your soul amen." Along with "Hoghead's huckleberry insouciance," hillbilly Harrogate now lives uptown as a city rat, country cousin no more.

Suttree rows out of the city to the north shore of fine homes and childhood memories, past river immersion baptismals, docking in his past with Aunt Martha t' home and a family picture album of the disremembered days. "Old distaff kin coughed up out of the vortex, thin and cracked and macled and a bit redundant." His mother's humble people claim him, though cast-off nephew Suttree keeps literary distance. "Blind moil in the earth's nap cast up in an eyeblink between becoming and done. I am, I am. An artifact of prior races." Uncle Clayton invites him to a drink, but like all McCarthy protagonists Sut is just leaving when he arrives. He's got to go. He visits the deserted and ghosted homeplace mansion with its ruined gardens, finding no solace or childhood anchorage for his skiff-and-houseboat life. Back on the river in town, Harrogate kills a shoat belonging to one Rufus Wiley and has to work off his theft for a "nigger," the beginning of this callow cracker's urban education.

The novel hoists ballast with a message taken by J-Bone that Suttree's old man wants him to call back. Sut responds that people in hell want ice water. He asks Jim who's dead, and J-Bone finally says, "Your little boy." Suttree is instantly on a train toward the Cumberlands bridging Appalachia to the midlands. "Fencerails, weedlots, barren autumn fields sliding blackly off under the stars." The reader drops into the character's grief-mute boyhood. He has been visited nightly by "gibbons and gargoyles, arachnoids of outrageous size." Somewhere beyond the smoking millstacks on a gray barren plain the cold rain falls in a new dug grave.

Suttree approaches the family house of his abandoned wife, and horrified she begs him to go away. Her mother, "axemark for a mouth and eyes crazed with hatred," attacks and bites him as the father goes for a shotgun. Sut runs for his life. The funeral parlor tells him the burial will be that afternoon at McAmon Cemetery, and he paces mid-America to the Irish-American gravesite just as his son's coffin is going down. Choked with sorrow, our man lays his head against a tree. The writing is understated until a vestige of metaphysical voices speak to the dead gathering in the fiction. "And who is this fool kneeling over your bones, choked with bitterness? And what could a child know of the darkness of God's plan? Or how flesh is so frail it is hardly more than a dream."

Father himself fills in his son's grave as the diggers stand aside and a paunchy officer in tan gabardines orders him into a squad car. "You, my good buddy," the sheriff says, "are a fourteen carat gold plated son of a bitch." He gives Suttree five dollars bus fare to get out of town and never come back. A real smart boy from that university, Sut has ruined the life of a good friend's daughter and is no longer welcome around these parts. The sheriff does him the favor of dismissal rather than jail. Sut uses the money to buy a bottle of whiskey, as he thumbs his road-scrapping way back to the Knoxville slums by the river.

Low-life goes on in detail. Now the city mouse, Harrogate rows a tin coracle of welded car hoods about the river, ingeniously poisoning bats for bounty. Indian Michael catches a record eighty-seven pound blue catfish and makes turtle soup for his Irish pal. Ab Jones needs the dwarf voodoo healer Mother She to doctor his wounds from street brawling, but won't go to see his "nigger woman." Leonard's old man, unreported as dead for six months to keep drawing his family pension, is dumped into the river. More brawls and dead bats, broads and river burials, the endless deadbeat life of the lower city bridging "niggertown." Harrogate burrows the underground Civil War caves toward the city bank vaults and dynamites a sewer main and spends four days covered in absolute dark slime. Everybody has a vice story. The novel doesn't go anywhere in particular, just sinks deeper into the low-life refuge of the lost and forgotten, and down there it burbles and cusses on, McCarthy's personal Night Town. The voodoo crone knows Suttree's fate and says he should have come alone. "Give over, Graymalkin," the narrative goes high Gaelic again, "there are horsemen on the road with horns of fire, with withy roods."

So in fable fashion Suttree takes an autumnal retreat through Gatlinburg without booze to the mountains where he goes crazy feral to lose and find himself. The falling golden leaves rushing like poured coins in the tail water tell him something about the perishable currency of temporality. In the grandfather time a ballad spoke of a beautiful girl drowned here, looking up through trout bellies to "the well of the rimpled world beyond," a scene cached for the end of *The Road* thirty years later in McCarthy's canon. Suttree finds a viper under a rock, "little brother death with his quartz goat's eyes," and wild chestnuts and mushrooms "frangible, mauvebrown and kidney-colored" that may or may not be deadly. What's the difference? Sut ponders. The wind soughs long and wild, the dark is cold and indifferent, the stars blind to this hermit with a long beard and clothes hanging like fallen leaves.

Suttree begins to dream of elves and discourse with birch and oak, the "old distaff Celt's blood" stirring dead footsteps, scarce telling where his being ends or the world begins nor does he care. In a children's cemetery a raindrop sings on a stone. Another figure goes before him, "some doublegoer, some other suttree," his stillborn twin eluding and threatening to drive him insane. He sees carnival figures and harlots and phantasms until a small crossbowman appears, and Suttree doesn't know whether he's real or illusory. "You're lost or crazy or both," the bowman in overalls snarls and directs the mad outcast with a "baleful heart" down the mountain toward Bryson City, North Carolina. "In his darker heart a nether self hulked above cruets of ratsbane, a crumbling old grimoire to hand, androleptic vengeances afoot for the wrongs of the world. Suttree muttering along half mindless, an aberrant journeyman to the trade of wonder."

The pilgrim vision quester emerges in a town that won't have him or serve him soup, and he begins to cry old winter griefs, "half blind with a sorrow for which there was neither name nor help." Suttree takes a bus to Knoxville where Mrs. Long looks after him in the poor house. Tennessee kin to Hamlet, he contemplates suicide: "Could a whole man not author his own death with a thought?"

Homeless Cornelius Suttree is back home in lower Knoxville where life is pretty much the same as he left it some months ago—to a letter from his mother, left unread, and a three hundred dollar check from another dead uncle, which buys him new clothes and ox-blood zipper shoes, a drunk reborn. There follows a pastoral interlude of sorts with a shanty family picking mussels off low-water shoals upriver, replete with a whorehouse romp and a tender outdoor romance over his partner's lusty virginal daughter Wanda Reese, pregnant and killed in a slate rockslide wiping out their camp. Cornelius has had a moment of respite, at rest on earth touched by lowly love, his separate peace only to be torn violently away.

Back to a deserted shantytown where Sut tells the ragman, "We're all right," and he responds, "We're all fucked." Our man stands in a thunderstorm and calls down the lightning to char his bones. Billy Ray Callahan is shot to death, and Suttree winters in a coal furnace basement of a McAnally boarding house. Again he returns to tavern Redtop beer, a red-headed street preacher haranguing a crowd of wastrels over a turnip, and more of the same pulsing slums. "An emaciated whore eyed him as he entered, a stringy sloe-eyed cunt with false teeth and a razorous pelvis beneath the thin dress she wore." Sut goes outside and sits on a stone curb with his back against a pole, "a silent dweller in a singing wood."

Cornelius takes up with a Chicago whore named Joyce, "not unlovely" in his basement bed. Her "sheer outrageous sentience" proves "the very witch of fuck." Soon they are calling each other lover and baby, another set-up for Suttree's heart to shatter, love with a bisexual Kentucky hustler in a rattrap flophouse. With her nighttown earnings the prostitute finances their sodden tryst and in "womby lassitude" Sut submits to her pleasures. Suttree and his soiled dove live for a while in style. They buy a 1950 Jaguar roadster and drive to Ashville, North Carolina for an unlicensed honeymoon. Joyce soon ages fat and mad, kicking out the car window, and Sut walks away to his houseboat, fishing alone again in uneasy peace.

Suttree has a last-word conversation with his *doppelgänger* in an ovoid of lamplight. "I'd say I was not unhappy," he says if he died. "I believe that the last and the first suffer equally. Pari passu." Repenting nothing, Cornelius opines to his inquisitor double that all souls are one not just alone in the dark of death. Dreams of orgasmic toil show him that envy is the "color of her pleasuring, and what is the color of grief?" Not depressive black or angry red, he sees, "a bitter blue, rue-tinged, discolored at the edges." His dream vision of the blues concludes, "The color of this life is water." A transparent fluidity, base animate matter. Such are the lyric stirrings of illumination, rumination, and prophesy in McCarthy's middle fiction, the need to hold philosophic parley over narrative denouement.

Death and epidemic violence ensue with hellish realism. "And in the dawn a female simpleton is waking naked from a gang-fuck in the back seat of an abandoned car by the river." The desecration is uncensored. The narrator notes that her "cunt looks like a hairclot fished from a draintrap." The black geechee doctor, Mother She, gives Suttree a potion inducing dream visions of past and present misshapen worlds, the dreamer a medieval hero led by a small black gnome. He nightmares feverish erotics of a mother-lover's "shriveled cunt puckered open like a mouth gawping," the boy helpless "in the grip of a ghast black succubus." So as a younger Buddy he goes to see Aunt Alice in the madhouse where she recalls him as Grace's son, and he realizes ironically that he's the son of grace (so the author is "Grail's son" of Gladys McGrail). The family history is a string of names and mishaps well forgotten, tracing to a granduncle hanged publicly.

Back in Knoxville, cigar-smoking Gene is on the lam from a telephone scheme gone static, and Sut takes him in, only to have the country cousin arrested and sent up for his first robbery. Ab Jones, the black Ajax, is sick to death and apprehended on the streets where Suttree drives a cop car into the river. Cornelius has more fever visions and sexual nightmares, here typhoid hallucinations, and Mr Bones, or Father Bones, visits him from the dead. J-Bone takes him to the hospital where tavern ghosts visit him in dreams, a section recalling the Night-Town nightmare riot in *Ulysses,* "foul perverts one and sundry" at his bedside. There follows a nun's catalogue of his company with the damned, all the lonely alone and only one: "Thieves, derelicts, miscreants, pariahs, poltroons, spalpeens, curmudgeons, clotpolls, murderers, gamblers, bawds, whores, trulls, brigands, topers, tosspots, sots and archsots, lobcocks, smell-smocks, runagates, rakes, and other assorted and felonious debauchees." He confesses existentially to a dream priest, "I learned that there is one Suttree and one Suttree only."

J-Bone springs Sut from the hospital, and they return to find McAnally Flats being torn down for an expressway. Cornelius discovers a yellow maggoty corpse in his houseboat bed and reacquaints one last tramp, the black transvestite whore Trippin Through the Dew. "Best luck in the world baby," she says, and Suttree wishes him the same. Sut leaves Front Street heading west, trailed down the new expressway by death's hound and huntsman. "His work lies all where and his hounds tire not," the ending goes medieval. "I have seen them in a dream, slaverous and wild and their eyes crazed with ravening for souls in this world. Fly them."

Where Suttree wanders out west no man knows nor does the novelist venture to tell.

CHAPTER 7

Go Bloody West: *Blood Meridian*

He was broad-shouldered and deep-chested
with a clear steady blue eye.

—Captain John Fremont on Kit Carson

Blood Meridian, Or the Evening Redness in the West is a queer piece of fiction painstakingly researched from the southwest Mexican-American wars spilling across national treaties toward *The Border Trilogy* taking place a century later. The main documentary sources seem General Samuel E. Chamberlain's *My Confession,* John Woodhouse Audubon's *Audobon's Western Journal, 1849–1850,* and Mayne Reid's *The Scalp-Hunters.* In far west tone, prairie desert locale, horseback vigilante character, marauding violence, and big sky cataclysm, *Blood Meridian* departs from woodland hill country, as its main character leaves Tennessee at fourteen for the wild west. So, too, McCarthy divorced his second wife and left Knoxville for good in 1976, moved to El Paso, Texas, and quit drinking. He learned Spanish and road-researched southwest history, publishing *Blood Meridian* nine years later.

McCarthy's teenage protagonist is a kid who could be modeled on blue-eyed Irish, mule-riding Kit Carson born the same year as Abe Lincoln in Kentucky, or balladeer Billy the Kid (Henry McCarty/ Antrim) Bonney from New York City, or a fourteen-year-old pony express rider William Frederick Cody from Kansas, later known as Buffalo Bill of the Wild West Show. Hyperreal boys among cows, outlaws, and varmints are plentiful down west.

The subtitle as Victorian storyline marquee portends a bloody sunset romance of the prairies, and the running chapter taglines serve as plot markers for a dime novel. The fiction seems to rise from a black-and-white silent film with off-tune player piano and a grinding projector, just as Johnny Depp's naif William Blake and Gary Farmer's Native Nobody emerge from the film noir western *Dead Man,* a Jim Jarmusch underground classic. So, too, the introductory quotes seem odd for this book: Paul Valéry the French *symboliste* aesthetician and poet lecturing on "your" faint hearts full of "terrifying" ideas of "blood and time"; Jacob Boehme the medieval mystic prophesying that "death and dying are the very life of darkness"; the *Yuma Daily Sun* for June 13, 1982 citing archaeological findings of a scalped Ethiopian fossil skull 300,000 years old. The tag-line headers imply an artistic tradition of terrible massacre, a visionary history of dark blood sacrifice, and early Paleolithic proof of ritual mutilation.

"See the child," the story opens, a boy born November 1833 in the Year of the Falling Stars, as recorded all over North America in tribal winter counts and weekly newspapers. Is this our male American heritage? "He can neither read nor write and in him broods already a taste for mindless violence. All history present in that visage, the child the father of the man." Wordsworth's Immortality Ode notwithstanding, the oddly innocent-eyed boy lights out for the Western territories down Huck Finn's old man river from St. Louis, brawling "all races, all breeds" on a New Orleans gambling boat, to be stripped of his past. Cleansed of history, the lawless reborn hero faces an old challenge whether a man's will can shape creation or whether his heart is a different make of clay. The cards remain out on this debated charge of mind over matter, free choice over fated genetics.

At sixteen during the 1849 California gold rush and all other trails loaded west, the nameless kid sees a parricide hanged at a crossroad village and rides an aged mule to Nacogdoches, the oldest city in Texas, straddling the border of an uneasy peace between lone star cowboys and Old Mexico. The odd place name Nacogdoches comes from Caddo Indians in the old days. The founding tribe sent one twin brother three days east into Louisiana, the other brother toward the setting sun to mark their western boundary in Nacogdoches. A cigar-smoking, seven-foot, albino hulk "bald as a stone" called "the judge" treacherously fingers a witless, tent-meeting preacher for child molestation and bestiality, and during the necktie melee the giant accuser har-hars the kid with a drink in a rough saloon of fugitives, thieves, and murderers. In this beginning lies the end. How much good old boy abusive fun is this read going to be?

A gargoyle named Toadvine, with plastered mud coiffure, no ears, and the branded letters H, T, and F triangled into his forehead, mangles the kid in the street, then shoots Old Sidney and burns down the hotel, and runs away laughing maniacally. The kid looks for his escape mule, and in the backgroud we hear the first Spanish in McCarthy's new western terrain, "Hay un caballero aquí. Venga." The kid gallops madly past the smiling judge and the old stone fort west of town.

"Now come days of begging, days of theft." An unsteady time sense shifts to present, the evenly paced chapter breaks with running plot-tags marking the novel as faux pulp fiction for the common reader. "Days of riding where there rode no soul save he." Some medieval offshoot of older English, the writing takes on syntactic inversions, tightened cadences, carved edgings of barren plains rhythms, and dry local diction. The kid finds a demented anchorite who grants him a sup of water at the well hole and invites him to "bring ye possibles" into his desert hovel. This is a hungry land, he warns, so don't leave the saddle, "out yonder somethin'll eat it." The mad hermit stakes the ground of his denuded territory. "I take it ye lost your way," he says, meaning the boy must be lost to have come here. He himself was once a Mississippi slaver, but got sick of the business and carries a black man's mummified heart as talisman, claiming four things can destroy the earth: "Women, whiskey, money, and niggers." With such disgust was the West won. They go shares on the fetid kettle remains of a prairie hare, and the old man talks hardscrabble philosophy à la surrogate semantic author. "A man's at odds to know his mind cause his mind is aught he has to know it with." A man can know his own heart, but he doesn't want to know such a thing. When God made man, the hermit sneers, the devil bent his elbow, allowing humans to make self-perpetuating evil for a thousand years. The kid is not much of a believer. Next morning he splits without adieu and meets up with a cattle drive headed by a mix of "cross-breeds some, free niggers, an indian or two," followed by packs of wolves, coyotes, and Indians. Passing a deadcart of corpses, the kid finds a bar where no one speaks American and shatters a bottle over a barman's head, cramming the jagged neck into the man's eye as he falls. No puerile pushover or mommy's boy, the kid takes a bottle for himself and walks out the swinging door. Damnation awaits him.

A slick recruiter for Captain White's rebel army headed into Mexico tells the kid naked in the brush to hellfire come on out, he's white and Christian. The border war is over, the Alamo avenged, but these trueblood vigilantes plan to liberate Sonora from Mexicans and get rich on war spoils.

> Kindly fell on hard times aint ye son? he said.
> I just aint fell on no good ones.

You ready to go to Mexico?

I aint lost nothing down there.

It's a chance for ye to raise ye self in the world.

Captain White gives a rousing patriotic speech about freeing land rightly American and tags the Mexers degenerates. "A mongrel race, little better than niggers. And maybe no better." He argues the old imperial cant that outsiders will come to govern a people who cannot manage themselves. "Hell aint half full," a crazed Mennonite warns the armed adventurers setting out to claim their pirate booty.

Ten days out and four men dead on the desert, the sun as foretold in the subtitle rises flushed in the east as seeping blood, then from night's nothing "like the head of a great red phallus" flattens into a squat, pulsing, malevolent white ball. It looks like the high road to hell, a man says of the vast malpais flats. The landscape grows surreal and they ride at night under sheet lightning. "Tethered to the polestar they rode the Dipper round while Orion rose in the southwest like a great electric kite." A scalphunter kneels and prays under the thunder and wind, "Lord we are dried to jerky down here. Just a few drops for some old boys out here on the prairie and a long ways from home." Scattered drops do fall, then "heathen stockthieves" show up for a little sport that goes bad. Beyond the herd "there rose a fabled horde of mounted lancers and archers," and the Comanche attack begins, "a legion of horribles" that swells into roiling unpunctuated paragraphs of slaughter, screeching, scalping, mutilating, and gore-soaked savages "who fell upon the dying and sodomized them with loud cries to their fellows."

A handful of eight or so recruits survives the attack, and the kid sets out with the wounded Sproule, fugitive and bloody. They come upon a mesquite bush with dead babies hung by their lower jaws "to stare eyeless at the naked sky," then a blood-gouted village of corpses, on across "a terra damnata of smoking slag" with Sproule's arm maggoty and no place to "hide at." Mexican soldiers mock them and ride on. Attacked by a bloodbat in the night, Sproule lets out "a howl of such outrage as to stitch a caesura in the pulsebeat of the world." The kid only spits and says he knows his kind. "What's wrong with you is wrong all the way through you." They are captured by yet more Mexican nationals and dragged into a village where the eyeless severed head of Captain White, "lately at war among the heathen," is passed in a mescal jar around a bazaar. The kid spits again and says, "He aint no kin to me." At the end of the gore-cadenced chapter, the kid meets a fellow long-haired captive who grins and mutters, "You dont know me, do ye?" The kid spits again and growls at the skull-branded, earless Toadvine, and says he'd know his hide in a tanyard.

The prisoners sign up with makeshift captain Glanton, his sidekick giant Holden called simply the judge, motley black- and white-recruits, and their "reeking horde" of hideous Delawares. They are in some ways a hellish historical footnote to Ahab's crew aboard the *Pequod*. The head-hunters ride upcountry through the mesquite and prickly pear, cholla and nopal trailed by a gypsy family of clowns. With his new rifle-bore Colt pistol, Glanton shoots an old squaw through the head and scalps her for the $200 bounty offered by Chihuahua state governor Angel Trias to stop Indians from stealing horses, documented cross-border history of the times. An old man prays over his poor Mexican country, thirsty beyond the blood of a thousand Christs, and warns the glossed Tejanos, "When even the ones is gone in the desert the dreams is talk to you, you don't wake up forever." A knife-wielding, black vigilante named John Jackson decapitates a white drunk of the same name before the evening campfire, again a documented event. The crazed killing mounts, body parts litter the desert, and the bones lie mute though telling—a necklace of ears, creosote-tasting mescal, the "crumpled butcherpa-per mountains." Apaches attack in shrieks "like the cries of souls broke through some misweave in the weft of things into the world below." McCarthy's hyperreal terrors run full throttle.

The judge pilfers dark bone talismans and scalps a dead warrior, and the killers ride on all day. They find a ravaged carriage stinking bad enough to drive a buzzard off a gutcart, then a compound of dying prospectors who first ask for whiskey, next tobacco. Holden holds forth in epic blasphemy that God only "speaks in stones and trees, the bones of things," not books, and later that night under dry lightning declaims violence as he stands naked atop the walls. An undressed, preteen half-breed is found facedown in one of the stalls next morning, and the reader ponders the naked judge on the bulwarks. The kid stands forewarned.

The misfits ride on without farewell and encounter skin-dressed *ciboleros* returning with dried buffalo meat from the plains and ride on, "each passing back the way the other had come," as all travelers endlessly pursue inversions on other men's journeys. Such are the pointless peregrinations of amoral men without women, children, compassion, or reason, save hunting the skins and meat and scalps of living beasts and unlucky victims. The mindless violence begins to circle back on itself, the tale's low comic dialogue mute.

And so the narrative switches gears. The ex-priest Tobin begins his back monologue to the kid about meeting the "sootysouled rascal" judge perched on a rock alone in the desert. The Dutch-speaking Holden is devilish handy at anything, Tobin swears, ambidextrous with gun, knife, or pen, taking botanical notes as he kills and scalps Indians. He's a first-rate dancer to boot and an even finer fiddler. Recalling rumors of all-cultured Kurtz in *Heart of Darkness,* it's a Daniel Boone or Mike Fink brag out west. "He can cut a trail, shoot a rifle, ride a horse, track a deer." World-traveled Holden speaks with Glanton of "Paris this and London that in five languages, you'd have give something to of heard them." The judge's rifle is inscribed from the classics *Et in Arcadia Ego*—and death also in paradise. With twelve bounty-hunters he made fire-and-brimstone gunpowder from a volcano crown to slaughter a hundred Apaches below. The kids asks what's he a judge of and the ex-priest says hush, the hairless giant has fox ears.

The fiction's historical portrait comes straight from General Chamberlain's *My Confession,* unpublished until 1956, as an army deserter mercenary with Glanton's gang of a hundred or so terrorists after the 1846–1848 Mexican War:

> The second in command, now left in charge of camp, was a man of gigantic size called "Judge" Holden of Texas. Who or what he was no one knew but a cooler blooded villain never went unhung; he stood six feet six in his moccasins, had a large fleshy frame, a dull tallow colored face destitute of hair and all expression. His desires was blood and women, and terrible stories were circulated in camp of horrid crimes committed by him when bearing another name, in the Cherokee nation and Texas; and before we left Frontereras a little girl of ten years was found in the chaparral, foully violated and murdered. The mark of a huge hand on her little throat pointed him out as the ravisher as no other man had such a hand, but though all suspected, no one charge him with the crime.

Judge Holden was the best lettered man in northern Mexico, Chamberlain swears, conversing with everyone in their own tongue and several "Indian lingos." During a fandango he would take the musician's harp or guitar and "out-waltz any poblana of the ball." Darwinian naturalist, geologist, and mineralogist, he was "plum centre" with rifle or revolver and a daring horseman. The Judge knew more about Boston than the General.

A blond bear carries off one of the Delawares in its jaws, and the narrative pauses to praise nameless warriors who learn war by warring and know horrible cultures from afar and are no more alien to violence than to their own hearts. The wild entourage rides "in a narrow enfilade" through mountain passes, "continuing autonomous across the naked rock without reference to sun or man or god." The judge sketches Anasazi flint, potsherd, and bone tool into his leather ledgerbook, then pitches the shards into the fire. A Tennessean named Webster objects to his image being drawn, and the judge paraphrases evolution smiling, "every man is tabernacled in every other and he in exchange and so on in an endless complexity of being and witness to the uttermost edge of the world." Holden tells an Allegheny story of treachery, disguise, and father-son legacies, concluding of the ashen midden before them, "All progressions from a higher to a lower order are marked by ruins and mystery and a residue of nameless rage. So. Here are the dead fathers." And ex-priest Tobin asks the way of raising a child. If God wanted to interfere in mankind's degeneracy of mankind, the judge poses, wouldn't he have done so by now? Orphans all, the "predacious" race of mankind abides by no familial or social laws, says he, and falls silent as a stone icon before the fire.

Horsemen of the apocalypse and "haggard butchers," the bandits scourge the desert and mud villages, slaughtering Indians and Mexicans and scalping everyone. "If we don't kill ever nigger here," captain Glanton says at one point, "we need to be whipped and sent home." The judge plays for several days with a naked Apache boy-child, then serendipitously kills and scalps him like all the rest. Grizzled soldiers of fortune, indentured thugs, and thrill killers ravage the terrain like a plague of locusts. The bandidos enter Chihuahua as conquering heroes bearing war trophies with 128 scalps and 8 heads and fall to a feasting debauchery of yet more fighting and buggering and killing and squalling, then they leave. Ghastly and disgusting, the slaughter grows tediously redundant.

The warmongers ride on into a long red sunset where rainsheets lie on a plain below them "like tidepools of primal blood." Their horses are bedecked with human hair, skin, and teeth, their own clothing festooned with cannibalized body parts, huge pistols stuck in their belts and their skins vile-stained with blood, smoke, and gunblack. They take on a caged idiot eating turds and his keeper brother Cloyce Bell. The note-taking, fossil-sketching judge opines that whatever in creation exists without his knowledge exists without his consent. He would be the "suzerain of the earth," as a Faulkner dement would trace his sovereignty back to Adam's "dominion" over all living things in Genesis. "The freedom of birds is an insult to me. I'd have them all in zoos."

The troupe never brings in the head of Gómez the Apache rebel, but they meet and warily circle the giant Mangas Colorado's Chiricahua Apaches, losing and recruiting mercenaries from pueblos they ravage or destroy. The East Coast mercenary Delawares are finally all slain. Fictive brother to Melville's Captain Ahab, Glanton stares into the fire embers and swears "he'd drive the remorseless sun on to its final endarkenment as if he'd ordered it all ages since." The narrator holds by Prometheus that "each fire is all fires, the first fire and the last ever to be." Anything is possible, the judge vows the truth, and pontificates satanically that the world is but "a hat trick in a medicine show, a fevered dream." The dark sophist wagers that men are born for games, war being the ultimate contest, indeed, "god." The judge says it makes no difference what men think, war endures. "As well ask men what they think of stone."

Ex-priest Tobin does not gainsay that religion aligns with war. "Nihil dicit," the judge drawls, the priest "would be no godserver but a god himself." Finally Holden says they are all fools wanting to know the unknowable. Their heart's desire is to be told some mystery, but the true mystery is that there is none, only the judge's notes and judgments. He stands before them pharisee of hyperreal megalomania. They reach the Colorado River and prepare to cross toward California, then commandeer the ferry and build a fortress, and the judge naked at night pulls the drowning idiot from the waters, "a birth scene or a baptism or some ritual not yet inaugurated into any canon."

Yuma Arizona Indians counterattack, kill black Jackson in his flowing robes, and axe "the head of John Joel Glanton to the thrapple." With a cannon under one arm, the naked judge towers over an undressed twelve-year-old girl and the slavering idiot on his bedroom floor, then absconds into the woods with the idiot. The savages heap a cremation fire with the corpses of the slain scalp-hunters, including the less invincible Glanton.

Toadvine and the kid fight their way to open country where they stumble across the desert to find ex-priest Tobin at a well, still shooting at advancing Indians who finally withdraw. In the morning the judge, bandoliered with raw meat and a mud-straw hat, and the imbecile with a rag-fur bonnet, both naked, stagger into the camp. The judge buys Toadvine's hat for a hundred and twenty-five dollars and orates on the desert that they are all here together. "Yonder sun is like the eye of God and we will cook impartially upon this great siliceous griddle I do assure you." Toadvine hesitates, "You wouldnt think that a man would run plumb out of country out here, would ye?" The priest implores the kid to shoot the judge below in the well, but he

holsters his pistol and the two set out across the desert like bedraggled pilgrims, leaving Toadvine to his own devices.

With recently encountered Brown's rifle, the judge snipes at the
kid behind sheep bonepiles, and the kid fires back, the ex-priest
whispering behind his ear to shoot the fool, then disappearing into
the sand. By late afternoon the ex-priest stumbles back toward the
well with a ram-shin cross "like some mad dowser in the bleak of
desert and calling out in a tongue both alien and extinct." The judge
wings the priest through the neck, and the kid blasts the two enemy
horses, and the pair escape on foot in the night to another hiding
boneyard, trailed by the judge and the imbecile.

The judge arrives, passes, and returns under a rib-bone parasol
with the idiot on a rawhide leash. "You alone were mutinous," he
calls out to the kid. "You alone reserved in your soul some corner of
clemency for the heathen." Show no mercy, take no prisoners. The
surreal judge and his tethered charge pass a third time and disappear
into the desert.

California Diegueño Indians find the desiccated pilgrims and take
them home to San Felipe where they are fed piñole. The pair treks to
San Diego and the end of their journey at the sea, as much of migrant
America floods after. The kid sits watching the hissing sun dip in the
waves as his horse stands dark against the sky and the surf booms into
the night: "the sea's black hide heaved in the cobbled starlight and
the long pale combers loped out of the night and broke along the
beach." Soldiers arrest the kid, and he wakes to find the freshly sarto-
rial judge outside his cell. Holden calls the kid to come up. "Dont you
know that I'd have loved you like a son?" He claims the kid betrayed
a patriarchal killing trust and by law must hang, and then he harangues
again on the sanctity of violence. "If war is not holy man is nothing
but antic clay." The judge says what joins men is not sharing bread but
enemies. With that Holden closes his hasp watch and says it's time to
be going and disappears as he came. Only to reappear in the kid's
dreams when he is released and undergoes surgery for the arrow shaft
in his thigh. "Of this is the judge judge," the narrative says of worldly
matters affecting the kid, "and the night does not end." Satan, avenging angel, albino monstrosity, or hyperrealist of paradise lost, the
judge remains the most morbidly captivating character in *Blood
Meridian*. He is reminder alone that the American west was at times
a holocaust of Manifest Destiny and white supremacy, the devil's
genocidal shibboleths.

In Los Angeles the kid witnesses a hanging and discovers that the
dead men are Toadvine and Brown, alive as the judge swore a while

back, now not. The sixteen-year-old descends into the hellpits of *Los,* the angel-less city of murderers, whores, misfits, thugs, and thieves. With his last two dollars he buys the heathen-ear scapular that Brown wore to the gallows. The Tennessee kid wanders the homicide capital of America witnessing its foul deeds, somehow charmed in his still young years. At twenty-eight he heads east with pilgrims going back home, then breaks off and turns his horse north toward the mountains. He passes bleeding barefoot penitentes flagellating themselves with cholla cactus and a hooded man bearing a cross, the Easter party butchered down the trail. The traveler tries to rescue an old woman in a cave, but she had been dead there for years.

In the late winter of 1878, now aged forty-five, the veteran kid is back on the north Texas plains. He comes across an old buffalo hunter by his fire and they exchange stories of this and other worlds. The kid meets buffalo bone pickers who jest about whores in Griffen and ask of his hundred-ear scapular. "Them ears could of come off of cannibals or any other kind of foreign nigger," Elrod says. In self-defense the kid kills a fifteen-year-old Kentucky youth who tries to ambush him and leaves yet more war orphans on the Texas plains.

At Fort Griffin he finds a nondescript bar to parch his blood thirst, and there stands the judge "among the dregs of the earth in beggary a thousand years." The latter says little has changed since they last met, or nothing in all these years. The same story all over again, with more color, perhaps—garish whores, a circus showman, a bear dancing to a female barrel-organ grinder. Then it happens. "Shot the goddamned bear," says the barman, and the judge asks the kid if he thinks it's all over. He elegizes that they are the last of the true, "all gone under now saving me and thee." There's yet time for the dance, hyperrealist Mephisto says of the unborn, but the kid defers, "I got to go," the signature line for a McCarthy protagonist. The judge claims the kid's soul is at stake tonight and waxes poetic on blood rituals and death agony, the only point worth considering—a satanic nihilism of war, will, blood, power, play, rhetoric, and the devil's dance of life and death. The judge himself wants to judge the quick and the dead, and in his petite footwork flows the satanically sanctified blood of war heroes.

A dwarf whore takes the kid by the hand and says she's got to go too. As at his 1833 Tennessee birth, the stars are falling endlessly through the night, and the kid goes out to piss. The hairless, naked, towering judge embraces him by surprise in the jakes. "Good God almighty," a few minutes later a man says looking into the crapper. Whether the kid is dead or not is left uncertain, but certainly he's violated and probably finished. Remember the undressed preteen half-breed facedown in the stall and the naked Apache boy scalped in the judge's thrall.

Holden keeps dancing and will never die, a ballad refrain repeats at the ending. Is the Judge fate himself, lascivious evil, a terrestrial satan as anti-Christ, or just a hulking, albino, bald, pontificating, fake magistrate who takes the place of a slain dancing bear? It's a strangely giddy, ambivalent, endless, and ominous ending about who lives or dies, what dances or doesn't, which kills or is killed down west. Nietzsche knew the nihilistic riff.

In the italic dawn Epilogue, prairie bone-gatherers and hangers-on trail a flame-douser who bores the stone with a steel awl *"striking the fire out of the rock which God has put there."* The motley sparks and scattered bones lie beyond good and evil, a Manifest Destiny of Promethean madness and pointless westering fired from tragedy. As documented by Richard Slotkin and other cultural historians, here reified in fiction, the country regenerates through hellish violence. Like Ahab on the *Pequod* with his harpoon, the douser *"strikes fire in the hole and draws out his steel. Then they all move on again."* The kid is gone, the judge dances, a bloody sun passes east to west through solar meridian. Is the hyperreal penny dreadful done at last? *The Border Trilogy* follows into the twentieth century.

CHAPTER 8

Theater Grotessco:
The Stonemason

Amid a place of stone,
Be secret and exult,

—W. B. Yeats, "To a Friend whose
Work has Come to Nothing"

Hyperreality is grounded in deep earth mysteries. McCarthy has always been interested in stones and stonework, the solid, lasting terra firma in a homeland of restless change, a humanscape of dreams and illusions. The novelist scratches for a fixed base to earthly things, mineral to gaseous. From geologic strata and ancient petroglyphs to Greek middens and Roman walls, medieval roads and Gaelic forts to city gutters and nuclear winter rubble, McCarthy is fascinated with a history of stonework and admires those who hardscrabble the earth, however miserably. "Stacking up stone is the oldest trade there is," he told Woodward in the 1992 interview, "older than fire," and the literary archaeologist found "rather interesting" the loss of stonework to hydraulic cement.

Just so, consider dramatic chiseling as grist for the novels. McCarthy's artistry with stage speech pulls taut the reins on language and form, apprenticing the trade from Greek tragedy through Shakespeare, to Mamet and Pinter. Without much literary precedent, the first three novels drop into Gothic grottos and swell with country diction, everyday dialect, and over-narrative rush. By contrast, the writer's mid-career drama demands condensed action and minimal metaphor, or at least metaphor embedded in plot and action, as Pound argued for "stone-carved" *characters* and the sculpted natural object as image. McCarthy's early fictions tend to go where they will and italicize evil as God's misshapen metaphor. His more focused, select-stage characters and two-hour borders work within classical markers, more or less, of time and space. God stays off-stage.

To mid-career, McCarthy's novels sprawl across time and terrain with any number of major and minor characters. Less expansive, his dramatic action must be temporally arced and structurally crafted, the first act flowing unimpeded to the last words of the last scene. The apprentice fiction wobbles a bit, going here and there and circling back to a touchstone. In live traditional theater, actions engender consequences, and the gun on the wall must go off at the right moment. Guns go off anywhere anytime in the hyperreal fictions, and there don't seem to be identifiable consequences of good or evil. In theater there are observable boundaries of stage, set, and house. Fictive characters in the novels wander off the set and come back through the side door, or simply disappear. A live dramatic audience will walk out on chartless characters and a poor production. The fictional author has little knowledge of reader response, except marketing sales and peevish reviews.

Drama critic and actor-director Peter Josyph would that McCarthy had blotted and restructured considerably more in his hybrid five-act play on stone masonry, but readers can leave the staging to theatrical divas ("Older professions: the fourth wall of *The Stonemason*," *Southern Quarterly,* Fall 1997 and expanded self-referentially in Rick Wallach's *Myth, Legend, Dust*). The whole existential experience of theater pitches toward a focal point—who, how, what, where, when, and why all coming to an end demarcation of sorts. McCarthy's early fiction simply stops when it's played out. Thus despite unblotted complexities, drama is a cutting room for McCarthy's writing to restrict the variegated fictions, to cull his cast of characters to the plot bones, to focus his time-space sense, to restrain his polysemous diction and expansive imagination, to rib his structural through-line, to drill home his hyperreal themes. There is a sense of ending at the end of his dramas, moreso than in the fictions.

Published by The Ecco Press in 1994, *The Stonemason* comes without production credits. The 1992 premier at the Arena Stage in Washington D C was cancelled, due to staff complaints that it was dramatically messy and politically incorrect, and a $25,000 Kennedy Center grant returned. Specifics of the setting, Louisville, Kentucky, February 1971, midnight: *The Stonemason* takes place with four generations of the black Telfair family in an old Victorian house on the Mason-Dixon Line. McCarthy insists that he researched the story living with an actual black stonemason family. It's a five-act play with lower and upper stage levels and bedroom entrances leading off the main kitchen loft. Snow is falling softly in blue light. To the left and one floor below the kitchen set stands a lectern for Ben's monologues. His actor-double sits across the lower stage in a study, suggesting authorial distance and a "completed past," the playwright says. The two Ben doubles are not to Peter Josyph's dramatic liking, among other complaints about the over architected play.

So the drama features twin Ben actors, one for a staged dramatic story and another for an overvoiced reflective Chautauqua. McCarthy is explicit about the "world of the drama on stage" and a "separate space" for Ben the thinker. His full Hebrew name Benjamin, *binyamín*, means "son of the right hand" or favorite son. Black Ben is thirty-two, the martyr-prophet's age when the play opens. He will speak obliquely for the author, especially on stones. "Go forward and faith will come to you," McCarthy quotes the mathematician Gauss to begin the play. A bit cryptic, yes, but true to the dramatic end.

Ben wants to be like his centenarian grandfather Papaw ("pap-aw," the parenthesis directs), a stonemason for ninety years. Young and old man stay up all night talking about things, a wall or a barn foundation, a bridge or a chimney, morality or family. True masonry holds together "by gravity," not cement, Ben says, honoring "the warp of the world" or how things rest against each other and on the earth naturally. He says a wall is made the same way the world is made. There is sap and fire in the living stone, Ben insists, echoing his bible-reading Papaw.

The play begins at family breakfast upstairs. The old-fashioned kitchen has narrow tongue-and-groove wainscoting, the usual chairs and implements from the early 1900s, and a wood-burning stove. Papaw comes into the kitchen from his side bedroom to drink tea and read his bible. Ben's Mama joins the breakfast to keep her father from going to the farm today with his grandson. Her daughter Carlotta enters in high heels for work, followed by Mama's husband Big Ben.

Will there be school today or not, Carlotta's fifteen-year-old son Soldier wants to know and fakes a phone call that school is called off. Not much happens or is said dramatically in the beginning scenes, but the foundations are laid. This will be a four-generation family story with household matters to start, breakfast to supper, an errant fatherless boy, an ancient great-grandpa, two working generations between. The times are changing, but the manumitted Telfair family is still black and trying to tell things fairly, truthfully. Though some secrets are hidden, the deeper fault lines hold things tenuously together, they hope, their old house and older walls anchoring the foundations of family social structure. The play is a form of domestic sociology as dramatic history and finally spiritual prophecy, though some of the female black actors at the Arena Stage found their parts demeaning, and the ensuing ruckus canceled the production. McCarthy does not comment on the aborted production or political incorrection of his play. Thought police are not in his cast.

To the side Ben tells the audience that ten thousand years of masonry make it the oldest trade in human times. You learn things about that history by tearing a wall down and seeing how it is made, a deconstructive creativity, to borrow from critical talk that top-heavy Ben would favor. A mason is his stonework, Ben says, as God is His creation. The world is made of stone—think of it, fossils, gravestones, petroglyphs, roads and buildings and streambeds, hieroglyphs, mountains, ideograms, aboriginal talking rocks—and masonry is older than fire. A mason is the world's "final steward, the final custodian." Nothing lasts as stone lasts. Placing stone on stone by God's laws at the world's beginning and end yields a metaphor for writing the play that will never fail men. God lives in stone word walks, if anywhere on earth. So goes the soliloquy.

Act Two opens with Ben and his wife Maven studying for law school. Ben translates working class into collective knowledge by way of self-taught Marx—the laborer who thinks is a wise man, he says, bridging masonry with intelligence. Papaw adds a warning, "Stone aint so heavy as the wrath of a fool," and the audience hears the beginnings of a cautionary tale as working metaphor for crafted writing.

McCarthy by this time writes from three narrative coordinates in whatever he's doing: action, character, and reflection. His narrative arc tells a story, the what, when, where, and how of the action. His concern with the people's language from low to high adapts the true speech of a multilingual culture, the dialect to dialogue of who's talking about what. A classical play, distinct from a picaresque novel, must work drum-tight, the kind of fit a stonemason requires to set a foundation or wall without mortar. No wasted motion or words, all working together, a movement of all parts through one another to the whole. If not Aristotelian in the twenty-four-hour formula, McCarthy's drama is solid as Greek stonework and classic in its foundational roots, if a bit antiquated for some.

Act Three pivots the dramatic action on Soldier going AWOL from the family and Ben trying to make things right. The doubling of Ben through stage actor and reflective overview establishes an inner narrative and an outer persona, a kind of voice from the stone and off the stone surface, much the way mask and character work in a Yeats Noh play like *At the Hawk's Well*. Family legend has it that Richard Nixon wanted hundred-year-old Papaw to lay a cornerstone for his memorial, but the old man refused "hewn stone" because scripture says no. Actor Ben reads from his desk, taking notes, "And if thou make me an altar of stone thou shalt not build it of hewn stone, for if thou lift up thy tool upon it thou hast polluted it." No graven images, no bondage in Egypt, no religious persecution—the Masonic order claims the children of Israel took up masonry from Egyptian trial. And Ben insists that the trade is learned by doing, not in contemplation—hands-on, proletarian, communal work.

Ben's literate politics run into high gear. He says that all trades begin in the domestic and are corrupted by the state. He considers the Old Testament a revolutionary handbook and freestone masonry the liberation of the masses. No slavery or mortar or hewn stone, only freedom in a man's own hands and what he does with them. "What holds the stone trues the wall," a working knowledge not in mind but blood. Papaw's plumb bob runs true four thousand miles to the center of the earth, "a blackness unknown" to the faithful stone-building generations come before or following "and let the rain carve them if it can." Amen to that, brother.

Rewind to Soldier truant from school. Five years ago they put blacks in jail for sending our kids to school, stage Ben says in disgust, now they want to jail blacks for not sending them. He runs off to find his crying sister's boy and Mama scolds her truculent husband Big Ben. "Trouble comes to a house it comes to visit everbody." It makes her cry for her daughter and her boy, cry for everybody. "They sure aint no satisfaction in it."

Ben finds Jeffrey, a young blood and former Nighthawks hood who lips back to his do-good elder in street stink. "Shit. It's just brother against brother. Shit going down out there dont make no more sense than nothing." Jeffrey disses Uncle Ben, "Man I don't know how old you are. All I know is you livin in the past. I'm livin in the past. History done swallowed you up cept you dont know it." A Harlem street kid in the early 1990s could get a gun easier than a library card and told his arresting officer that you can't just expect to live the rest of your life. Back home, Big Ben needs six thousand dollars from his son, no questions asked or answered. Maven asks whether Ben would tell his sister the truth about her son. Are some things better left unsaid?

Act Four, oddly enough for the transitional dramatic ligature, has all the action and an intermission after the first scene. Podium Ben says absence is the worst suffering for those left behind (as with an unexpected dramatic break?). Soldier's absence is a pall of humiliating guilt to the family now enslaved to the runaway boy. Ben can't fix everything, he's learning, and some walls come down, even whole houses and cultures. Human history including scripture is clear on that point, what goes up must come down. The plot turns on unraveling secrets, loosening foundations, tearing up roots, the nay of the yea in worldly aspirations, politically correct or not.

A claims adjuster named Mason Ferguson shows up to court Carlotta, and brother Ben grills him. An interesting name, Mason, another slave stone-builder now a white-collar insurance clerk, and son-of-Fergus, Gaelic king of the Red Branch heroic cycle in the old days of McCarthy's oppressed ancestors on both sides. "Who Goes with Fergus?" Yeats challenged the "filthy modern tide" of modernist history and state technology.

From his lower stage pedestal Ben lectures on the journeyman's trade as the old meaning of journey, a "day's" travel, one day at a time—a day's work means the mason quits at quitting time. Ben shows prospective clients Papaw's ancient walls, cellars, chimneys, houses, springhouses, and bridges where there are no two stones alike and laid without mortar eighteen levels high. Here Ben has learned from his grandfather's faithful working hands rhythm, pace, and wholeness leading to truth, justice, and peace of mind. Now the "stones come to hand for me."

Just so rise the art of words laid end-to-end in lines or sentences, as Frost writes of mending walls and minding gaps—the patient constructing of paragraphs and scenes, acts and chapters, and whole living works of speech and silence. "So I begin to live in the world," Ben says for the artist, where "Nothing is ever finally arrived at." This is a key point in McCarthy. Bear on with no ending, for to end things would be death, that is, an end to storytelling, literary masonry, or reading pleasure. True mastery is unselfconscious acceptance of the doing alone. Form, design, scale, structure, and proportion run dramatically and kinetically all of a piece. Design rises out of necessity in making the wall stand up. The author's surrogate voice concludes, "He becomes a master when he ceases to wish to be one." The writing is all, the reading or witnessing a reconstructive journeyman's labor. Somewhere someone wants to know, Ben pleads with himself on stage. "Nor will I have to seek him out. He'll find me." In the audience, perhaps here dramatically, or in the study, library, park bench, even school. The monologue seems a bit much to some critics, as with the winding disquisitions and end soliloquies in the novels, still the author strikes his through-line.

Yes, opportunistic evil exists in the world, stage preacher Ben admits, but the spirit resides in all things rather than in none. Knowing nothing explicit of God, the favored son Benjamin knows that "Something knows or else that old man could not know." Something that knows will tell you and also tell you when you stop pretending that you know. Suddenly his wife Maven calls "Ben! Ben!" from downstairs. Their first son is about to be born, named Edward after his great-grandfather Papaw who dies in the next scene. "Oh Papaw," Ben whispers as he holds the old man's lifeless hand. "I didnt want you to go." Papaw is laid to rest out of Egyptian bondage, and Big Ben locks the bathroom door and shoots himself to end the act, consistent with a shattering of tender illusion and momentary grace in all of McCarthy's work.

Act Five opens with the house boarded up, fire dead, kitchen bare, stage Ben leaving, and podium Ben saying the big elm and old dog died and the family moved. "Things that you can touch go away forever." When we die "*will* that namelessness into which we vanish then taste of us?" Man lives in this world only, he says. "Ultimately there is no one to tell you if you are justified in your own house." Orphic as Rilke, dark dreamy as Keats, tender as Fitzgerald's night, Ben rises to elegiac dialogue with himself, a double speaking to his inner brother. "Papaw. Papaw," he grieves his father and his father's father. "Why were you everything to me and nothing to him?"

Ben goes to the porch of a small frame house owned by Mary Weaver, a mid-forties "not unattractive" woman who appears to have been his father's mistress for a decade. "I caint do nothin for you child," she says. Let the dead sleep. Are you here to know about him, she challenges, or about yourself? The old crossroads Oedipal dilemma. "Caint get around that daddy." Ben wanders into anchorite and avatar talk, getting remorseful about the daddy he never really knew and now obsesses on. He's had a cautionary dream of waiting at the door of ultimate justice, his masonry job-book beneath his arm, the pages yellow and crumbling, the ink faded and accounts disappearing, and a deeper voice asks, "Where are the others?" Gaze into your innermost soul "beyond bone or flesh to its uttermost nativity in stone and star and in the unformed magma at the core of creation." Know that "we cannot save ourselves unless we save all ourselves." Ben feels that he did not heed the tribal avatar dream and lost his way.

Soldier, now nineteen, shows up wearing flashy clothes around town, saying he wants to get married and needs the family blessing. Does the girl know about you, his Uncle Ben asks, and Soldier snarls, "She knows all about me, sucker. She knows shit they dont nobody know." All he'll say about her name and age is that "she aint from here."

Without warning Soldier dies of a crack overdose in Room #212 of the Louisville Fairfax Hotel, and Ben is grief-stricken, irate, and denying. Maven tells her husband he has to acknowledge the death to the authorities and his sister Carlotta. "He's still a part of this family, Ben." So the favored son phones the police about his nephew. "Telfair. *His* name. Benjamin. His name was Benjamin." All the plotpoints turn ironically on this recognition, Big Ben, Ben, Benjamin, son of the right hand of God, the favorite son, the dead nephew. And so the minister at the family cemetery among the stone markers quotes scripture that encapsulates McCarthy's key themes around a prodigal son: terrible events, displaced hope, voluntary homelessness, redemptive wilderness, makeshift shelter from the stings of reality. "And horror hath overwhelmed me. And I said, Oh that I had wings like a dove, then would I fly away and be at rest. Lo then would I wander far off. I would lodge in the wilderness. I would hast me to a shelter from the stormy wind and tempest."

Stage actor Ben confesses his guilt for Carly's loss of her boy, and stage-manager Ben dreams of Papaw in a cemetery with a great boundary stone. Recall Moses carrying the tablets down off the mountain, Sisyphus pushing his rock up the slope, Christ's boulder rolled away from his tomb by angels. Ben's sermon concludes that he most needs to learn charity and that small acts of valor are great courage. We each among the elect are on "a journey to something unimaginable." We have nothing but our fathers' counsel to sustain us.

Naked and alone, Papaw appears in the family cemetery, as remaining Ben weeps for joy and his grandfather smiles and holds out his hands. "Shaped in the image of God. To make the world. To make it again and again. To make it in the very maelstrom of its undoing." The Greek root *poeta* means "maker," and modern art is the unmaking of false promises. Holding out his hands in Christian charity, the risen Christ tells Mary Magdalene *noli me tangere,* "you cannot touch me."

Ben falls to his knees and prays for the first time, as ancestors ten thousand years ago prayed for guidance from their dead kin. Again, the oldest word for art comes from the Proto-Indo-European root *ar-,* to "connect," as in arm, arc, arch, articulate, architecture. At the play's end Ben wishes that his grandfather would "guide me all my days and that he would not fail me, not fail me, not ever fail me." It's as close to patriarchy and God as Cormac McCarthy, a fallen Irish Roman Catholic and family black sheep, ever gets. The play may be structurally flawed for some critics, politically incorrect for other audiences, old news for a few postmodernists, but McCarthy like Faulkner goes on record as he understands cultural history personally trying to dramatize black character, family, masonry, pain, and grace in America.

CHAPTER 9

Vacquero, Ride On:
All the Pretty Horses

Cast a cold eye
On life, on death.
Horseman, pass by!

—W. B. Yeats stone epitaph

Begun as an aborted screenplay that no film company wanted ("Cities of the Plain" in the Cormac McCarthy Collection at Southwest Texas State University), *The Border Trilogy* opens with a runaway cowboy picaresque kin to *Don Quixote* and *Huckleberry Finn*. At sixteen John Grady Cole and his father Wayne attend his mother's father's funeral, the rough Grady patriarch unnaturally groomed in death. A headstrong actress, John Grady's mother went missing when he was an infant, but now "she" owns the ranch and wants her boy in school, so he splits on horseback with his granddaddy's satchel full of personal effects—clean shirt, socks, toothbrush, newly acquired razor and shaving brush—wearing his daddy's blanket-lined ducking coat. Little does this teen cowboy know what all he's leaving, but one thing is certain: a gender disruption has fractured generations of postwar ranching families, the women quitting a working man's world for social life in cities like San Antonio, the theater and dinners out, courting and finer things. Not everyone thinks a cattle ranch in west Texas is the second best thing to dying and going straight to heaven, the family lawyer explains the Cole divorce and his mother's control of the ranch. "She dont want to live out there, that's all." A sorry piece of business, "the way it is is the way it's goin to be." A gendered hyperreality holds the boy in check.

The narrative runs objectively neutral with few personal names, "he" and "she" and "father" and "son," a west Texas funeral in a cold plains wind, the weather all sideways. Wayne Cole tells of a man "come back from up in the panhandle" who said when the wind quit, the chickens all fell over. The hacking Second World War vet now lives smoking in a town hotel room and can do little about the way things are, including quitting cigarettes. These may seem small disturbances in the West, joked about laconically among men without women, but there's trouble afoot and overhead. "The wind was much abated and it was very cold and the sun sat blood red and elliptic under the reefs of bloodred cloud before." This wounded sunset, as stated, bodes no good in a McCarthy story.

The young hold out for dreams of unrestrained action and moving freedom in the unfenced aboriginal west. John Grady rides the old north Kiowa road and dreams of young blood-pledged Comanches riding wild mounts spirited as circus riders hazing wild horses with their dogs trotting along lolling their tongues. The riders chant as they pass on, "ghost of nation passing in a soft chorale across that mineral waste to darkness bearing lost to all history and all remembrance." From *Blood Meridian* we've heard a more horrific marauding tale of savage Indians, blood thirsty vigilantes, and Mexican bandits all slaughtering each other. As he goes along in the fictions, McCarthy's vision of the West deepens tragically, darkening elegiac over all the stories to the cannibal holocaust of nuclear winter in *The Road*. The last thing John Grady's father says is that the country will never be the same. Wayne Cole looks back sadly and reflects stoically that they're like the Comanches two centuries ago. "We dont know what's goin to show up here come daylight. We dont even know what color they'll be."

An old cowboy soul, young John Grady Cole is born to sit and ride a horse. What he loves in stallions he loves in men, the blood heat that runs them. Early on, he asks his maternal grandfather about the kitchen sideboard horses oil-painted from a book, and old man Grady says they're "picturebook horses." Are the boy's dream steeds real or made up, school a better place than a working ranch, a book the real thing? The title *All the Pretty Horses* comes from a slave lullaby in a minor key, a black mammy singing a white child to sleep while her own infant "way down yonder" lies crying for his mother, bees and butterflies around his eyes. *Hushaby, don't you cry, go to sleep my little baby. / When you wake you shall have all the pretty horses. / Dapples and grays, pintos and bays, coach and six little horses.* Something's wrong here, racially and historically and socially amiss—natural mothers in the wrong houses, fathers enslaving and splitting families, children crying out, all the pretty horses disillusional or damnably unreal.

In many ways a man and his horse redefined Western history. Consider the horse-and-stirrup that changed the whole of Europe, and equestrian heartland Indians who challenged homesteaders for several centuries, and the centaur soldiers who bucked civilizations, from Genghis Khan to Napoleon, Crazy Horse to Kit Carson. In *The Border Trilogy* especially, think of horse trading and trickster barter, the cowboy fun of horsing around and the horsey bodies of working men, the wild horses of prairie freedom and the mustang crossings. In addition, there are no-name working horses, cow horses, and quarter-horses—pack horses and horses of instruction and the Four Horses of the Apocalypse. Pale horse, the Book of Revelation prophesies, pale rider. The West could not be won without "sky dogs," as the Plains Indians called them. In this European import lay the seeds of tribal destruction, the plains centaur's tragic fall. McCarthy records the dying years of the cattle-horse culture as cities swallow the plains, the archaic role of the mythic cowboy in America's history.

On their last ride together father and son scarcely speak all day, the man's sunken eyes searching the sere prairie for fractured changes and desiccated lucidity. Even if there were no horses in the world, the boy would have wandered until he found one and known it for what he sought. John Grady Cole rides an anachronism that defines the American west as machines fly over and gouge the prairie garden. In this first of three twentieth-century border stories, McCarthy tells a straight-forward, mostly plain-style narrative of western history with lyric arpeggios, watching and overhearing characters lay out their lives as chosen destiny. Jump cuts cross-tie actors and scenes, fathers and sons, runaway cowboys and the land they are leaving. Lying on the blacktop road with his truant bud Lacey Rawlins, a dreamy John Grady stares up and says, "I'm already gone." So in the year 1949 they set out at predawn "like young thieves in a glowing orchard" among the early morning stars. Teen picaro cowboys, they simply "dont give a damn," as Rhett Butler tells Scarlet O'Hara after the fiery Civil War and romantic betrayal. Theirs is an easy-going, tight-lipped, good-natured recklessness and disregard for adult restraints— an old American story, epic as *Paradise Lost* and endemically western as *The Odyssey* or *The Adventures of Tom Sawyer*.

Looking south to Mexico by oil company roadmap, Rawlins sniggers, "There aint shit down there," exactly where the lads are headed with their Vienna sausage, crackers, koolaid, and hot sauce. They are soon trailed by a boy who calls himself Jimmy Blevins, a thirteen-year-old, barely pubescent gunslinger with a 32.20 Colt pistol. And why should they let him tag along? "Cause I'm an American," Jimmy defends his place among teen desperados, showing them he knows how to shoot the stitching out of a wallet. "You never know when you'll be in need of them you've despised," Blevins paraphrases a radio evangelist whose name he's taken.

John Grady never shoots anybody, but he knows cowboy tricks with guns too: how to use a rifle butt to pound out a boot nail, how to cauterize a bullet wound with a heated pistol barrel. John Grady's gun is a working tool and peace enforcer, not a killing instrument, unlike the ill-fated boy-child Jimmy Blevins who fancies himself another Jesse James. The cowlick trio crosses the Rio Grande naked to Coahuila, Mexico and picnics on the riverbank, a landscape of ocotillo, cholla, creosote, mesquite, and nopal soon to turn more treacherous.

The Rio is the border, and water on the desert is crucial to human survival. *Agua es vida,* natives say. There are no medians: when it rains, it grays and floods and doesn't quit. When it's hot and doesn't rain, the world dries up and dies. When it's cold, the snow and freeze drive every living thing inside or below ground. Best be prepared.

Jimmy's clothes and horse are swept away in a flash flood as he cowers from the lightning sure to strike him by blood curse. He steals back his horse but not his pistol from a mud-hut villager and rides away madly over the horizon. Always one to worry, Rawlins knows something bad is about to happen. These young-hearted hipsters swagger like men, question reality like boys, and talk big in the juvenile wake of words overheard elsewhere. "A goodlookin horse is like a good lookin woman, he said. They're always more trouble than what they're worth." He says a man needs just one to get the job done. John Grady is a bit more respectful. Chewing their first wild deer meat, they campfire-talk of dying and heaven. "You aint fixin to quit on me are you?" asks John Grady, a bit sore on the subject of abandonment. Rawlins says he said he wouldn't and won't. The latter wants to know if God looks out for people, and his bud guesses so. In anapestic rhythms that cluster spondees and grace slack syllables, they lope to their destiny riding on a workman's prose poetry. "They *rode* all *day* the *day fol*lowing *through* the *hill coun*try *to* the *west.*"

McCarthy is not unloading the full darkness of western tragedy just yet, but tracking the callow fall into early sorrow, the verdigris romance of boys running away to behold a new country old with history. Theirs is a southwest paradise momentarily regained in Old Mexico, soon to be lost again: "the country of which they'd been told. The grasslands lay in a deep violet haze and to the west thin flights of waterfowl were moving north before the sunset in the deep red galleries under the cloudbanks like schoolfish in a burning sea and on the foreland plain they saw vaqueros driving cattle before them through a gauze of golden dust."

The first of the novel's four picaresque movements ends with a dark-haired beauty passing on a black Arabian saddle horse, touching her crop to the felt brim of her flat-crowned black hat, and smiling coquettishly. Tired sentimental trope, perhaps, but after *Blood Meridian* a welcome soft spot in the plot. The ranch *gerente* hires them and the *vaqueros* ask respectfully innocent questions of U.S. life north across the border. "Some pretty good old boys," Rawlins whispers, falling asleep in the bunkhouse. "This is some country, aint it?"

The Hacienda de Nuestra Señora de la Purísma Concepción is aptly named after the virgin birth, eleven thousand hectares of New World Spanish land grant in Don Héctor Rocha y Villareal's family for a hundred and seventy years. Fish, birds, and lizards unknown elsewhere abound in this valley. The *hacendada* runs a thousand head of cattle, overlords several hundred wild mustang mares in the high country, visits his wife in Mexico City by red Cessna airplane, and guards his seventeen-year-old daughter like a suspicious king. The story verges on knightly allegorical romance. John Grady talks horses with the *hacendada*, knowing through his own patriarchy the thoroughbred pedigrees and legendary breeders. He breaks *mesteños* by roping and speaking to them in whispers that would calm a skittish lover, cupping their eyes and stroking out the terror. "What good do you think it does to waller all over a horse thataway?" Rawlins carps, but John Grady masters the wild mares in record time. The story sways between *mesteños* and alluring horsewoman as the blue-eyed, fine-boned beauty again rides past John Grady by the laguna. "He'd half meant to speak but those eyes had altered the world forever in the space of a heartbeat." She disappears beyond the willows, small birds passing over and calling, and the boy's fate is sealed. Perhaps uncharacteristically, McCarthy shades toward a young western romance with love at first sight, not without dark cultural precedent or troubling consequences that mark the *picaro* for the rest of his short life.

In the high country rounding up wild mares, Luis the bandy-legged *mozo* discourses on horses and war around a wind-tattered fire, the first of McCarthy's extended inset ruminations. Revolution destroyed Mexico, Luis says of his fighting days, and some men believe to cure war with war, as a curandero advises the serpent's flesh for its bite. Equine souls mirror those of men, he says, and both love war. No man can understand a horse who has not ridden to a battle, his father told him. The souls of horses are terrible to see in death, all sharing "a common soul and its separate life only forms it out of all horses and makes it mortal." John Grady asks, "Y de los hombres?" and the old man says men have no such communion. The idea that men can be understood at all is probably illusory. The boy slides off into one of his many freeing dreams of open country herds. "Horses still wild on the mesa who'd never seen a man afoot and who knew nothing of him or his life yet in whose souls he would come to reside forever."

Which leads into further talk of Don Hectór's daughter, as later around their campfire embers John Grady and Rawlins stare up at the burning stars: "in that coldly burning canopy of black he slowly turned dead center to the world, all of it taut and trembling and moving enormous and alive under his hands." Rawlins asks her name. "Alejandra. Her name is Alejandra," the Spanish feminine of Alexander the Great, conquering Macedonian horseman. Her name is his fate.

With their first pay and the prospect of a village social, the young riders race down the road to La Vega in muted fury to get haircuts and new clothes trailed by "dust, sunlight, a singing bird." The dance will call the young lovers out. Alejandra flirts boldly with the American cowboy and christens him "a mojado-reverse, so rare a creature and one to be treasured," but warning that she will always change her mind about everything. He inhales her perfume over his shirt on the canter home.

A pedigreed chestnut stud sixteen hands high arrives from Lexington, Kentucky to sire all the mares on the ranch. "Le gusta? said the hacendada. John Grady nodded. That's a hell of a horse, he said." Horses are put on earth to work cattle, the hacendada says, and besides cattle there is no other wealth for men. To be seen by the elusive Alejandra, John Grady rides "caballo padre," the twice-a-day paternal stud, and whispers obscene Spanish phrases "almost biblical" to the stallion. "While inside the vaulting of the ribs between his knees the darkly meated heart pumped of who's will and the blood pulsed and the bowels shifted in their massive blue convolutions of who's will and the stout thighbones and knee and cannon and the tendons like flaxen hawsers that drew and flexed and drew and flexed at their articulations and of who's will all sheathed and muffled in the flesh and the hooves that stove wells in the morning groundmist and the head turning side to side and the great slavering keyboard of his teeth and the hot globes of his eyes where the world burned." With equestrian passion and Nietzschean will to live, the pounding diction and pulsing sensuality call to the seventeen-year-old girl among the lakeshore tules with her skirts above her knees. Redwing blackbirds circle and cry, as she gathers waterlilies beside her black horse by the lake. This is McCarthy's single hyperreal scene of romance.

John Grady takes to riding the stallion bareback and the dark beauty says that she wants to ride him. Erotic heat suffuses the scene, his trouser legs wet and hot, and he worries, "You're fixin to get me in trouble." Sexually way ahead of him, she says, "You are in trouble." He sees her for the last time this time, erect and distant riding the patriarchal Father Horse, regal and disappearing in a rain squall. An older man might know better, but still relinquish: "real horse, real rider, real land and sky and yet a dream withal." As lightning is about to strike, the novelist teases his reader with a romantic trope in a cowboy western, a feral come-hither yet without consummation.

Dueña Alfonsa, the girl's grandaunt and godmother, quizzes John Grady by playing chess with him, both left-handers on guard, she the more experienced and skilled in piercing to matters of the heart. He must respect the girl's honor, she says, they can only ride together supervised. Of course Alejandra comes to his bunkhouse room unannounced late at night when he's sleeping, bearing steamy sorrow in her indignation at being talked about and harnessed by convention. They go for a moonlit bareback ride and he does what she tells him, wading naked into the lake where she asks if he really wants her. "Me quieres? she said. Yes, he said. He said her name. God yes, he said." Her rebellion, his vulnerability, a dangerous role reversal in a foreign country.

McCarthy sketches a love scene to draw the reader in erotically, watching and listening and feeling like the voyeuristic cranes on the lakeshore. Nothing goodwill come of this. "She thinks you got eyes for the daughter," Rawlins says of the Dueña's suspicions. "I do have eyes for the daughter," honest John Grady says. His bud warns that he isn't holding any aces.

> Did you give your word? said Rawlins.
> I dont know. I dont know if I did or not.
> Well either you did or you didn't.
> That's what I'd of thought. But I dont know.

What lingers yes or no, black or white in the cowboy naif's eyes is darkening erotically to gray, the shadows of worldly romance gathering around him. Five Mexican rangers ride ominously through the encampment, and Alejandra comes to his bed for nine nights nakedly crying that she doesn't care. The studded mares graze pregnant, Alejandra goes back to Mexico City, and John Grady plays straight pool in the converted family chapel with Don Hectór Rocha. The boy is badly beaten. "Beware gentle knight," the hacendada echoes Cervantes. "There is no greater monster than reason." Alejandra will be sent to France, he says, as the red Cessna flies off, and the cowboys are arrested in the night and led away by soldiers.

The novel's third movement follows the three-day manacled ride to Encantada or the Enchanted where Jimmy Blevins stole back his horse. John Grady, ever the stand-up, gutsy cowboy, protests his innocence and swears to his bud Lacey he's the same boy who crossed that river. How he was is how he is and all he knows is to stick. Contrary to his mother running away, he's adamant with get-down loyalty. "You either stick or you quit and I wouldnt quit you I dont care what you done." Blevins is shackled in the jailhouse with broken feet for shooting the man who stole his pistol and wounding two *rurales* with self-same pistol, killing one of them. Jailed John Grady can still dream himself free with horses that run in the resonance of the world itself, "and which cannot be spoken but only praised."

Lacey has to bare his naked back and butt for the lascivious police. "You must co-por-rate, said the captain. Then you dont have no troubles." Rawlins specifies his birthdate as September 26, 1932, his height as 5'11", and his weight as 160 pounds. Against these bared particulars, his still featureless bud insists, "There aint but one truth, said John Grady. The truth is what happened. It aint what come out of somebody's mouth." The thirteen-year-old Blevins is executed summarily in the trees en route to the Saltillo prison where readiness to kill is the only thing that keeps a man alive. A *cuchillero* knifes Rawlins in the stomach three times, and Pérez the yard boss talks his own philosophy of mankind and the devil, good and evil, Mexico versus the United States. The world wants to know if he has *cojones*, the boss says, if he is brave. John Grady survives a vicious knife fight in the mess hall, killing the hired boy assassin, and the Dueña Alfonsa buys the Texans out of prison. John Grady can't make things right about killing the *cuchillero* and leaves Saltillo on a truckbed, as Lacey goes home on a bus. "I reckon I'll see you one of these days," Rawlins ends the third section.

The goodwill of fellow Mexican travelers helps to restore John Grady who returns to the Dueña pleading his love for her niece. She believes tragically of the Spanish heart "that nothing can be proven except that it be made to bleed. Virgins, bulls, men. Ultimately God himself." The Dueña speaks sadly of the heroic courage of the revolutionary brothers Francisco and her lover Gustavo and vows that she will be the cowboy's hated enemy in the end, having extracted a promise from her niece never to see him in exchange for buying his freedom. The closest human bonds are bonds of grief, the deepest community that of sorrow. Heedless of the warning, John Grady impulsively arranges to meet Alejandra in Zacatecas, recalling his father's advice that "scared money cant win and a worried man cant love." They make love in the Reina Cristina Hotel on Mexico's Independence Day, and having broken her father's heart and her lover's dream, she leaves forever on a train.

John Grady has but one thing left to do. "I come back for my horse," he tells Raul the police captain who shot Blevins, riding before him double like a store dummy on his father's horse Redbo, that is, "redbone" or mixed-blood, as they make a desperate comic escape. By this time the reader gathers that McCarthy has written the tale into romantic thriller with a flaming shootout in the end, an adventure story of the lone cowboy's revenge and sadly comic denouement. He just wants his horse back. Cauterizing a rifle bullet wound through his thigh with a campfired pistol barrel, John Grady talks through his pain to his horse Redbo, leading the captain on Rawlins' horse Junior. He dreams of never ending order in a horse's heart that the rain cannot erase.

The noisome captain Raul is taken away by revolutionary countrymen, and the story begins to close down with the sacrifice of a doe to keep the boy alive. John Grady remembers Alejandra riding along the ciénega road and equates the deer's dying eyes to his sad first love. "Grass and blood. Blood and stone." Perhaps the Dueña was right. The world's heart beats at a terrible cost, its pain and beauty intertwined. He also knows instinctively that his father is dead. A gray crepe-paper, monochrome wedding in Los Picos reminds this seasoned seventeen-year-old that God hides life's truths from the young starting out or they would have no heart to start at all.

He rides the darkening plain north by polestar, the narrator recalling an exodus from Egypt, and crosses the Rio Grande baptismally naked in the rain into Langtry, Texas and weeps for his dead father on Thanksgiving Thursday. What pilgrim thanks can be given in the Hispanic southwest where Indians were almost eradicated, where Mexicans gutted each other, and where the Anglo cowboy culture has become an anachronism?

The local judge awards the boy Rawlins' disputed horse. He's heard many things giving him grave doubts about people, the judge says kindly, "but this aint one of em." Shadows of windmills and Spanish pilgrims, Don Quixote as John Grady on Redbo or Rosanante, Sancho Panza as Lacey Rawlins on Junior some time ago crossing the border to their youthful destiny. "John Cole," the judge calls him for the first time, initials JC without his mother's maiden name. The boy says he doesn't feel right about the girl back there. The common sense judge gives him some needed fatherly advice to keep going and put things behind him. "My daddy used to tell me not to chew on somethin that was eatin you." John Grady finally confesses that he killed a boy in prison and maybe there isn't an answer, but he doesn't want to be considered "somethin special. I aint." The judge counters the young boy's humility, "Well that aint a bad way to be bothered."

On Sunday morning radio John Grady hears Jimmy Blevins Gospel Hour from Del Rio and rides to the evangelist's house for chicken and dumplings. The preacher gives a softly comic blessing for most countries and mentions war, famine, missions, and other worldly matters "with particular reference to Russia and the jews and cannibalism and he asked it all in Christ's name amen and raised up and reached for the cornbread." Radio called Jimmy Blevins to the ministry, a Georgia cracker first to have his listeners put their hands on the set for healing. Over buttermilk and peach cobbler, the self-broadcast preacher's wife says her husband testifies through the air in China and can be heard all the way to Mars and all over Mexico. The reverend Blevins lies snoring in the next room. "The Lord dont take no holidays." John Grady is back in the United States: a kindly judge in wise country grace forgives a cowboy sinner, a buffoon preacher of divine salvation feeds the boy on his way home to a funeral. The village stalwarts of social rule can offer but humble comic grace to an endless rider of the southwest plains.

"Sum buck," Rawlins caterwauls when he gets his horse Junior back, and John Grady heads out again. This isn't his country anymore and he doesn't know where it is. "I don't know what happens to country." This boy without country or people goes home to his surrogate mammy Abuela's burial at the Knickerbocker Mexican cemetery, as the novel began at his grandfather's funeral. The slave lullaby *All the Pretty Horses* closes around John Grady Cole who grew up without his mother and stands holding his hat and calling goodbye to his Abuela in Spanish. He turns and puts on his hat and turns his wet face to the wind and holds out his hands "as if to steady himself or as if to bless the ground there or perhaps as if to slow the world that was rushing way and seemed to care nothing for the old or the young or rich or poor or dark or pale or he or she." The end of innocence, the beginning of dark wisdom that can cause a man to wander homeless all his days.

The novel closes near the oil pumpjacks by Indian wickiups on the Texas plain, a pale copper rider passing in bloodred sunset. "The *des*ert he *rode* was *red* and *red* the *dust* he *raised.*" The loping iambic hexameter turns in chiasmic rhythms that reverse and cross back upon themselves, a lyric narrative ending that rises into the next story, *The Crossing:* "rider and horse passed on and their long shadows passed in tandem like the shadow of a single being. Passed and paled into the darkening land, the world to come." The first of *The Border Trilogy* closes portending darker song-tales, stories where John Grady Cole and Billy Parham will cross and recross fates until one of them dies and the other keeps passing on through the millennium.

All the Pretty Horses is a lullaby for lost innocence, an elegy for a young nation of cowboys and New World breeds, a lament for first love and last chance, a love-song for a southwest border landscape of severe beauty that brings out strangeness, cruelty, and kindness in men and sorrow, compassion, and inconstancy in women. At their best men and women are courageous and passionate, at their worst they act cowardly and behave unfaithfully. It is no country for John Grady Cole who can't *act* like his mother or malinger in a hotel like his father, but is only what he is blooded, a southwest horse whisperer whose mother's father ran the last west Texas ranch in the family.

John Grady is a true *picaro,* a wandering pilgrim whose ancestors walked to Canterbury, Seville, or the Holy Land, through the Cumberland Gap and down the Santa Fe Trail. His cowboy persona is a man of few words in a drifting narrative that goes where it will, ruminating on character actions and social values, worldly verities and the human condition through time into eternity: life and death, courage and truth, God and an animate universe. Tracing a lineage back through Zane Grey's four-legged tales, Bret Harte's *The Outcasts of Poker Flat,* and even Hamlin Garland's Middle Border Series, this cowboy embodies horse sense or savvy, the heart and soul of the mount, the spirit of the beast, the simpatico of the hoofed warrior who in turn knows the truths of its rider. John Grady Cole speaks truth to power, courage to the soul, endurance to pain, humility and humor to survival. How will the heart's wounded honesty carry this man through millennial history and worldly sorrow?

CHAPTER 10

Star-Crossed Cowboy:
The Crossing

how do you like your blueeyed boy
Mister Death?
—"Buffalo Bill's defunct," e. e. cummings

Borders define boundaries as they demark crossings. In the natural world borders are generally porous, more gradations of contiguous fractals such as crumbling coastlines or cloud flows or weather fluctuations. Bioscientists like Lynn Margulis are exploring Serial Endosymbiosis Theory (SET) that posits the evolutionary interconnectedness and fusional reciprocity of all life-forms crossed and crossing into each other from the beginning. As with microbiologists tracing life to a single protoctist, geologists like Vladimir Vernadsky argue for a global hypersea of continuous living matter, "animated water," including rocks that give off vital elements hydrogen and oxygen. Just so, aboriginals the world over believe the cross-connected animacy of all things, interdependent and living stones, plants, animals, and humans among them.

The hybrid crossing of fractal Southwest borders is a set theme of a writer inhabiting office space at the Santa Fe Institute where related scientific discussions take place daily. The novelist serves as interdisciplinary translator among the heavy thinkers, including his friend the Nobel physicist Murray Gell-Mann—not without true empirical skepticism, ironic honesty, and agnostic need to track a god unknown (see *Atlantic Monthly* 2005 and Oprah Winfrey *Book Club* interview 2007).

In *The Crossing* Billy Parham passes over the U.S.-Mexico border with a wounded, pregnant she-wolf on a rope, as he will pass back four years later in the third of such crossings with the desiccated bones of his younger brother Boyd over his saddlepack. The narrative bilingually crosses Spanish and English, as the reader peers through scrims of dialogue searching for what men say in strange tongues, cowboy and *vacquero* speech native and foreign in their respective border lands. U.S. citizens are strangers to a Spanish-speaking world, aliens south of the border, true *joven*. Just so, Americans would be forever young with the isolationist insistence on cow*boy* youth in a monolingual, mixed-blood country where migrant homesteaders stay half feral and never need grow up. America's hyperreal youth may prove the world's curse.

Modern times are hard on all our relatives. Kinships fray, families are broken by violence, war, betrayal, hardship, and heartbreak. Men cut loose and go wild as loners on the road, wandering. All life-forms live at risk as the world loses an organism every few minutes. At the present rate a quarter of all extant species will be extinct by 2050, half of all living things forever dead by 2100. Crossings may save or destroy life-forms. Rootless, southwestering pilgrims from Anglo Europe cross with migrant Spanish colonials into Mexico where a thin overlay of Hispanic culture, history, and religion stretches across deeper-rooted Indian civilizations. Beleaguered peoples all, homesteaders struggle to reroot their migrations, orphaned loners hit the road and ride on, mestizos duck into the camouflage of poverty, Indians scatter into the mountains and deserts. In the 1930s when the novel opens, a global Depression brought on by overproductive greed takes away what little is left, leaving a Dust Bowl West, and hard times grip everyone into the Second World War. Some never make it back home.

The obvious crossing interdependencies of human and animal pervade the storied landscape: cowboys with their stock, men with their horses, boys with their dogs tracing back to wolves, coyotes yapping on the horizon, game animals in the mountains, birds in flight. *We are all related,* Native peoples say against Western diaspora, all one including our kinship with the four-legged, two-legged, winged, crawling, rooted, and swimming beings. Evolutionary scientists stand in agreement, tracing all life-forms to oceanic protoplasm.

After shooting his beloved totemic she-wolf, chained in her dog-pit misery, Billy Parham ferally regresses as a wild child of Old Mexico. For two years the boy lives off the land and the generosity of strangers and vagaries of fate, losing all sense of self, time, and place, until he is hardly recognizable as a human, carrying a bow and arrow, dressed in rags and tatters. Like Suttree retreating into the Great Smokey Mountains, Billy runs "gaunted" as desert chaparral, wild-eyed and wary of human contact. As Natives say of new-comers, the boy loses his tribal soul sacrificing guardian spirit and family home.

Billy Parham, too, is cross-bred, as we overhear four hundred pages into the novel. His maternal grandmother was "fullblooded Mexican," which includes the Indian and Spanish mix all over Latin America, hence he fuses many sides of Western hemispheric borders. The reader senses this racial crossing through Billy's maverick character and native actions. As mentioned, McCarthy shows things by detail and indirection. The genetics of character as fate are clear enough to the unlettered, and an alert witness need not be told things, rather draws out cross-truths in the storytelling. Some say it's the Indian way—watching, listening, learning quietly by example—perhaps the frontier way learned in part from Natives, being shown, not told survival skills.

Even Hidalgo County holds crossings where the immigrant Parham ranch sits under the Peloncillo Mountains. *Hidalgo* is Spanish for mustang or cross-bred horse, and the mountains are named for pelts or skins that interconnect inner beast with outer world. A crozier is a pastoral staff and sign of a herder, and the Parham ranch is called the SK Bar whose branding insignia, a heraldic cross, would be SK with a bar through it. And for the unlettered, as in *Outer Dark,* the X-cross is the ancient mark for an illiterate.

To cross is also to betray. Sixteen-year-old Billy abandons his role as his younger brother's keeper to return the mother-wolf to Mexico. Twelve-year-old Boyd witnesses the shotgun murders of their parents, then is left orphaned by parricide and fraternal loss. So only a year after their reunion to retrieve their father's horses, Boyd in turn leaves his brother for a homeless Mexican girl his own age and dies an outlaw, his fate crossed. Suicides and murderers are buried at crossroads where bandits lie in ambush, and the cross is anciently a gibbet for torture turned into a crucifix honoring Christ's *agon* for all mortals. Christ's crossing from god to man, from earth back to heaven, signals the trial, the sacrifice, the resurrection of flesh and spirit. Hence to cross oneself or another is to bless them in the name of the martyred god, and ironically in common use, to cross someone is to betray a trust.

In McCarthy's Southwest, everyman as avatar appears in the broken cowboy of border ballads and *corridos*, village tales and bar fiction, young men of heart who die defending others, civil justice, and passionate truths. With folk overview the novelist surveys all this through the distantly cocked eye of a dispassionate observer. Billy and Boyd have no designated facial or racial features in the novel; rather we know them by their clothes, hats, boots, horses, and gestures (forefinger to the hat brim). Parham is vaguely Anglo, as are Cloverdale neighbors like Parsons, Echols, and Gilchrist. Hispanic surroundings shadow them—the names of mountains, rivers, plains, and cities—as Spanish engulfs southwestering flotsam. A dark sparseness and humble poverty hovers about the young gringo runaways who appear ghostlike in streets or on vast bajadas or over plains horizons. Displaced Tarahumara and Yaqui Indians, homeless gypsies, desert isolatoes, and wandering riders seem to understand the wild boys' orphaned dilemma, perhaps sensing their Mexican maternal kinship, certainly sharing this homeless dislocation. Each must find home in his heart on the endless road.

History is a crossing of time past into present. With border wars and territorial disputes roughly quiescent since the Alamo, the Mexican people's unending revolution remains futile. Religion provides thin solace in the figure of Guadalupe, the mother of sorrows with a flaming heart. To take up the cross is to shoulder Christ's burden of sacrifice for others, to accept mortality and the need for grace, to face death with courage and eternity with humility. These are old values not limited to Christianity but folded into the complex spiritual strata of trial and faith, integrity and betrayal, endurance and suffering that make up Native, Hispanic, and post-Columbian beliefs of the Latin Americas. At risk of literary cross-purposes, note that one can suffer crossbirth, a fetus turned by fate and ill-born; be cheated by crossbite; be crossed in a dishonest contest; use a crossbow or cross guard as a weapon of defense; or simply be cross with the world. The old cautions are ever current in *The Crossing*, and the consequences hyperreal. A cross wind is generally an ill wind, and a crossway or walk can be perilous, as a cross word may elicit trouble and a crossword frustration. The warnings interlace McCarthy's canon: don't be caught in the crosshairs of a hostile enemy, avoid cross bones, look out for cross-currents, and learn to cross-examine stories and advice and directions that may lead a traveler astray.

As an unacknowledged avatar, an unheralded traveler all his days, Billy weeps three times in the story: for his murdered parents, over his dead brother's bones, finally on the last page for the road itself, all lonesome travelers as one without end or home. He wanders his own endless path among men journeying to a new day, another step somewhere, more sorrow and witness and pain. As men say in minimal talk, there's not much to say, finally, and everything to say tragically, the stuff of myth and song, heroes and losers. Men cross borders as fate crosses them, the wooden slats, for example, over Boyd's foreign grave. Humans are travelers on storied roads winding toward death. And yet nothing changes as all changes shape: the witnessing and hearing and telling and acting of stories comprise men's lives, and that is all they are, words like wind or water that add up to nothing substantive—everything men have in their hearts and voices, but can't have in their hands. God is not out there, some savants argue, but inside, if anywhere, skeptics say, or nowhere or somewhere unreachable, crazed prophets fume. Crossing is all—to pass, to mark, to sign generically, to counter, to erase, to interbreed, to intersect, to oppose, to double-cross or betray.

Dubbed "a miracle in prose" by former poet laureate Robert Hass in the *New York Times Book Review* (12 June 1994), *The Crossing* is a whip-lashing long narrative without chapter breaks, a four-part coming-of-age *Bildungsroman* of the cowboy native Southwest into Old Mexico, a border still mostly wild and sparsely inhabited. In the opening paragraph we hear Billy's narrative over-voice. "You could ride clear to Mexico and not strike a crossfence." The ambling cowboy story patiently details pace and accretes scenes in conjunctive prose full of limpidly compounded declarative sentences. McCarthy's prose cuts loose from Appalachia and lopes across the Southwest prairies. Actions and particulars, from tracking predators to digging postholes, are strung together as a man works them in smoothly continuous rhythms riding the borderlands, herding the range, taking it all in before sundown.

The ostensible plot kernels the romantic pilgrimage of two brothers to avenge their parents' murders, fraternal love down west, against the epic sweep of the landscape and the wrenching twists of character and time. The names of mountain ranges toll like bells over the parched desert, Peloncillo Peaks, the Animas Range, the Guadalupes. On the second page we hear Billy's dream witness of the wild freedoms of wolves and all natural things, an epiphany akin to Isaac McCaslin's first encounter with Old Ben in Faulkner's *The Bear:*

> They were running on the plain harrying the antelope and the antelope moved like phantoms in the snow and circled and wheeled and the dry powder blew about them in the cold moonlight and their breath smoked palely in the cold as if they burned with some inner fire and the wolves twisted and turned and leapt in a silence such that they seemed of another world entire. They moved down the valley and turned and moved far out on the plain until they were the smallest of figures in that dim whiteness and then they disappeared.

This canticle is as close to animistic religion as the story gets, and Billy "never told anybody."

Early on, a generic Indian drifter nears the Parham homestead to extort food from the boys. He calls Billy a little son of a bitch. Checking a sentimental stereotype, the Native drifter is what is left of a wild, fugitive border culture decimated of wolves, now only extant in Mexico. We learn hundreds of pages later how the generic Indian, a kind of Magwitch to Pip in *Great Expectations* or even the devilish Pap in *Huckleberry Finn,* is right about Billy—a bastard breed mix of races and cultures and wildness without home or parentage for much of the story.

Where are the women? The matriarchy is always frustrating and troubling for McCarthy's men. In the beginning the boys and their father in the snow track a pregnant she-wolf who's been killing calves. They have no luck or skill in the hunt. In old man Echols' abandoned cabin for killing wolves, the boys find the bottled inner parts of beasts calling up the hundred-thousand-year slaughter dreams and realities that undertow McCarthy's fictions: "Dreams of that malignant lesser god come pale and naked and alien to slaughter all his clan and kin and rout them from their house. A god insatiable whom no ceding could appease nor any measure of blood." Indeed, Adam was given deadly dominion over all the Garden beings, destroying them wantonly.

A thickened biblical cadence churns the telling, and there is less dialogue than in novels to come later, more narrated detail and working action. Talk between characters lends human texture, rather than advancing plot. Don Arnulfo, the dying savant who knows wolves, some say a *brujo* oracle, pronounces in the alien tongue that all is "Una historia des desgraciada." Of the wolf he says, "El lobo es una cosa incognoscible." Made the way the world is made, the wolf alone knows and accepts death's order, the blood of skin that vanishes at a touch like a snowflake. A man cannot touch or hold a world made only of breath. And at a sudden plot point several pages later, destiny crosses the family path. Without premeditation Billy leaves home to find and follow the she-wolf, riding out the ranch gate before his father wakes, "and he never saw him again."

After many misses, Billy catches the pregnant loba in a trap, wounding her leg, but even with a greenstick bit and lasso he cannot drag her home, as he cannot rope the wind, the stars, the rivers, the lightning, the sun or moonbeam. Back to Heraclitus, Lao Tsu, and Native wisdoms, no one can grip life in hand. The campfire flames burn in the wolf's blazing ocher eyes and reflect a "world construed out of blood and blood's alkahest and blood in its core." Only blood has the power to resonate against a void that threatens hourly to devour it.

Dragging a pregnant she-wolf into Sonora, Mexico reverses the trails of Coronado, de Soto, Oñate, and Cabeza de Vaca, as Billy Parham acts on instinct and blood, not forethought. "Adónde va? the man said. A las montañas." He waters and calms the wounded wolf by talking and singing to her, and he talks to no human this way. The tale fends the border mountains south in grinding pace and trail stink of a writer who has ridden through the rugged malpais landscape, seen Mexican poverty and dignity and mescal carelessness, noted the Indian distances of survival and secrecy, including the countless Native petroglyphs and pictographs and blackened tribal campfires. Everywhere in McCarthy's landscape scatters rock-scarred evidence of ancient habitation, struggle, and death.

The wounded wolf is precipitously stolen from Billy, and he tracks her to a Mexican fair, chained for the curious to stare at and torment. She watches him with yellow eyes of no despair only "that same reckonless deep of loneliness that cored the world to its heart." This author has watched wolves watch him and noted Sam Fathers heeling the wild dog Lion in *The Bear*. In one of his many prophetic dreams Billy sees his own father's eyes turned toward the darkness to search the coming of cold night and terrible silence before a solitary bell tolls and he wakes.

Unarmed Billy walks directly into the fighting Mexican dog-pit to free the wolf, saying simply "Es mía," and then shoots the spent animal after three hours of unreprieved battle, the pregnant wolf about to be torn apart by murderous Airedales. The boss man, the *gran chingón*, says to the men with their drawn pistols and knives that it's "finished." Billy trades his father's rifle for the wolf corpse and rides away with her on the pommel like a dead mother-child, singing songs all night long in Spanish and English as a nighthawk cowboy for the heroic fallen. The scene prefigures his ride back home with his brother's bones.

The first of four chapter-sections ends 127 pages along with Billy at sunrise holding what cannot be held, only dreamed, the wild life of the cold reality of dawn. Her eye turned to the fire gives back no light and he closes it with his thumb. He sits by her and puts his hand on her bloody forehead and closes his eyes and sees her running on wet grass under the starlight as the sun has not yet dissolved night's matrix of animals among which she belongs. In death we are all interrelated kinship species, as biologists and Natives contend, no one alone and all as one, despite individual destinies, animal fates, tribal dislocations, family losses and personal griefs. "He took up her stiff head out of the leaves and held it or he reached to hold what cannot be held, what already ran among the mountains at once terrible and of a great beauty, like flowers that feed on flesh." She is made of blood and bone that cannot be made again on any altar nor by war. "What we may well believe has power to cut and shape and hollow out the dark form of the world surely if wind can, if rain can. But which cannot be held never be held and is no flower but is swift and a huntress and the wind itself is in terror of it and the world cannot lose it." The falling blank verse cadences echo scripture and classic literatures, a canticle of animate freedom. "Yea, though I walk through the valley of the shadow of death, I will fear no evil: for thou *art* with me." The narrative sweeps to a peak in the first of a four-part set of symphonic movements with musical themes and cadenzas, harmonics and lyrics, here building to the crescendo of the wolf's death and the dream of freedom, man's last wilderness in the dying eyes of his oldest and best canine friend, still wildly free in death.

McCarthy's threnody records a deeply sorrowful lament for the feral terror and perishable beauty of all living things. Billy shoots his guardian mother-wolf to save her from an ignoble death, to rescue her spirit from men, and to dream her forever among the ferocious animacies of the mythic world. These canticle sadnesses are informed by the Psalms of Solomon, Keats' Odes, Faulkner's elegies for the Old South, Melville's awe of natural powers, and Dostoyevsky's respect for dark things that cannot be controlled or contained, including beasts of the human spirit.

Billy buries his mother-guardian with her unborn pups and rides on through environmental calamities, natural courtesies, human reciprocities, common decencies, and the violences of men. Villagers and fellow travelers feed the stranger and ask if he is an orphaned American cowboy.

> Ay, vaquero.
> Adónde va?

Mountain *huérfano* with a broken spirit, Billy has lost all sense of home or kinship. He travels through men, not with them, as the narrative comes to insist on its journey through words. Passages flow like wind and water that cannot be held or stepped into twice. He says he didn't come here, he's just passing through. The ancient Chichimeca petroglyphs chiseled in stone speak to him of a world they would endure and a world dead in their hands.

And so the storytelling winds fugally between narrated scene with prerequisite dialogue and wildly philosophical, hermeneutic monologues by savants, idiots, pilgrims, gypsy singers, and highwaymen. The narrative modes shift between conventional plot and heuristic commentary, character in action and extended advisings on human life and reality. Paralleling the oral traditions of older cultures, Native and Western, the story changes registers from cowboy brother ballad with wolf and horses to philosophical disquisitions among odd characters—hermits, blind men, road drama queen, town stranger, unknown rider—commenting on life, home, wandering, storytelling, dreams, prophesy, history, and mortality. It's the classic way Homer enters his lyric narrative through a character like Tiresias, or Melville comments on epistemological seeing through the mad cabin boy Pip, or Faulkner off-stage rises to elegiac crescendo over the wilderness fall of the bear, or Dostoyevsky lets a mad priest seize the story, or Conrad speaks through Marlow. Story, character, and action are followed by inset reflection, deduction, and proposition that shadow the story's circling advance back to dialogue, scene, event, and character. "He was just a word for me," Marlow says to his chums at anchor aboard the *Nellie* in *Heart of Darkness.* "Do you see him? Do you see the story? Do you see anything? It seems to me I am trying to tell you a dream—making a vain attempt, because no relation of a dream can convey the dream-sensation, that commingling of absurdity, surprise, and bewilderment in a tremor of struggling revolt, that notion of being captured by the incredible which is of the very essence of dreams...." McCarthy's narrative voice shifts in fugal form and large phrasing curves of action—point, counterpoint, call, response, question, answer—crossing paths and weaving stories and ruminations altogether, as the ballad of Gregorio Cortés or *corridos* of Billy the Kid interweave narrative and lyric genres in folk tales across the border.

Hermit keeper of a fallen church, an ex-Mormon holds forth about miracles of destruction, the search for God's handprint, apocalyptic cities of the plain, and stories that take place, that is, *are* the place they tell in the world. Of all the imperishable tales and folk *corridos* in this perishable world there is only one canticle to tell, the nameless prophet swears—that of death, and the telling is all, all tales but one, as stone, flower, and blood are nothing if not a tale. The hyperreal seams are hidden. God is not out there, he ventures, but in men's hearts, witnessed in tales of ruin, sorrow, wandering, rubble, aging, and inevitable death. These are endless words of an endless pilgrimage, for when the words end, life stops. Can one reckon God's boundaries? the hermit questions in an inset stand-off rant with a priest outside the fallen church. The deranged anchorite, perhaps a lunatic hermit as holy man, has a Dostoyevskian obsession to talk back to God and the tragic need to query fate. "If the world was a tale who but the witness could give it life?" The witness bears God in his heart, he swears, into the world. Half-wild cats cadence and channel his tale-telling with their silken movements.

Like a mad Stein of Conrad's *Lord Jim,* this authorial persona offers stoic life-reasons for telling stories in a tale embedded in the simple narrative of a nonliterate cowboy growing up to tragedy and sorrow, betrayal and death. "All is telling," the anchorite tells the reticent boy, and all are one, every man's path every other's. All men are one, he says for good measure, and there is no other tale to tell. Immanuel Kant's theater of the mind crosses with Walter Benjamin's indefatigable Storyteller into Homer's blind faith canticle—singing the tale of the heroic moment and epic loss, the fall of kingdoms and corruption of men, the betrayal of lovers and violence of strangers. God is everything outside man's witness, the hermit says, all that he cannot name and tell, the ultimate Other and the Whirlwind's admonition to Job. "Out of whose womb came the ice? and the hoary frost of heaven, who hath gendered it?" (Job 38: 29). McCarthy sketches an Orphic parting with the idiot savant in the church ruins, Billy deciding on his advice to ride home in early spring *nostos,* still and always the *joven.*

Billy crosses and recrosses the river many times on his journey back north. At the border-crossing he speaks to a kindly man named John Gilchrist who loans him half a dollar to get home and is asked how he likes the country:

> I like it fine.
> The boy nodded. I do too, he said.

He touches his hat brim and thanks the man, then heels his wild horse and gallops "up the street into America." Billy rides his father's horse Bird to an empty house and discovers the darkened, bloodstained crime on the underside of his parents' mattress. He weeps the grief of an orphan, his second heart loss of the tale. The boy rides into Cloverdale to find his brother, as the sheriff sums up the plot thus far: "You just got a wild hair up your ass and there wouldn't nothing else do but for you to go off to Mexico." His parents have been shotgunned by horse thieves and his brother Boyd is detained with a mute dog whose throat was slit by the murderers. The sheriff adds not to get crosswise with the law over this. The narrator casts Billy to this point, a wild renegade that people envy and revile and sometimes kill for small cause, boy martyr to the heart's witness, ballad hero of border *corridos*. When he walks into the sun to untie his horse from a parking meter, folks passing turn to look. "Something in off the wild mesas, something out of the past. Ragged, dirty, hungry in eye and belly. Totally unspoken for." The parking meter jolts the reader out of border myth into present history.

Then the story grants a moving, minimal-word reunion in the language brothers share—callow laconic speech Billy has not heard or used for two years.

> I reckon you thought I was dead, Billy said.
> If I'd of thought you was dead I wouldn't be here.

And the boys set out together straddling their father's horse on the road to redemption and perdition and death's reckoning.

> Are you ready to go? he said.
> Yeah, said Boyd. Just waitin on you.

Teenage cowboys ride as outlaws now, of necessity not romance, and they don't talk about vengeance or justice, just do it, perhaps to talk later. "It is what it is." And Boyd refuses to look back. "It aint no use you askin me a bunch of stuff." Like the dog with its throat slit trailing their dead father's horse, Boyd remains mute witness of the family tragedy, his pale hair almost white and looking fourteen going on an age that never was. "He looked as if he'd been sitting there and God had made the trees and rocks around him. He looked like his own reincarnation and then his own again. Above all else he looked to be filled with a terrible sadness."

In Bacerac after a week riding south, they find the roan gelding Keno in front of a dead woman's house and steal him back and ride into the country, only to turn back for directions to Casas Grandes to find the remaining horses. A crazy old man draws a map in the street dirt. "Un viaje pasado, un viaje antiguo." An aged street chorus dismisses the loco dirt mapper and proceeds to discuss right and wrong maps, crazy and credible guides, journeys and actions, phantasms and reality. Whether good or bad directions, one local instructs them helpfully, luck, kindness, and events will determine the crossings. Learn to read warnings and stories, know sound advice from ill will, find the way in the going.

Crossing the Chihuahua plains, they brush against Tarahumara Indians whose provisional and deeply suspect view of the world sets telling example. The beleagured Natives show wary absorption for all about them. Having seen too much and worrying too often, Boyd is "all sulled up" with voiceless grief. The ragged boy pilgrims ride gaunted horses and trail a mute dog and grow into figures of ballad, Billy Boy and Billy the Kid, *jovenes* marked by fate and honored in folk *corridos*. They come up against a horse trader's simple advice to go back home. Boyd says they don't have one to return to. The boys rescue a fourteen-year-old, unnamed Mexican girl from rapacious "sumbucks" at a campfire, and they become in the narrator's purview "storybook riders" with a "stolen backland queen" as silhouettes on the plain. The second hundred-page movement ends on this winsome romantic note.

Consider the characterizations thus far. The Western cowboy doesn't say anything he doesn't know, legend goes, or isn't true. Keep your mouth shut until you must speak and save it for the right time. Spitting is preferable to needless talk. Be polite, say hello, please, thank you, sir or mam. Touch your forefinger to your hat brim in respect. Be watchful and alert with all your senses. Act from the heart and true knowns. Against these sparse codes, hyperreal violence builds for over two hundred pages—calf killings, dogfights, drunks, wary strangers, rapists, horse thieves, family murderers, road assassins—a slow, steady, sure reckoning of the trail to justice, to vengeance, to redemption or death. No home, only the passing through. No past, only the serpentining present.

In picaresque mode the three come upon an opera troupe of gypsies, and Billy tells the primadonna that they seek their father's stolen horses "For ever how long it takes." She in her center stage command warns, "Long voyages often lose themselves." The cautionary tales of the country advise that the shape of the road is the road. The shadowland path seen through her opera glasses contains "only what was needed and nothing more," a sere hyperreality. Boyd sees her at sunrise "buck naked" in the river, and feminine sensuality throws a new curve into the boys' road. Erotic women are another world altogether. "You aint about just goin with her. Are you?" Billy asks his brother of the Mexican girl who wants to go home. The growing-up break is seeded.

All three of the missing paternal horses rise up miraculously in the road, Bailey, Tom, and the favored Niño, only to be repossessed with their papers by a jefe and his vaqueros, then given back inexplicably by an Indian ranch boss to the boys. "It aint like home down here," Billy says to his brother who looks like a breed of child equestrian left after war, plague, or famine. In rounding up the stolen horses Boyd shows that he knows roping despite his youth—diamondhitch, hackamore, jimsaw loop, hoolihan configurations familiar to the narrator. These are thin, ragged, capable boys aging daily who need to "cut back on the cussin," Billy says, just before Boyd is shot by a rifleman and taken by Mexican workers in a truck, as Billy escapes on horseback. He talks and sings to his mount Niño, that is, Boy, and prays to Boyd. "Don't be dead, he prayed. You're all I got."

Billy finds his wounded brother attended by mud-hut villagers. With painstaking detail and the pace of a field dressing, he watches Boyd heal from a mortal chest wound, only to ride off with the Mexican girl Billy brings to his bedside. A simple, staggering, unaccounted event in the night, the hyperreal way it is, the way betrayal often happens, as his parents were shot, just as he left three years ago for Mexico with the she-wolf that he shot in a single gesture.

The final fourth-part movement opens with a declaration of the Second World War. "Hell fire, boy," the border guard says, the country is at war. U.S. history keeps interrupting the border pilgrimage. Billy sleeps in a Deming bus station with his boots on and strangers feed the penniless drifter. He tells a recruiting officer that he's just seventeen and has no next of kin. A heart murmur excludes him from service, and he commences to drift all over southern New Mexico, touching the worn landmarks and greeting old men such as Sanders reading scripture on his porch.

By the age of twenty, the war over, Billy heads back to Chihuahua still a *joven*, the people say, looking for his lost brother. All traces are gone from the old places just three years back with Boyd. A wedding and a funeral take place interchangeably in the Mexican girl's abandoned home. Billy hears rumor of his brother the *güerito* killed as a revolutionary bandit and buried in the cemetery at San Buenaventura or Good Journey. The *corridos* are gathering about the storied brothers. A sixteen-year-old beauty shells pecans in a courtyard and sings the heroic deaths of a boy and his beloved dying in each other's arms.

Quijada, the Yaqui trail boss who gave the Parham boys back their horses, shows up to say that Boyd is indeed dead, the revolution defeated again, and an American investor named Hearst employs him as ranchhand, but that's his business alone. The *corrido* is a poor man's history, the Yaqui Indian says, honoring the solitary man who is all men and death's truth. The hermit priest and gypsy singer underscored these points earlier of a world that has no true name. Man's lost world is named in futility since humans are the lost ones who choose their death as unnamed fate.

The "exquisite" desolation of Boyd's grave, dated 24 February 1943, lies under the Sierra del Nido or "nest" peaks. Billy digs up his brother's bones and wraps them in a soogan tarp, carrying the wooden cross and carcass in a packframe on his horse Niño. A drunken bandit stabs his father's horse in the chest and cuts open Boyd's shroud, scattering the bones in the road, and a further wounded Billy weeps a second time over the ghost of his brother.

Hyperreal *deus ex machina,* an airplane float drawn by oxen appears on the road with Durango *gitanos* who save the horse with herbs. "Los huesos de mi hermano" in the tree, Billy tells the gypsies, and they tell him the made-up truth in a wild story of biplanes from the mountains, splinter tales to defray the novel's sense of an ending. For homeless gypsies movement is a form of property, and their stories go on and on, as do people. Reality runs in the telling, the going, not the getting on or getting done with. Death is the only end of man's fate, the vanished mortal husks of past knowings, all we know or can say. Reality runs inexplicable except in the presence of witness, as the path is not there except in the going. "Fugitivo. Inescrutable. Desa pía-dado." No payment, no thanks, just do what you will, the way of the road rule for all.

In the wake of the biplane gypsy parade trails a well-dressed stranger on a horse who asks Billy what he's doing here in the guts of Mexico. Minding his own business, Billy says that he got what he came after on this third trip, but not what he wanted. He reveals that his mother's mother Margarita was a "fullblooded Mexican didn't speak no english." Highway stories are mostly faux, the fellow traveler says, especially gypsy tales, bringing this story fictively down to the road underfoot. Billy answers, "There aint but one life worth livin and I was born to it," his most reflective moment in the story. The rider says the world will never be the same, and Billy replies, "I know it. It aint now."

With an Indian travois for Boyd's bones, Billy crosses the border again at Dog Springs and enters Animas on Ash Wednesday. The reappearing Cloverdale sheriff says at the cemetery where Boyd is buried, "There aint much to say, is there?"

From there Billy Parham rousts about the Southwest, leaving places for no reason he knows, and as the novel closes, he's doomed to wander forever. He chases away a sallow, crab-walking, arthritic old dog and feels the shadows of passing birds and tries to call the crippled dog back against the alien dark and dusk settling over the road. His only road friend seems to be the she-wolf ghost, sorry companion of his brother Boyd. With head bowed over the tarmac Billy weeps alone for the third time. "He sat there for a long time and after a while the east did gray and after a while the right and godmade sun did rise, once again, for all and without distinction."

Inexplicably in loss, the sun also rises, as Ecclesiastes prophesied of waning light and Hemingway echoed ironically in the postwar West, for each and everyone, pitiless without favor or accusation. The reality of the open road charts Billy's ongoing life-story, a new day and another step into destiny, wherever he may cross damned cities of the plain.

CHAPTER 11

Horse Sense and Human Fate:
Cities of the Plain

Most of them marry, and love their wives sincerely, but since
their sociology idealizes women and their mythology excludes
her, the impasse which results is often little short of tragic. Now,
as then, the cowboy escapes to the horse, the range, the work,
and the company of comrades, most of whom are in the same
unacknowledged fix.

—Larry McMurtry, *In a Narrow Grave: Essays on Texas*

Cities of the Plain shadows El Paso and Juárez with cursed biblical
sites below a blood-drenched desert horizon. "Then the LORD
rained upon Sodom and upon Gomorrah brimstone and fire" (Genesis
19: 24). The plot builds like an ill-omened storm, the characters
dwarfed by time and events, the setting ringed with real mountain
ranges called the Sierra Viejas, Guadalupes, Cuesta del Burro, and
Presidio on the border. The first note of color comes formulaically
twenty-six pages into the narrative, a "blood red" sky over the
mountains. In the natural world we are taught to be wary of red
tints—eyes, spiders, waters, wounds, veins, sunsets, moons, dreams—
where black destruction is never far behind. The warnings are ancient.
Old Testament vengeance is swift, God's justice immutable. "And he
overthrew those cities, and all the plain, and all the inhabitants of the
cities, and that which grew upon the ground" (19: 25). A saturnine
Yahweh is neither pleased nor merciful with transgressions of His
Word.

McCarthy's modern-day blemish on Old Testament vengeance
features border-crossings between a southwest frontier of ordinary,
English-speaking surfaces with out-of-the-ordinary cowboy stories,
the pimp Eduardo snidely tells "farm-boy" Billy Parham. On the

other side lie Spanish-speaking, Indian-bedrocked cultures of strange surfaces and the old familiar tragedies overlaying temporality, fated choice, and human folly. Few want to plumb the hyperreal strata. Old beneath new history, Anasazi petroglyphs litter the stories everywhere as backdrop to ancient tales. "But his wife looked back from behind him and she became a pillar of salt" (Genesis 19: 26).

Calle de Noche Triste references Cortés's retreat from Tenochtítlan, today's Mexico City, giving Robert Frost the title of his first published poem in a high school newspaper. *Street of the Sad Night* canticles the main boulevard of Juárez where the heroine walks bloody-footed to her slit-throat death into the Rio Grande River, where later the hero's cowboy bud carries him knife-slashed to his blood-rags end. A twice-told tale of tragic lovers—Adam and Eve, Orpheus and Eurydice, Son of Man and Mary Magdalene. Billy Parham grieves the same "old story" all over again. Half a century later under a freeway overpass his articulate double, a hobo philosopher, says of all predestined pilgrims that they contemplate choices but follow only one path.

McCarthy has read the Greek tragedians and modern existentialists. So if each man is bard of his own life, who bears witness? The man standing there before you, the hobo waxes humanist in the closing pages, do you love that man? Will the reader honor his path and listen to his tale? Still homeless and unwed, Billy at seventy-eight begs his shadow hobo just to end the story. He still got a ways to go, he says impatient with the word-clouded dream-tale. Billy tells Betty, putting him to bed on the penultimate page to dream of all the pretty horses, that he "ain't nothing," echoing John Grady's confessional to the border judge that he "aint" anything "special."

The novel opens gritty with jejune cowboys in a Juárez whore-house across the footbridge from El Paso. The muddy Rio Grande may well be the southwest River Styx. Drinking whiskey with beers back, the boys joke in nasty bar-fuck talk, but a last-year teenager isn't adding insult to affection. "You all go on, said John Grady." Reversely in the bar glass, John Grady now nineteen sees a prostitute "school-girl" of "no more than seventeen" sitting demurely. The plot is set from backdrop to *All the Pretty Horses,* Romeo and Juliet, Tristan and Isolde, Rhett Butler and Scarlet O'Hara—grief crossing backstory, nostalgic romance, and regressive tragedy. Add to these hyperreal pairings the cross-border romances of Cortés and La Malinche, John Rolfe and "Lady Rebecca" Pocahuntas, Lewis and Clark and Sacajawea.

Back on the ranch we learn that the Foreman Mr. Johnson lost his daughter three years ago when John Grady got his cheekbone cicatrix from a knifefight. The old man's near crazy, and the boys are drifting the dry arroyo behind him. Johnson, John's son, Juan—Everyman's son in any language, harlot's john, the jakes or john, the universal degradation in male loss of the feminine. John ironically needs his mother's maiden name Grady to be respectfully surnamed Cole, an Irish-American vaquero in an old romance damned to heartache. Mac the patrón says of his dead wife that you don't get over a woman like that. "Not now, not soon, not never." His dead wife is the son-of-John's daughter, Margaret Johnson McGovern. Grievous woman loss defines all McCarthy's men of the West.

The story gathers slowly around desert-leathered, love-starved, one-woman cowboys going "crazy as a shithouse rat" for lost home affection and a woman's touch. We read these characters looking back through a distant sandstorm of history, a desert mirage twisting their images in get-down frontier dialect. A fine rough wind all but silences common thoughts of a cowboy myth passing, times bygone, lives rusted and postheroic and sad.

"Where's my by god coffee at?" Billy says the morning after the whorehouse, as minimalist Socorro the cook, surrogate mother of another tongue, warms the boys by the woodstove. Spanish is the neighbor language of the border others, a reminder that words are but sounds signing the world strangely, never ends in themselves. Billy asks the fallen beauty schoolgirl her name in the bordello, and she says she cannot speak English, but that her name is Magdalena. "Y usted?" she asks demurely. John Grady doesn't answer, since his name doesn't measure up to the mythic allure of the biblical prostitute and Hispanic epileptic of cinders. John Grady remains the humble suitor, the horse whisperer, the unheroic cowboy in love with a teenage whore who knows her own reality. "Como una princesa, she whispered. Como una puta, said the girl."

Backroom bar talk lays the story to buy Magdalena across the border in ballad romance—a slow, wide-stage build-up with operatic gravitas to the obvious fall, but nothing too fancy, an ancient romantic tragedy told in down-home ranch dialect. Billy can't believe what John Grady tells him about Magdalena.

> You are shittin me aint you? he said.
> No. I guess I aint.
> What the hell's wrong with you? Have you been drinkin paint thinner or something?

John Grady confesses his love for the seizuring prostitute, and all Billy can say is, "Aw goddamn, he said. Goddamn." Their bunkhouse talk is as real as it gets.

> What in the goddamn hell would you do with her if you did get her away from down there? Which you aint.
> Marry her.
> Billy paused with the cigarette half way to his mouth. He put it down again.
> Well that's it, he said. That's it. I'm havin your ass committed.
> I mean it, Billy.

Billy leans back in his chair and eventually throws up one hand. "I cant believe my goddamn ears." He thinks he's the one gone crazy and is a son-of-a-bitch if he hasn't. "Have you lost your rabbit-assed mind? I'm an absolute son of a bitch, bud. I never in my goddamn life heard the equal of this."

With ancient Greek pacing in bunkhouse dialect, the storyteller's genius lies in how the tale is told and played out, cowboy Orpheus, prostitute Eurydice, pimp Eduardo Dis. The boy-hero's beloved is lost forever with a glance back, and sere winter rules. We know the tale from ancient days and watch how it figures in our tales and own times as outrider to *West Side Story, Porgy and Bess, Aida, One-Eyed Jacks,* or *High Noon.* Western and Southern writers Louis L'Amour, Zane Grey, William Faulkner, and Eudora Welty flank filmmakers John Ford, Sam Peckinpah, Sergio Leone, and Clint Eastwood. Some stories never slack.

There is horizontal tension in the plotting, the signature steady accumulation of detail, jump-cuts increasing as the plot picks up speed. Many stories old and new gather into one Orphic legend of fallen love and grounded knight-heroes. All the boys are busted at the ranch house. Old man Johnson says he was never in love with the cattle business, but it was just the only one he ever knew. Few choices, fewer chances, an elemental destiny. McCarthy assembles an ancient camp-caste saga of men alone on the sundown plain—tooth-pickin, dirt-spittin, horse-breakin, posthole diggin, cowshit-booted, cold-grubbin bunkhouse boys on a western border makin do with the animals. Are there any options? "Daybreak to backbreak for a god-given dollar, said Billy." He loves the ranch life and wants his bud to love it too. "Cause by god I love. Just love it." Billy's speech carries a touch of tender-edged irony and stoic sentiment through the hard-core American theme of where the all-American cowboy's at. It's a fencepost heaven and hell, a national and lingual and gender-harsh wasteland border, beautifully destitute mystery on the south side, restless and ill-fated innocence on the north.

Before the girl, the all-American cowboy's either "kneewalkin drunk" or riding a squirrel-headed sumbitch colt to the ground and spraining his ankle. "I reckon he just don't like to quit a horse," the middle-aged ranch-hand Troy says—nor drop a woman. The plot slowly congeals around antique tone and aged subject, an old revolver or a handmade hammer, a tin coffee pot or an iron horseshoe, roll-yer-own breath and scrub-scarred hands. Epic legends of loss overshadow Western free will and individual character and family ties. Billy tries to serve as big brother to John Grady and tells him nobody can tell anybody anything. You just use your best judgment. John Grady says the world doesn't know anything about his judgment, and Billy says it's worse than that, the world "don't care." There's horse sense to all this, the basic four-legged American truth of seeing plainly what you get, the "justice" in a horse's heart and passion in a horseman's.

Nightmare slaughter frames the other side of the Orphic cowboy story, from roping off a wild dog's head, to a knife fight to the death, to flooring an Oldsmobile at 110 miles-an-hour to a Dimmitt, Texas gas station and discovering the front grill studded with decapitated jackrabbit skulls sending a woman into hysterics. Homeric-named Troy tells the story of a hundred rabbit heads jammed sideways into the car bumper covered with blood and guts: "I reckon they'd sort of turned their heads away just at impact cause they was all lookin out, eyes all crazy lookin. Teeth sideways. Grinnin." With pointillist dark humor of dry arroyos and salt flats and moonless night skies, McCarthy sketches a postwar critter diaspora. You've got to laugh with the rangy dialect through men's sweat and tears. "He's beat me like a rented mule," Mac says playing chess with John Grady. "I aint got a weeping dime," John Grady says headed for town with a horse trailer.

The novel honors the working details of repairing a truck inner tube for broke-down Mexicans in the night driving to Sanderson, Texas looking for work, the setting for McCarthy's next novel. "Hay trabajo allá?" The plot layers with manly courtesy and working manners, as Billy tells the story of such a Samaritan favor extended long ago when he and his dead brother Boyd broke down in Mexico in McCarthy's previous novel from Hidalgo County. The Mexican men and boys in the truck bed stand and raise their hands, and Bill can see them above the dark cab hump against the burnt cobalt night sky, "The single taillight had a short in the wiring and it winked on and off like a signal until the truck had rounded the curve and vanished."

When an owl shatters the pickup windshield like a giant moth caught in a web, Billy asks Troy what's wrong. "Just ever goddamned thing. Hell. Don't pay no attention to me." He says he shouldn't drink whiskey anyway. It doesn't help thinking about things, Billy says, his dead brother Boyd, unfaithful girls who run off, the run-down homestead of his childhood, the ill omen of a dead owl that is a dread harbinger to Native thinking. And all around scatter lost unknowable hieroglyphics, Ancestral Pueblo mysteries as backdrop to the all-American tales of unsettling the West.

You can't go back, Troy knows, because back home everything you wanted different is still the same and everything you wished the same is different. All you know finally is that "beauty and loss are one"—what all have all must lose, the Orphic legacy of love. Following their first night together, John Grady holds his sleeping love Magdalena at dawn and has no need to ask her anything. The story becomes a simple tale of plain-spoken lyric and heart-breaking pain across desecrated cultural borders, low tin shacks and cratewood skirting the city, barren gravel lots and sage and creosote plains beyond. Roosters call the dawn and the air stinks of burning charcoal. John Grady meets a man driving a donkey with firewood as the distant churchbells begin to toll. The man smiles with their shared secret of age and youth, the justice of their claims and the claims upon them, a world past and to come and common transience. "Above all a knowing deep in the bone that beauty and loss are one."

The canticled moral will be earned by the story where working prairie life proves raw and feral. A respectful love scene in a whorehouse is followed by a stallion mounting a one-eyed mare, sex a complicated bestial act with the overlay of human care and courtesy. The legend builds in a mock border ballad. "John Grady Cole was a rugged old soul," Billy sings along a red-dirt trail through a wash. "With a buckskin belly and a rubber asshole." These are greenbriar Western boys who don't know what they want and never did, really, Billy adds a few pages later, since the Second World War changed everything. Things "aint the same" anyway and never will be again. The good old days are always what was and is no more, stories of the West that was.

With the mention of history, a blind piano player in the White Lake whorehouse describes Magdalena as a visitor who does not belong here among them. The whorehouse Tiresias, a blind Mexican pianist, speaks Old World English from another place and time. This ancient matchmaker prophetically circles the role of the father who knows the fate of Eurydice and will not sponsor the ill-fated suit, even when he knows it must be. The Homeric Maestro has seen too much of this and he can only speak to the tragedy. "The girl," the waiter says. "She say you no forget her." Ancient cliché, the theme is still true for romantic tragedy, *The Odyssey* to *Troilus and Crissida*, *La Bohéme* to *Gone with the Wind*.

There's something uncanny about the shadows to this tale, whispering geese blacking out the moon over the Platte River. "I aint talking about spooks," Mr. Johnson recalls his cattle drive days up the Chisholm Trail to Ogallala, Nebraska. He says it's more just the way things are if a man only knew it. The old man respects a limit to human knowledge, always a stranger to the hyperreal world out there. His is a precivilized regard for things you don't know, the humility and courage to face them. "I just meant I'd seen things I'd as soon not of," John Grady confesses. Mr. Johnson says he knows it. "There's hard lessons in the world." And John Grady asks what's the hardest, and the old man answers truthfully that he doesn't know. "Maybe it's just that when things are gone they're gone. They aint comin back." John Grady seconds the notion, "Yessir." The story's fatal touchstone seems the Orphic fatality of desire in an ephemeral world of shadows and echoes and ghostly silhouettes of the living and the dead.

Facing the devil personified and speaking for his buddy, Billy Parham stays absolutely honest and point-blank innocent, all guts and angel wings. He says that you can ask anybody that he works for old man McGovern at the Cross Fours out of Orogrande, New Mexico. The devil speaks the damning truth too about a dream that will always be lost, adding that his friend is in the grip of an irrational passion. Nothing said to him will matter because he has a certain story in his head. John Grady's illusion of happiness with Magdalena is not a true story, unfortunately, but like all men he desires a world that can never be, the world he dreams. The crux of the story is whether men should dream a world forever lost. The satanic pimp sneers that his longing realized is no longer the dreamed world at all. Men can't have what they want, and with that Adam is hooked to barter his soul for a lost paradise and fallen lover. "He's in trouble, aint he?" Billy asks. Eduardo smiles and says that is not a question.

Billy later boils things down for his bud John Grady:

> She aint American. She aint a citizen. She don't speak English. She works in a whorehouse. No, hear me out. And last but not least—he sat holding his thumb—there's a son of a bitch owns her outright that I guarangoddamntee you will kill you graveyard dead if you mess with him. Son, aint there no girls on this side of the damn river?
>
> Not like her.
>
> Well I'll bet that's the truth if you ever told it.

And through all this talk stand timeless petroglyphs above cities of the plain recalling Native creation and destruction stories and biblical days of talking rocks and totemic animals and an all-knowing God punishing the wicked with end-times of swift justice and pitiless retribution. "They crossed gray bands of midden soil from ancient campsites washed down out of the arroyo that carried bits of bone and pottery and they passed under pictographs upon the rimland boulders that bore images of hunter and shaman and meetingfires and desert sheep all picked into the rock a thousand years and more." The rocks are etched with the tragic love, hardship, courage, and ghostly dreams of ten thousand fathers, the heart's desire against time itself, as with Keats' Grecian urn.

The blind Maestro refuses a padrino's honorable duty because he knows the heart's truth, "what was flesh and blood is no more than echo and shadow." Speaking with authorial oversight, Maestro mixes philosophy and prophecy in accepting fate and embracing destiny. The Tiresian seer knows that men are free to act only on what is given them and conversely that every act without heart will be found out in the end. Gentleman of deep thought, however humble and human, the blind musician cannot see the future, only bend to past fatalisms. The tragic hero and heroic moment are all. Our fated options? Trust the heart that forbids having and love the loss for itself. A man is always right to follow what he loves, Maestro says, even if it kills him.

And so John Grady tells Magdalena of his childhood dreams when Comanche ghosts passed on their pilgrimage to another world "for a thing once set in motion has no ending in this world until the last witness has passed." Eurydice will be lost, again and forever, and Orpheus will sing canticles of it. It is the last time John Grady sees his beloved. "Para todo mi vida." From there the bleeding-footed penitente, fated Magdalena, walks down the Calle de Noche Triste on Ash Wednesday to her wedding death in the river, met by Charon crossing the river Styx, the pimp's street thug, smiling Tiburcio.

Meanwhile back at the ranch, Travis tells John Grady don't do nothin dumb over some girl. "It aint too late if you aint done it," but it is too late. In the Juárez morgue "the girl to whom he'd sworn his love forever lay on the last table" with a severed throat in a twisted blue dress like shoeless Rinthy in *Outer Dark*. John Grady sets out to kill the pimp devil and swears to ride until he dies. "I'd ride and I'd never look back. I'd ride to where I couldn't find a single day I ever knew. Even if I was to turn back and ride over ever foot of that ground. Then I'd ride some more." Here is the beginning and the end of mounted Orphic Western myth from Eden to Armageddon.

First he must kill the evil that kills what it loves but cannot possess, the cigarillo devil Eduardo. The forty-year-old pimp wields a knife like a torero and carves an E into John Grady's thigh. He mocks the gringo farm-boy's lust to find "a thing for which perhaps they no longer even have a name" in a whorehouse, Americans carrying their "pale empire" across the border with an "unspoken labyrinth of questions." Perhaps the devil protests too much. The last one to speak will be the loser, Eduardo warns, and a knife fight worthy of all chivalry and chicanery ends with John Grady Cole's ancestral hunting knife slammed through the pimp's lower jaw. "His jaw was nailed to his upper skull and he held the handle in both hands as if he would withdraw it but he did not."

Mortally wounded, John Grady staggers down the Calle de Noche Triste to a boyhood packing crate hovel where Billy finds him the next day. "You daggone fool," Billy says to his bud and carries his blood-soaked body down the Calle, "and the children followed and all continued on to their appointed places which as some believe were chosen long ago even to the beginning of the world." Adam loses his Edenic innocence and curses working the earth. Orpheus loses his beloved Eurydice and dies in a singing river of tears. Tristan never returns to Isolde, and Romeo collapses beside the corpse of Juliet. In this heart-broken tragic romance of the West, love is forever lost with all the innocence and hope of the world.

Except for the updated coda: Taking up John Grady's cowboy pilgrimage, Billy rides on the rest of his life to El Paso in 2002, finally a 78-year-old drifter finding refuge under a concrete overpass somewhere in Arizona. Everyone is dead and gone, his parents, his brother Boyd in Mexico, blue-eyed Alejandra the heart-breaker, his bud John Grady, his sister, even the epileptic prostitute. Their dream ghosts do not turn or answer but only pass down the empty road "in infinite sadness and infinite loss." Billy swears he's been wrong in everything he's ever thought about the world or his life. Then the hobo existential shows up, and they share Billy's crackers and talk philosophy, a place for the authorial ghost to unload his burden, whether the cowboy wants to hear it or not.

Lessons learned: consider the coda a campfire wrap-up with the fire out. Think of a happenstance conversation with a prescient guy in a bar, a derelict woman singing on a bus, a wizened driver at a truck stop where guys stop and rest and talk. This cowboy Billy has become a movie extra, superhighways have braided the west to parking-lot urban centers, and the old ways that never were certain are no more, or changed irrevocably. The overpass hobo speaks fatefully in an ancient sophist tongue that "all knowledge is a borrowing and every fact a debt." Every event reveals itself to us only at the surrender of an alternate course. There are myths, but no systems, no predeterminations known. The blind Maestro's warnings prove highway-concrete storyteller's craft now, the traveler's life converging at this place and hour.

Every story begins with a question, the hobo says, a hesitantly anticipated step into mystery where there is no end or beginning, only ongoing story. Spanish and English struggle across opposing lingual borders to parse the dream-tale, and words prove only partly and provisionally helpful. "Pero desaparesido? He shrugged. Where do things go?" Billy prods his literate double just to get on with the story. Imagine drifters Don Quixote and Sancho Panza on the dark vacquero plain under a highway overpass. "Listen," the philosopher says, and "Got to go" the traveler rejoins.

The prelanguage of dreams appears a calculus of storytelling that precedes words, the hobo offers. If there is no sound, there can be no language, only a dream in a language older than the spoken word. Men have only the instant of the journey they are on in this strangest of all worlds, the philosopher-novelist opines. "Before the first man spoke and after the last is silenced forever." Faulkner, Dostoyevsky, and Melville in the wings, surely, the hobo knows how little is known and how poorly a man can prepare for aught to come, but he keeps talking. The novel mutates into a densely mentalist narrative thickening with dream talk, the elemental Orphic cowboy canticle after the singer has lost everything and his head continues to float down the river. What more should a reader of such frontier tales expect? "Each man is the bard of his own existence."

Impatient with all this, Billy repeats he's got a ways to go, but the Zarasthustrian hobo goes on talking. "I think he saw a terrible darkness looming." Billy's double continues narrating his dreaming a dream, all ghost-travelers driven by terrible hunger to traverse the ancient landscape debris of ten thousand father cultures. Not without regenerative faith and brotherly counsel. Perhaps, despite the human plunge from grace, there are terrestrial spirits, mysterious strangers, and saintly drifters among us, the fiction risks, barefoot prophets and philosophers in rags and savants of death. Perhaps these are our dream keepers, our soul guides, our voices of conscience. Perhaps. "Every man's death is a standing in for every other." The answer, if there is one? Love the man-traveler before you. To repeat from the beginning, "Will you honor the path he his taken? Will you listen to his tale?"

And so Billy treks on past ancient Spanish missions and radar tracking stations to Portales, New Mexico where a hardscrabble family takes him in, as half a century ago the Cross Fours ranch house proved refuge for Mr. Johnson in his lost-daughter grief. Like the mother he lost, the wife Betty pats Billy's rope-scarred hand veined to his heart, a map for anyone to read, and puts him to bed. "You go to sleep now." As the slave mother ballad promises, *When you wake you shall have all the pretty little horses.* Broken Billy confesses he's not what she thinks he is. "I aint nothing."

> Well, Mr Parham, I know who you are. And I do know why. You go to sleep now. I'll see you in the morning.
> Yes mam.

Humbled pilgrim, quieted child, or lost cowboy bum?

Cities of the Plain ends with an inverse ballad Dedication in rhyming tetrameter and lyric dimeter verse:

> *I will be your child to hold*
> *And you be me when I am old*
> *The world grows cold*
> *The heathen rage*
> *The story's told*
> *Turn the page.*

The novel's essentials current in talk-singing measure: parent-child love, crossing from innocent youth to wizened age, entropy of all things, apocalyptic end-times, story's denouement, the next page blank for going on. We end where most stories begin, the author dedicating the story told to the next tale to be heard, *No Country for Old Men.* The biblical cities of the plain, Sodom and Gomorrah, are destroyed in Genesis so the people can go forth and multiply and continue with all the other Orphic loss stories to come. El Paso and Juárez still adjoin across a southwest border that cradles the last cowboys in America.

CHAPTER 12

A Sorry Tale: *No Country for Old Men*

An aged man is but a paltry thing
A tattered coat upon a stick, unless
Soul clap its hands and sing, and louder sing
For every tatter in its mortal dress

—W. B. Yeats, "Sailing to Byzantium"

"No country for old men," W. B. Yeats defied death and opted for timeless classics in hammered metal and chiseled stone. The Irish bard left "those dying generations" of crass modernity for a place beyond time. How old is a thirty-six year-old veteran like Llewelyn Moss in *No Country for Old Men?* Aged as he gets to be when he dies, and so with Carla Jean his wife of nineteen. "But he wasn't nothing compared to what was comin down the pike," the sheriff says opening the narrative at a child murderer's state execution. It's an old story told by older men to anyone who might make it this far: a little man up against lethal odds and forces much bigger than himself, huge fortunes and ruthless powers, bets his life, stash, and love against overwhelming odds. He is fated to fail. How he fails is the hyperreal story, the drama of everyman against destiny and ill winds and corruption. McCarthy crafts an ancient tragedy without epic overbite, no heroes or romances that can be saved, men "ignorant as a box of rocks," the old uncle says.

An aged man wonders if things have gotten worse over the years. Possibly, but how would anyone know the difference staring down the devil's cobalt barrel? "By the time he got up he knew that he was probably going to have to kill somebody," our man knows, but he just didn't know who. The narrative refuses to sentimentalize the fall into willed violence nor does the story suck on melodrama. Characteristically for McCarthy by now, there's a page number every other page, missing apostrophes in the local speech, no quote marks and acres of white space around the dialogue, big gaps and jump cuts between scenes. The whole is a spare, clean, objective rendering of unwilled pain and willed endurance, minimalist figures against a staggering backdrop of space and eternity where the chase is seen from above and afar, sniper-fashion.

There are no psychological plumb-lines into the characters, more a flat analogical sheen all on the outside—in voices and gestures, cars and guns, boots and shirts, ill-lit streets and listless motel beds. What you see is what you get, and what you get is minimal talk, maximal distance from what's talked about. It's a kind of tunnel focal intensity that bores forward scary and seductive, like scoping prey with a high-powered rifle. Watch this book closely, the craft seems to say, your life depends on it. The story moves quietly, feline feral, through characters and actions laid out as body riprap across a desert mountain pass—murderers, clerks, war vet, cops, wives, hit man, hired killer, uncle. Poker-faced, people guard their names as they do their backs and checkbooks and innards—game fare worth protecting from low critters and circling vultures. The devil is in the detail. The narrative patiently accretes daily particulars, local dialects, small thoughts, short actions in the face of grand slaughter through drug trade and institutional greed, futile stupidity and satanic killing.

Mostly McCarthy's fiction is a man's world, whether socially bad or good, women sidelined in grief. All turns on masked words for things and a lucky mastery of things, even reversed gender roles: How to pour coffee and wait for someone to speak. How to watch the sun rise or set knowing the odds of difference and survival. The bore, carry, drop, scatter, and explosive shatter of guns and bullets. "The box of shells contained exactly the firepower of a claymore mine." The horse power, thrust, crawl, traction, handling, and societal regard for engines, cars, and trucks. A Ramcharger is not an imported pickup, and a black Plymouth Barracuda or a patrol car has to go places where only horses used to go. People ride through off-road terrain, but you've got to know who to trust, what will carry you where. "Nothin wounded goes uphill, he said." The studied, slow-mo chase and murder scene seen in exacting detail. Chigurh says that anything can be an instrument—small things you wouldn't notice passing hand to hand. People pay little attention, and then one day is an accounting, and after that nothing's the same. Like coins or bugs or viral cells.

Specifics tell all: when Moss buys clothes to replace his blood rags at mid-point, we know him literally—Wrangler jeans 32" x 34", which gives him a small waist, long legs, a tight midriff fit. Large shirt and ten-and-one-half Nacona boots, which makes him broad-shouldered, just shy of six feet, and accustomed to workingman's footwear. A seven-and-three-eighths Stetson hat silverbelly gray for a largish head needing coverage. White socks and medium Jockey shorts. "I aint been duded up like this since I got out of the army." Dressed to kill, or be killed, a coroner couldn't be more precise.

As a representative American, Moss is on the run through the entire narrative, a veteran Vietnam sniper with a good heart, everyman caught in the crosshairs of hell. "Do not, he said, get your dumb ass shot out here." Bell, the fifty-seven year-old middle-man peace officer and makeshift narrative stage-manager, does his best with the mess, hangs on to his own self-respect, and walks away from war as work at the right time. He's a public servant on a low rung of law enforcement in a violent land. "You care about people you try and lighten their load for em," he says toward the end of the storyline. Family-protective Bell seems to know when to hold and when to fold his cards. Foreign scented and "faintly exotic," Chigurh shows the devil's mastery of weapons of destruction, from slaughter yard tools, to trucks and a transponder the size of a Zippo lighter, to rifles and handguns and sawed-off shotguns. He knows exactly how to strangle a deputy with handcuffs cutting into his own wrists. He is Nietzsche's will to deadly power through force, cunning, and know-how: the certitude, efficiency, and indifference of a highly tuned executionist. Malign will gone rancid, he enjoys doing it right.

The utility of things, as bluntly useful as a rusty double-bladed axe or efficient as a 30.30 rifle or immediate as a monosyllabic name. For starters, how to write a true sentence, as Hemingway worked in a Paris café with a lead pencil in a blue notebook. "He'd of set there till hell froze over and then stayed a while on the ice." How to pace a plot and set a story. "If the heroin is missing and the money is missing then my guess is that somebody is missing." How to draw character from single detail. A clerk looks into Chigurh's eyes. "Blue as lapis. At once glistening and totally opaque. Like wet stones." Satan plays on the thousand-meter-stare of soldiers who have seen too much. *Lapis negra* cobalt eyes—you won't look into them twice. The craft of all this shows in the words to tell a story clean as picked bone, brackish as a festered wound, ominous as desert talus obscuring a horizon of red-eyed jackals. Slow, accretive, local detail inches toward action with real human characters in all their working, small-town class, or lack. The real talk is nasty, brutish, short, and deadly honest. Telegraphic sentences. Abrupt fragments. "No you never done no such a thing," the young wife says of her man's purported cache of 2.4 million. Colloquial West Texas wryness, the way folks say things, or don't if they don't feel like talkin'.

This country is a land where the good die young and the bad seem to prosper forever, hyperreal themes as old and scoured as tree stumps and fading stars and hardpan winter graves. Minor characters go down at center stage preemptively—deputy, driver, desk clerk, child, cop, hired killer, boss, girls, kids—one by one, staring into the devil's slate eyes. The major characters die in the wings, off-stage, without high drama, simply blown away, or gunned down dead between the eyes. You use birdshot to kill a CEO if you don't want to break the window behind him.

Why should we care? *No Country for Old Men* scripts an old morality tale in a new context of precision weapons that replace bows and arrows and atlatls. Petroglyph to power tool the consequences remain the same—hunter hunts the hunted and in turn is hunted down by a more lethal killer. "The rocks there were etched with pictographs perhaps a thousand years old." Moss knows the men who pecked these images were hunters like himself and this their only trace left. Perhaps little has changed but the tools.

The reader gets to be spotter, tracker, sniper, translator, and executioner in this tale. Death is the final word, sooner or later. What men do between innocence and extinction marks their place on the stage: Llewelyn Moss the average man with a marksman's eye caught stealing the devil's ransom; Carla Jean his child-bride, patient in the trailer, or tending her dying grandmother in Odessa, waiting for the phone call; Ed Tom Bell the good sheriff with his own war-conflicted conscience and Loretta his better half ("Marryin her makes up for ever dumb thing I ever done"); Carson Wells the bad-ass bounty hunter and hired corporate killer killed by his old killing partner from clandestine operative work, perhaps government Special Forces or the CIA; Anton Chigurh the devil's croupier who flips fate's coin and enforces the sentence, live or die. "Every moment in your life is a turning and every one a choosing." He does not drop into local dialect and he overvoices philosophy as he kills.

Chigurh stands up to God with an unflinching, uncompromising belief in predetermination—no free will or human choice, no mercy or sentiment, no giving in or letting go or giving up. Principled in the purity of his work, he defies sentiment and falsehood and betrayal. A pure born-again agent of death, anti-Christ Calvinist Chigurh is a man of his deadly word, a relentless avenger, an implacable killer defying God, no less than the diabolic Judge in *Blood Meridian*.

"How to prevail over that which you refuse to acknowledge the existence of." Iago was never so clear-minded, Ahab no more manically fixated, Kurtz no less obsessed with his mission to exterminate losers. "The horror! The horror!" What more can a man say of pure evil?

Anyway, the old uncle says, you never know how bad luck has saved you from worse. It's a cautionary moral fable of sorts worthy of Hieronymus Bosch sketching hell in color or Goya's war scenes. Shakespeare's tragedies and histories were as blood-sopped. How to and how not to get along in mortal life may be the moral, and deadly consequences are all. Characters are pitted between fate and free will, chance and choice, love and indifference, all caught before the knurled hammer of mortality's firing pin. Little guys and big evil forces—we don't see the power brokers or the drug dealers or the users center-stage, but we witness the societal meltdown all around them, the wastage, the carnage. Finders-keepers, losers-weepers depends on what you find, and there is a dicing fatality to it all.

Keep talking, as Faulkner said accepting his Nobel Prize, man's puny voice through the blood-meridian end of time. Americans have heard it before in Ahab's vehemence toward the white whale, in Thoreau's civil disobedience during time of war, in Whitman's bar-baric yawp at scented armpits and shorn pubes, in Poe's manic glee over serial killing, in Hemingway's dead-eye clarity at a bull fight, in Faulkner's inebriate passion with Southern families gone to seed, in Berryman's mad brilliance from the fatal bridge, in Kerouac's brash candor on the open road, in Ginsberg's beatific howl at repression, in Kesey's edgy physicality around a lunatic asylum, in Carver's tawdry romances within backlit motels. But never with such unblinking min-imalist precision. World-weary, mortal-heavy renunciation of all things human beyond survival. Have matters changed for the worse, or were they always this grim? Tell me the truth, the young man implores, his innocence the old man's scar.

By the millennium, hunter becomes warrior in defense of family and country, and drafted warrior falls to foot soldier, grunt, hump, swinging dick. What if he's sent overseas to foreign wars for foreign powers where he doesn't know what he's fighting for, just trying to stay alive, as with Llewelyn Moss in Vietnam, then comes home to fight for a living and fail daily? Stiffed, men say. Some like Anton Chirgurh and Carson Wells turn their second-amendment weapons into wanton killing tools. Kill or be killed would seem the bottom line of American manhood, the raison d'etre for his hunting instincts soured from the old frontier days when feeding and defending a fam-ily defined manhood. His moral choices are whittled down to brute survival or massive robbery or corporate slaughter. Vietnam cost 58,000 American soldiers and 4 million Vietnamese, mostly civilians. Back home by Memorial Day 2007, according to news reports, 180,000 Nam vets had committed suicide and 190,000 wandered the streets homeless, and the United States has been at foreign war again for over five long years.

Uncle Ellis fought in the First World War, and his brother Harold died in that war. The dead brother's son Ed Tom Bell fought in the Second World War, distinguished himself dubiously in battle, and came home to the Texas-Mexican border as sheriff to protect the spit-dirt town of Sanderson. Llewelyn Moss was a sniper in Vietnam and came back to work as a welder, marry a child-bride of sixteen, and find 2.4 million dollars in a drug deal gone bad on the desert. What can be done?

Obviously Moss, against his better judgment, takes the bait knowing there's hell to pay, but willing to gamble with the devil, as he tells his child-bride in their Desert Aire trailer park. "I'm fixin to go do something dumbern hell but I'm goin anyways. If I don't come back tell Mother I love her." Carla Jean says his mother is dead, and Llewelyn mutters he'll tell her himself then. The young wife sits up in bed and says he's "scarin the hell" out of her. He says go to sleep and he'll be back in a bit. "Damn you, Llewelyn," she scolds, and he steps back into the doorway asking if he doesn't come back, are those her last words.

How check the Apocalypse? Bell-weather Ed does what he has to do as sheriff, none too heroically. In the wake of unsolved carnage Bell finally moves on, retiring from the force rather than pursue the pure evil of Anton Chigurh who watches the capillaries in his victim's eyes congeal as he shoots them through the forehead, either with a gun or a cattle euthanizer. The point may be obvious—people mean no more than stock to death's handyman. Society fattens them in herds to kill and eat and be replaced by more feed-lot meat. Cattle and chattel come from the same Latin word through capital, or "of the head," crowning the false riches of Mammon. A stun gun works better than a sledge hammer.

Colonel Carson Wells hires out to the highest bidder to recover the lost money and heroin for the Matacombe Petrolem Group, probably a front for border-crossing drugs. Acosta's people, or Pablo's Mexican men, come after the illicit stash as well. And Moss, who'd like to have small leverage to rescue himself and Carla Jean from the trailer-trash shithole of Sanderson, scatters bloodstained bits of the money behind him and runs hard across the border and kills pursuers and finally is machine-gunned coming out of a seedy motel with a teenage hitchhiker headed for the morgue, "kind of a skankylookin little old girl" from down in Port Arthur. If not the way it seems, perhaps it's much worse. And we don't even see the final shoot-out or really know who kills Moss, probably the drug thugs. High noon is low sundown.

Page after page of quick-cuts from pursuers to pursued, a child murderer executed in the beginning, a troubled sheriff who's never seen nine county homicides in a week, wives back on the dirt-poor ranch or trailer park, motel clerks snuffed with the cattle bore, patrolmen blown away, taxi drivers and border-crossers giving rides and coats to wounded runaways with bloody wads of cash, pubescent girls snuffed, doped Mexican kids killed joy-riding an old Buick through an intersection, Anglo teens aiding the devil for a few bucks in his get-away, and finally Bell's ghostly dream of his father riding a horse past him with a fire-horn to carry civilization somewhere else, a nighthawk father-son vision portending another story. Not a pretty picture, not a romance, not for light-hearted readers.

Civilization? Conservative urban legend has it that teachers in the 1930s worried about chewing gum, teasing, cutting class, and talking back, sheriff Bell says, and these days they list rape, arson, drugs, murder, and suicide on their educational checklist. Evil is relentless and unending, since Euripides and Aeschylus wrote of Oedipus and Orestes, since the Old Testament prophesied the destruction of Sodom and Gomorrah, cursed cities of the plain. But is evil more pronounced or more equipped today when the Christian right is ascendant and the devil has an end-game? There's a man goin' round takin' names. "For the great day of his wrath is come; and who shall be able to stand?" (Revelation 6: 17). Should we all be put down for good and forgotten? God could just bag things and call it the Rapture. "If any man have an ear, let him hear" (Revelation 13: 9).

The decent man perseveres. The bad man gets his way. The women in the way get killed. The man at the crossroads of good and evil reads the coin the wrong way and gets gunned away. The old uncle tells the sheriff to ease up, don't be so hard on yourself. The good wife goes riding into the sunset trailed by her retired peace officer. The drug lords service the drug addicts, the border gets crossed no matter, the old guys die or fade off or get killed violently, and nobody knows where it all ends. In the end Chigurh (pronounced shi-*gúrr* in the movie?)—not sugar, someone says, more like a blood-sucking chigger or redbug flea—is still on the loose, always, and precisely, since God's fallen angel is there to keep providence honest, and us.

But none is hardly deserving of mercy, and none gets it. Carson the hired killer dies calling Chigurh a "goddamned psychopath. Do it and goddamn you to hell." Carson closes his eyes and turns his head and raises his hand to fend off the gunshot, but his lifeblood drains slowly down the wall behind him—mother's face, first communion, forgotten women. He remembers men dying on their knees in front of him and a child's dead body in a foreign country roadside ravine. As Carson lies with half a head on the bed and his shredded arms akimbo, Chigurh stands and picks the empty shell casing off the rug and blows into it and puts it in his pocket and looks at his watch, a minute before midnight. Hyperreal death comes swiftly, all of a motion like swatting a fly, by surprise and in the instant, uneventful before and after the fact, perhaps no more than a small bullet hole in the forehead or a two-and-a-half inch indent from the cattlegun cylinder or a shotgun blast in the face. Is it too much in a land of broken warriors come home to hell?

To the book's tough love credits: there's unrelieved page-turning dramatic action about who will get it next. Dialogue to die for. Character motivation on a horizontal plain, again almost allegorical in a medieval plane sense, but micro-cosmically and grindingly real to all of us who have flipped a coin, stolen something, taken a chance, tried to do the right thing, hitched a ride, shacked up illicitly, crossed a border, or stared into the devil's black lapis eyes with no quotation marks. The child-bride has to die because Chigurh always keeps his word and he won't "second say the world." He asks if she sees this, and she sobs that she "truly" does. He says good, then he shoots her.

McCarthy records the truth of fiction and the story as historical myth, not to be forgotten. Pictographs are chiseled in the rocks from thousands of years back of hunters, always the hunters, the game and the gaming, the pursued and the pursuing, the relentless wearing down of life. It's a brutal chase around Keats' Grecian Urn. Sheriff Bell is the story's wizened Lone Star stage-manager. "Good hunting, as we used to say. Once upon a time. In the long ago." To what end? The telling is all, the words, the picturing of a vast arid wasteland, shot-up trucks, dead bodies, missing stash, guns, blood, flies, choices, fate. A hard, flat, flinty bajada hyperrealism with fragments of thoughts and actions, small noticings. "Less aint none." And the chase into the river, down the road, into the motel rooms, the dusty cafes, the hitchhikers, the bloody-footed walkers. "Ever step you take is forever. You cant make it go away." Travelers all.

Maybe that's the most of it, wanderers, seekers, trackers, fugitives. The Spanish poet Antonio Machado had inscribed on his tombstone,

"*Caminante, no hay camino / Se hace camino al andar,*" the ancient image of *homo viator*. "Traveler, there is no path, / You make the way as you walk." One footed word in front of another with enough interest to keep walking through the dead-tired dusk of a gut-stained receding frontier, bloodred against the washed-out caliche and creosote bush and cholla cactus. "Your life is made out of the days its made out of." Truth-telling pilgrims on God's plain, but what's God got to do with it? "Long reefs of dull red cloud racked over the darkening western horizon."

Yes, it's an old story of a desiccated wasteland, a deafening horizon, an unbearable burden, a tarnished memory, a broken heart and cracked mind, a conscience that can't stand to make choices anymore. "I didn't think you'd do me thisaway," the young wife protests over the phone. So characters give in to destiny, or fate, or dumb luck, or a cursed existence whose only grace is that it will end someday. Not pretty, true though hardly desirable. Consider any options. The one good thing about old age, the elder uncle says, is that it's short.

Beginning with *The Orchard Keeper*, are there no more heroes in our time? War gives men license to hunt and kill other men. The short gaps between wars equip them to do it unlicensed. Most try to live by rules against violence without reason—what the rich, the mercenary, the desperate, the addicted, the evil, and the insane among us too often get away with. Some working stiffs get caught in the grey zone between license and lawlessness.

Why do we read *No Country for Old Men*? This may be a book you love to hate, but can't put down, like chocolates, fries, or drugs. You've got to respect the hyperreal truth of what it is. "This country has got a strange kind of history and a damned bloody one too," sheriff Bell admits. The story rubs an aged wound of injustice. Most of us like Llewelyn Moss don't get rich and we work hard and we try to make the right choices, and what do we get for it? Or people think they've struck it rich, only to be torn apart by the rabid dogs of greed, dominance, and lust. The sheriff laments the erosion of respect and thinks the trouble starts when you begin to overlook bad manners. "Any time you quit hearin Sir and Mam the end is pretty much in sight."

Unholstering second amendment, gunbarrel justice, we have an old romance with violent American "heroes," from our founding revolutionaries to frontier gunslingers, mobsters to marines. The sheriff claims most folks will run from their mothers to hug death by the neck. Billy the Kid notched his gun twenty-one times for the number of men he killed until his violent death at twenty-one. Kit

Carson killed hundreds of Indians and Mexicans. Davy Crockett wrote in his diary, "I was rathy to kill a bear" and slaughtered many. Cotton Mather preached on a Sunday that he had sent five hundred heathen souls to hell on the gift of smallpox blankets. In 1864 Methodist Minister Colonel Chivington with his Colorado Volunteers eviscerated the sexual organs of Cheyenne Indian men and women at Sand Creek and wore body parts in their hats at the Denver opera. In 1876 Lieutenant Colonel George Custer got himself and two hundred men killed chasing glory along the Little Big Horn.

New World freedom fighters love the feral sentiment of the outlaw, the killer patriotism of the soldier. Bonnie and Clyde shot up the bank and then got all shot up. Al Capone ruled the Chicago South Side, and General Patton stormed Europe with pearl-handled pistols. In 1945 Oppenheimer saw hell in his mushroom cloud over Trinity Site, New Mexico, and Truman dropped "Little Boy" on helpless Hiroshima civilians. General Westmoreland slaughtered 4 million Vietnamese with napalm, rockets, defoliants, and hand-to-hand terror as Oliver North won his stripes and returned to bootleg Iran-Contra and tote the Football, the red nuclear strike telephone for President Reagan. Lieutenant Colonel Ollie even ran for President. Hannibal Lector ate human liver with fava beans in the movies.

Ah, the hyperreal Rapture. Robert MacNamara set the faux war stage for Don Rumsfeld, and Lone Star George Bush the Second rushed to war with WMD lies about Niger yellow cake, phony terrorist connections, and a Christian Crusade to retake the Holy Land. Wyoming's Dick Cheney oversaw shock-and-awe carpet bombing of the biblical House of Abraham, authorized torture at Abu Ghraib and Guantanamo, outed a CIA agent to cover a White House gaffe, and peppered a Texas politician in the face with a quail shotgun. The buck stops here. On his better days the sheriff thinks there is something he doesn't know or that he's leaving out. "But them times are seldom." He wakes late at night and knows certain as death "there aint nothing short of the second comin of Christ that can slow this train."

It all takes place in the longhorn state of Texas near the Alamo, the Pecos River, and Mexican border. This writer was born in Lubbock during the second Great War and grew up with hardscrabble dirt farmers and broken-down cowboys in the Nebraska Panhandle, just south of the Wounded Knee massacre site. The Chisolm Trail connected respective state Panhandles, and homesteaders scratched a living much the same at both ends. My brother did his basic Vietnam training in Fort Bliss, Texas, where the military is buying up Mac's cattle ranch in *Cities of the Plain*. Notwithstanding well-meaning and decent citizens, Texas is the highest carbon-polluting state in the Union, though smog and traffic lie off in the cities and along the interstate highways of *The Border Trilogy*. Global warming seems light years from the hardpan survival of a dying cowboy culture or drug wars across the border, but mega-business and federal politics are extensions of local injustices and regional tragedies, witness the Metacumbe Petroleum drug fence and the Vietnam War in *No Country for Old Men*.

Working-class people like Llewelyn and Carla Jean Moss take buses over long hauls, write letters home, and say howdy over the dial telephone. "Real" men and sheriffs roll their own smokes, hunker down on their heels to jaw, tip their hats, open doors, and two-step at the saloon. Caricature or not, working men say *ain't, he don't, aw shucks,* and *tarnation* while they slaughter stock, gush oil, cyanide prairie dogs, and hang Jesus from their pickup rearviews. From Appalachia to the Texas border, guys go by nicknames like Slim and Shorty, Bubba and Junior, badges of youth club intimacy.

Church is a must for most, as Jimmy Blevins the born-again evangelist preaches over the radio in *All the Pretty Horses,* and freedom codes anything you damn well want across an unfenced prairie. Chigurh's license to kill is based on an American brand of predeterminist nihilism rooted in Puritan advent. If all's fated, nothing's consequential and anything goes. The chosen rule all, exaggeration be damned. Big talk, bigger brag, biggest swagger. *Wanted Dead or Alive, Bring It On, No Way, Mission Accomplished.* LBJ and Vietnam, GWB and Iraq—despite Molly Ivins, Bill Moyers, Kinky Friedman, Lance Armstrong, and millions of good Catholic Hispanics and recent Asian refugees, die-hard Texas is the heart of born-again, Anglo-Republican, Christian-crusading, antiabortion fervor and stem-cell abomination, gay bashing and ethnic discrimination, extra large hats and boots, loaded guns in the bedroom.

McCarthy's novel layers in more firepower data than Tim O'Brien's Asian war saga *The Things They Carried*. The state flag menaces *Don't Tread on Me* with a rattlesnake hiss, while the Dixie Chicks, ashamed of their bellicose NRA President, stump London singing "No Time to Make Nice." On shock jock TV shows and country-western radio, the Lubbock girls were defiled as traitors. *Shut Up and Sing,* the documentary goes.

Make no mistake, the Tex-Mex border desert of *No Country for Old Men* is a place where proud people like Ed Tom and Loretta Bell still ride horses, raise families, work hard, and lead decent lives. Others like Pablo's men fly drug-cargo planes and carry Uzis, or blue-collar workers slaughter stock in feeder lot herds and resent wetback immigrants and believe in capital punishment big time. The novel opens with sheriff Bell remembering the state execution of a teenage murderer. How far will the Great Wall protect the Lone Star folks? *No Child Left Behind* means public education gives way to faith-based credos of Creationism, blind patriotism, mindless jingoism, end-times hysteria, and an endless war on terror that allows America's own licensed terrorists to get away with murder. Who will take the rap?

McCarthy knows all this and writes hyperreal fictions documenting history, local dialect, and regional behavior. Extrapolate the results. From Dallas to the White House, calculate the war-profit billions made by Haliburton and Blackwater, the bandit tax cuts for one percent owning half the country's wealth, the swelling Supreme Court repeal of Roe v Wade, stolen elections, the erosion of civil liberties under the Patriot Act, the guttering of public education, unclean air and water and foods, denied global warming, and a new arms race with North Korea, Iran, China, and India. "If you killed em all they'd have to build a annex on to hell," the sheriff says under his breath. Jeremiah and Ezekiel would have a Texas field day today. Religion has invaded politics and science, and the everyday citizen doesn't get up the gumption to figure differences. So much for public schooling, reality TV, advertising, tent meetings, malls, and lobbyists. If we leave education to the media, the sheriff reflects, we get what we get, green hair and nose rings.

Why from the Dark Ages are humans drawn to witness violence, corruption, bloodshed, betrayal, and all the deadly sins? A question perhaps too big to answer. Maybe we want the God's truth, terrible as it might be, and we fear the worst. We want to see the coin flip played out and weigh the consequences all over again since the Expulsion. *Wheel of Fortune, Strike It Rich, Power Ball, Who Wants to Be a Millionaire?* The country kills you in a heartbeat, the sheriff muses, and his people still love it. Americans want to consider what they would do with any windfall, legal or otherwise, given the odds and choices and possible rewards and punishments. *Survivor, American Idol, Desperate Housewives, CSI, Miami Vice.*

Characters cross into other countries or states of mind where the codes are different, or simply applied differently. It's a debatable question of human justice and international rule of law. The poor stay poor, the rich feed off the lesser, and the rest take what they can get and hang on to what doesn't get stole back. "Never have so few taken so much from so many for so long," goes the "liberal" bumper sticker.

Oil pollution, cyanide poisoning, cultural meltdown, and political chicanery take place in the caliche hardpan between storylines. Wars ravage *other* lands, the politicians say, as they once ravaged this land in border and civil wars, and the wounds stay with us. "You cant go to war without God," the sheriff swears. The Alamo, the Mexican War, the Spanish-American War, the Civil War between North and South, global wars to end all wars, foreign conflicts of slavery, conquest, territory, imperial power, faux democracy, oil, uranium, outsourced productivity, our righteous War on Terror. And the Southwest keeps resettling, or unsettling, as hard-working folks like Llewelyn Moss or Uncle Ellis hunker down and scrape out a living and fight for the fatherland and come home to trailer-trash misery and sour dreams of no country for old men. And the world doesn't tell a man "nothing about how it's fixin to get, neither." The sheriff used to feel that he could somehow put things right, but he just doesn't feel that way "no more." One man knows when to quit.

Neither fantasy nor improbable fiction, McCarthy's most recent novel *The Road* forecasts even more dire news, a father-son pilgrimage to the coast during nuclear winter when all's gone down, winning the Pulitzer Prize for Fiction in Spring 2007.

CHAPTER 13

Live or Die, Brother?
The Sunset Limited

Nobody knows you when you're down and out.

—Bessie Smith

The Sunset Limited, the title-page states, *A Novel in Dramatic Form.*
Character development, dramatic action, and story arc funnel through
conversation on a circumscribed stage with two live actors, premiered
May 2006 by Steppenwolf Theatre Company of Chicago. One
continuous act with two men in one room, no breaks, no interruptions,
no commercials, like the midnight A-train through Harlem. The text
can be read in a sitting, as in the earliest Greek drama of just two
actors, *alazon* and *eiron* sans chorus—dialogue between the believer
and the skeptic, human subject and biological object, yea and nay.
The play boils its plot and characters down to a fundamental question,
to be or not, and a timeworn trope, white existential despair and
black chthonic salvation. It's a far reductionist cry from *The Stonemason*
aborted at the Arena Stage, compassionate distance from the violent
degradation of *Suttree* or *Blood Meridian.*

The "Sunset Limited" is an underground train, probably through
the Columbia University district of Harlem, the urban commuter as
pilgrim in a lonely black-and-white city where the subway is dubbed
the Underground Beast. Sundown end of the road, the third rail to
nowhere, the limits, margins, and erasures of things—white boyz
Angst, black bro rap. The drama is limited to a select and nameless
two, Black and White, a born-again, no longer violent ex-con and a
suicidal professor with no personal history—for better and worse,
spiritual optimist and colorless nihilist. Black-on-white chronology
comes down to a freed slave who finds unlikely salvation through
repenting crime and comes to Jesus in the ghetto, a dark son of the

deadly sins who wants to save others while addicts and criminals steal him blind. He says he's just a homeboy Louisiana "nigger" come north to redemption. Black temporarily rescues White and brings him home, a motiveless, anemic academic who has no friends or family, who despises others, who loathes his academic colleagues and sputters existential nihilism like a guttering Nietzsche. Academic caricature or no, for him there's no story, no people, no love or desire left to live—he simply wants out.

Think basic color. White optically as the spectrum of colors, purity and innocence and rainbow promise, the colorless all-color hope of the New World, mythologized albino legend in Herman Melville's *Moby Dick*. Black as chromatically every color, cursed through darkness as satanic antilight, and so personalized in Ralph Ellison's classic *Invisible Man*. From 6 to 10 million Afro-American slaves were brought to our shores in chains by privileged prodigal Puritans looking for a new life. God's Chosen beached the Edenic cliffs to overlord by Divine Right the sons of Ham and Shem, through White Man's burden, Manifest Destiny, and eugenic fallacy.

Prodigy of all that *Paradise Lost* cultural history gone squalid, the suicidal White steps out of the Old Testament conscience-stricken and soured to judge and to curse and to self-destruct. The good neighbor Black rises hopeful from the New Testament to accept and to bless and to save others. An old stand-off, Jesus versus Jehovah— Christ humoring the disciples at the Last Supper, Job's dialogue with the Whirlwind: "Before I go *whence* I shall not return, *even* to the land of darkness and the shadow of death; A land of darkness, as darkness *itself; and* of the shadow of death, without an order, and *where* the light *is* as darkness" (Job 10: 21–22). Hyperreal terror is good Christian history, tiresome or no.

Have audiences not seen these tragic characters elsewhere? Blind Oedipus on three legs at Colonus before Tiresias, Philoctetes left to die of his stinking wound only to kill Paris with a poisoned arrow, Prometheus strapped to a rock facing the vulture, Sisyphus rolling his destined stone up the mountain. Art is barbaric after Auschwitz, as Theodor Adorno said—Hart Crane jumping ship, Paul Celan drowned in the Seine, Papa Hemingway with shotgun barrels to his temple, Virginia Woolf stone-weighted in the river, Primo Levi broken down the stairwell, Sylvia Plath placing her head in the oven. "Daddy, Daddy, you bastard, I'm through." Has overcivilized humanity seen enough misery? Those who have want no more, those who have not get more. "Then the Lord answered Job out of the whirlwind, and said, Who *is* this that darkeneth counsel by words without knowledge?" (38: 1–2).

The wrath of God is silencing, the violence of mankind deafening, the white-black dichotomy ageless.

McCarthy's one-act opens to a locked tenement room with formica table and chrome-plastic chairs, a bible and newspaper, glasses with pad and pencil. A large Black man sits opposite a middle-aged White in running pants and T-shirt. "So what am I supposed to do with you, Professor?" the wry Samaritan asks.

Pinioned to philosophical rejoinder that goes nowhere, the head-tripping nihilist answers rhetorically from his abject cul-de-sac, "Why are you supposed to do anything?" Black takes no credit for the hyper-real plot. "This aint none of my doin," the dark brother says, "But here you is." And narcissist White typically answers, when he chooses, that nothing means anything.

The audience hears illiterate street sense and literate despair, the witnessing voices of divergent cultures stereotyping each other. "Mm hm. It dont." Interjective mumble corrected by high-brow jibberish. "No. It doesnt." Thoughts before words, words before thoughts—rhetorical sincerity and sincere rhetoric. White abhors the do-good keeper of perfect strangers, and Black says to himself with softly ironic compassion, "Well, he dont *look* like my brother. But there he is." His is a revisionary corrective to xenophobic isolation, a reformed cross-racial care for the *other* other whose people did him grievous wrong. Christ's mercy gives Black second judgment. "Maybe I better look again." The country may not want to hear this over, but White Man's Burden and oceanic slave trade hyperrealize American history to this day, what James Baldwin calls the kinship of "bitter possessed and uncertain possessor" in *The Price of the Ticket.*

Our insomniac suicide admits that today is his birthday, but nothing special, adding tonelessly that Christmas is not what it used to be. Deadpan Black vouches that to be a damn true statement. Immediately White has got to go, but Black will not let him go alone. Serious as a heart attack, he wants to talk.

Compelled by Jesus and "the lingerin scent of divinity," a phrase Black heard on the radio, he reads a single book, the Bible, to White's some four thousand books and forty thousand fellow curses over four decades. Black draws from street culture, White from study hall conundrums. The talk sidles into a literary seminar with a born-again solicitor and a snippy suicide about a fiction, *War and Peace,* and a true story, *The Decline and Fall of the Roman Empire.* Theirs is a form of cultural *occupatio,* as Black buys time against a train schedule, while White lets on that he's lost all faith in culture, books and music and art, fragile civilized things. Saint John of the Apocalypse sensa the Rapture, White says in compound syntax that civilization went up the chimneys at Dachau. Soon it will all be gone, he prophesies in gossamer jargon: "I've been asked didnt I think it odd that I should be present to witness the death of everything and I do think it's odd but that doesnt mean it's not so. Someone has to be here."

Both characters forage for one true sentence, any right word, negative or no. Suppose he were to give his word, Black cuts to the chase, "that I wouldnt listen to none of your bullshit." Astonished that White would not go to his father's dying deathbed, Black scratches for solid familial ground. "That's the way it is. Aint it?" And White answers that he supposes so. Black insists on the stone truth, "No you don't suppose," and that family is not relative. "Is it or aint it?" Their truncated dialogue bleeds a cross-cultural male exchange, the power struggle of faith and faithless reason that echoes Beckett Pinter, Stoppard, Mamet, Camus, Carver, and Sartre against every true word of a blues wail canticled by Bessie Smith or Robert Johnson. Black says "us old country niggers" try to call things for what they are, the "jailhouse," for example. He commences the story of his seven-year sojourn of prison life, pointless violence, loss of family and faith. To what end?

White thinks Black's is a horrible life in Harlem and junkies not worth saving, and Black admits the futile bottom line, but holds out for brotherly love. His street smarts and get-down humor ground survival in the basics, a poor life worth living, even when "the sun dont shine up the same dog's ass ever day." The talk teases out character, motive, and story from each, and Black finally breaks down telling his "bonafide blood and guts tale from the Big House." Skirting criminal violence, White objects to the n-word, as Black gets to his prison awakening on the surgical table. This time White bottom-lines the narrative: "The story of how a fellow prisoner became a crippled one-eyed halfwit so that you could find God." Suffering is human destiny, White holds, and Black counters that pain teaches happiness—hardly new insights, still engrained in history.

Changing strategy from his mojo trick bag of tales, Black considers fortune's dregs, the sorry lot of addicts, and sums up an alcoholic's dilemma. "Because what he really wants he cant get. Or he think he cant get it. So what he really dont want he cant get enough of."

Pimping Jesus versus Jack Daniels returns White to his positivist axis. "God is just a load of crap." But no, Black argues, if God spoke to a "nigger" in jail, the Creator can speak to anyone that biblical truth "is wrote in the human heart too" and Jesus "just told it." Faulkner notwithstanding, White brings Kant and Hegel to their knees. "I think the answer to your question is that the dialectic of the homily always presupposes a ground of evil."

Whoa, Black says reaching for his pad and pencil, that's "strong as a mare's breath," and White asks why he keeps calling him honey. Old South talk, Black says. "It means you among friends. It means quit worryin bout everthing." That's hard for a White academic on his last day, so Black instructs his brother in doing the dozens from street corners. A man can learn to take insults from the others without getting pissed off, but no, he's never stopped an addict from taking drugs.

"Then what is the point?" White interpolates his story and doesn't get it and thinks it's hopeless in this "moral leper colony."

Wow, Black says, he likes the sound of that, but "aint writin no book." Black is culturally vaccinated in bullshit detection against White's top-loaded dreck. For McCarthy talk consistently supercedes text, the spoken word made flesh and blood, as body holds out against brains.

Don't be "facetious," White says, and Black asks him to explain the word. "I guess it means that you're not being sincere." Yet White doesn't mean what he's saying and is just being cynical.

Hoist on his own petard, White defers to Black's talk of life everlasting that gives off light and carries a little weight, though not much, and stays a little warm to the touch. "And it's forever. And you can have it. Now. Today. But you dont want it." Just stay a while, brother, we'll talk about something else, maybe baseball, and share a bite.

White leaks some "personal" information about detesting group therapy and loathing university colleagues, then consents to black coffee while shunning the idea of talking with fellow commuters.

White	Speak to them?
Black	Yeah.
White	About what?
Black	About anything.
White	No. God no.
Black	God no?
White	Yes. God no.

God no, no God—an inverse conversation in shards, full of feints and reversals, exposes little in detail, all of tone and character. They get down to soul food, a stew with bananas, mangos, and rutabagas, and oddly enough the professor likes it. The play stays basic, going nowhere fancy or new, repeating ancient dialectic as New World Noh theater.

Do unto others as you would have them do likewise, Black suggests of breaking bread together, and White slings back that it's just symptomatic of larger issues that he doesn't like people. Spiritually bankrupt as "Kafka on wheels," White says he always gone his own way. *"Ich kann nicht anders."* Husserl and Wittgenstein flip phenomenological ears in subject-object discourse. *Mann ist nie allein,* Kafka also said, *aber immer einsam.* One is never alone, but always lonely

White isn't buying the rap, German or Judaic. "So you come to the end of your rope and you admit defeat and you are in despair and in this state you seize upon this whatever it is that has neither substance nor sense and you grab hold of it and hang on for dear life." He asks if that's a fair portrayal in his longest monologue thus far, so Black admits existential summation could be a way of saying it. White goes on to argue the darker picture, the world's history as a saga of bloodshed, greed, and folly. The tag could cover *Blood Meridian* or *Outer Darkness, Child of God* or *The Road,* echoing the blind Maestro's summary of things in *Cities of the Plain* or Chigurh's justification for cold-blooded execution in *No Country for Old Men.*

Black makes up his own newspaper byline for White's human *jus bellum.* "You couldnt tell the son of a bitch nothing." And the tables reverse momentarily.

White	Now I know you're being facetious.
Black	This time I think you're right. I think you have finally drove me to it.
White	Mm hm.
Black	Well, the professor's done gone to layin the mm hm's on me. I better watch my step.
White	Yes you had. I might be warming up the trick bag.

So Black comes to his point abruptly, love one's brother or die, and White counters that the world is a forced labor camp where death row coughs up a few each day, hence his desire to be done with it.

Holding on for grim death, Black won't give up, and he searches for the words to the Professor's heart. Put another way, "If you can jack you own self around nine ways from Sunday I'd like to know what chance you think I got."

White won't relinquish his lethal will. "The one thing I wont give up is giving up." Line by line, he's lost everything, courage, love, hope, pity, but can't say how or why.

Black sticks to his point: stay on the platform with his fellow commuters. "All of them is travelers too." McCarthy's *homo viator* speaks up, from Tennessee white trash, to Texas crackers and New Mexico cowboys, to Harlem commuters and nuclear winter pilgrims. And Black objects to the condescending futility of White's pessimism.

"Mn. If I'm understanding you right you saying that everbody that aint just eat up with the dumb-ass ought to be suicidal."

Yes, that's the point, White says, the mind's rightful self-annihilation over the soul's heavenly pipe dreams. Village atheist versus town idiot. "The shadow of the axe hangs over every joy. Every road ends in death. Or worse."

Death is the wake-up mother. Parroting Marlow's frame in *Heart of Darkness*, White concludes: "You tell me that my brother is my salvation? My salvation? Well then damn him. Damn him in every shape and form and guise. Do I see myself in him? Yes. I do. And what I see sickens me. Do you understand me? *Can* you understand me?" A Dostoyevskian night rider in daylight clothing, this self-appointed "professor of darkness" turns white into black, a racial appropriation and reverse ethnic slur at the end of a long dramatic road. "I've heard you out and you've heard me and there's no more to say." White turns to walk out the door off the stage into "the hope of nothingness."

—leaving Black alone swearing White doesn't mean what he says and that he'll be there in the morning commute for his brother. He collapses to his knees, asking God why He didn't give a loyal believer the right words to change another's self-destruction. But it's alright, Black backs off, "I'll keep your word. You know I will. You know I'm good for it." He can't help lifting his head and asking the Lord deferentially, "Is that okay? Is that okay?" Will the word save a man, or simply stall death?

Forty years ago, John Berryman constructed a blues lyric dialogue between middle-aged, suicidal, white academic Henry and his alter-ego, a shadowy blackface brother in *The Dream Songs*. The tragic poet futilely split his mainstream self into many selves trying to save itself through cross-racial, darkly comic, hip jive. "—Try, Dr God. Push on me. / Give it to Henry harder." Berryman's black mask wondered out-loud, "What bad could happen to Mistah Bones?" Victim of "the thinky death" at fifty-nine, the tragic poet sprang nimbly off a Mississippi bridge waving to the crowd. "Kitticat, they can't fire me—."

Nobody knows you when you're down and out, Bessie Smith sang way back in Harlem, and Louis Armstrong blew *What did I do to be so black-and-blue* in Carnegie Hall. You may have heard it all before, white cynic and black survivor, but the interethnic crux is no less true. The white man is left with the strange fruits of his own racial guilt and dubious material success, the suburban spoils of his toxic mind, greedy pockets, and affluent suffering. And he can't take it anymore. Hold on, the Black brother says, finger the jagged wound, as Ralph

Ellison talked out the blues in *Shadow and Act*. Squeeze out a comic lyricism, an affirmation through suffering, that sings through the pain beyond the chains of slavery or cultural betrayal, at the end of a lynch rope or a logical argument, at the bottom of the pile of institutionalized racism or stuporous labor force. "These songs are not meant to be understood, you understand," Berryman chanted his own canticle. "They are meant to terrify & comfort. / Lilac was found in his hand."

Postwar urban laments are legion. Elizabeth Bishop wrote a poem of "The Man-Moth" commuter who rides backward into the suburban night, stealing across the pavement and up the sides of buildings to the illusory hole of light called the moon. If you catch him with a tear in his all-pupil eye, steal it quick, the poet advised, or he'll swallow his salt-life sentiment and disappear lidless into the shadows.

Black is left pitiful with White's exit, imploring the Lord like Job crestfallen, getting no answer. The departing Whirlwind speaks in riddles or falls silent. "Where *is* the way *where* light dwelleth? and *as for* darkness, where *is* the place thereof" (Job 38: 19). The born-again Good Book isn't all that reassuring, and McCarthy's one-act ends with Black on his knees.

CHAPTER 14

The Final Story: *The Road*

The first angel sounded, and there followed hail and fire mingled with blood, and they were cast upon the earth: and the third part of trees was burnt up, and all green grass was burnt up.

—Revelation 8: 7

No one wants to talk realistically about the end of the world, and for that reason we may just hasten the fire next time—fomenting war with lies and political machinations and imperial overreach; masking nuclear holocaust in the Rapture or Islamic terrorism (destroy a culture to save it); hiding Global Warming behind Creationism or job loss rationalizations; dismissing pandemics as mythical plagues in faraway places; blaming gays and liberals and scientists and soft politicians for antipatriotic bad news and sentimental social programs and godless biological research (see Nobel Peace Prize Winner Al Gore's 2007 *Assault on Reason*). Ronald Reagan said we could survive nuclear winter if there were *shovels enough to go around,* and the Second Bush administration wants to restart a Star Wars first-strike shield for Homeland Security that a trillion dollars won't make right. "Blessed *is* he that readeth, and they that hear the words of this prophecy, and keep those things which are written therein: for the time *is* at hand" (Revelation 1: 3).

Is the "journey" in this last book somehow its significance? Oprah Winfrey probed Cormac McCarthy in her Book Club interview, June 2007. "Oh, it's just a boy and a man on the road" McCarthy deflected. "You can obviously draw conclusions...depending on your taste. It's a pretty simple story, I think." The novelist had no idea how *The Road* would end when he started. Oprah asked where the "apocalyptic dream" came from, but Cormac didn't exactly know that either. He was staying in a mid-American hotel with his young son John, and he looked down at the sleeping boy and out the night window and heard the lonesome sound of trains passing. He wondered what the town would look like in fifty or a hundred years. He thought of fires up on the hill "and so I wrote this page and another, the end of it." Four years later in Ireland he knew "that man, that little boy" was his story. The novel is dedicated to McCarthy's son John Francis, now eight. "A love story, I suppose," Oprah said and the author blushed, having ventured that his son "practically co-wrote" the book.

"Write hard and clear about what hurts," repeating what Hemingway advised, a male aesthetic seasoned in wounds, bent on survival, all too human. Who will cross the earthly truth about end-times with telling narrative, gauge industrial-military blowback against mean survival, detail the charred aftermath of denied global consequences? Possibly the hyperrealistic novelist, if anyone is listening, the artist, the filmmaker, the truth-teller, if we have the stomach to attend. So, what if, what "rough beast" slouches toward Bethlehem?

The Road begins in ballad lyric prose under the ashen graylight of a nuclear winter: "When he *woke* in the *woods* in the *dark* and the *cold* of the *night* / he'd *reach out* to *touch* the *child sleep*ing be*side* him." The anapests, reverse spondaic feet, and alliterative rhythms give fine classic cadence to the tale's opening, a father-son love story at the end of the world, all balanced in blank verse couplets turning back on themselves to Shakespeare, Milton, and Yeats. McCarthy classically cadences a lyric narrative to tell a terrible journey: "Then they *set out along* the *blacktop* in the *gun*metal *light, shuf*fling / *through* the *ash, each* the *oth*er's *world* en*tire." Waiting for Godot* crosses with *Pilgrim's Progress* and *King Lear* heading south to warmer climes and the origins of life in the sea, the "effigy magnolias" of the singing New World Carolinas, perhaps. The sojourners hold a plastic tarp against the sooty snow and rain of Puritan New England, pushing a shopping cart of scavenged provisions. The golden-haired boy of possibly eight proves the father's "warrant" for living through end-times. "If *he* is *not* the *word* of *God God nev*er *spoke,*" again in grim lyrical hexameter worthy of Homer. It's not that McCarthy is straining to write well; his words must set up with edge, heft, rhythm, and resilence against the despoliation of the setting, the despair of the characters, the reader's fatigue. The language labors epically to redeem a fallen world, a humanity gone rabidly insane, a father-son survival barely to be told. How else could a reader get through the story?

The man drains trashcan corners of oil for a slutlamp to light the grey pall and read his son a story of the "good guys" giving essentials to others and saving the world. A ghost world of things stands intact, lifeless, the mummified residue of a neutron bomb possibly that kills all living organisms and leaves objects standing. "*Everything* as it *once* had *been* save *fad*ed and *weath*ered." The world as we knew it, now without life. The boy, aged for his age by death-march witness, asks elemental questions throughout the journey. "Are we going to die?"

The ashen scabland infects everything including pilgrim lungs, and walkers wear makeshift mouth scarves of torn sheets. The writing settles into a postholocaust grammar of scree, shards, smoke, fractals, bits and pieces of charnel, dead flesh and sallow bone. Pointillist paragraphs without indentations, scattered thoughts of survival or death. There are no chapter reliefs for 241 pages, no plot line or story arc of character development, just two shrouded figures walking the road and running for their lives, dark figures on a darkling plain. "A colorless world of wire and crepe." Is this a survivor's handbook, barely numbered, unstructured observations of the days after? "Cold to crack the stones." The fear is palpable and growing, real terror, true postwar nightmare, a book to be read seriously, if at all, as a survival manual in the way Hemingway taught his readers to make camp after the war, or to tie a fishing lure, or to elude a sniper. Ralph Ellison in *Shadow and Act* said that by reading Hemingway during the Depression he learned to wing-shoot flying birds to feed his mother's Oklahoma brood.

The pilgrims come to the father's childhood homestead, tangled dead lilac in the yard, and see the pinholes in the Christmas mantle for stockings forty years ago. The boy knows nothing of this ritual. Imagine no Christmas or New Year's Eve, no Easter, no Independence Day, no Thanksgiving, no birthday or even work-free Sunday. The light through a hole in the roof is as gray as the man's heart in this grayhearted story. The man says they should not have come, and the reader wonders who should be reading this book. Goggled refugees trudge on as fevered migrants with barrows of shoddy, everything frail and dissolving. These are end-time vignettes worthy of Hieronymus Bosch, the Rapture manmade, Halloween for real, and there is no more time called ever. "Ever is a long time. But the boy knew what he knew. That ever is no time at all."

The man pledges to euthanize his son and himself with his last two bullets, if he must, the boy all that stands between life and horrible death. Can you do it when the time comes? the father asks himself. He is coughing a mist of blood on the gray snow as the forest fires burn still higher in the mountains. He ponders how the never to be differs from the never that was. Philosophy at ground zero: what never would be is now past, the never that was is with us. What could never be imagined details the unimaginable present. "By day the banished sun circles the earth like a grieving mother with a lamp." It's a desolate lyricism, curiously moving in lamentation like the Book of Job or Ezekiel, showing that the wounded voice can make music of hell itself. "Let the day perish wherein I was born, and the night *in which* it was said, There is a man child conceived. Let that day be darkness" (Job 3: 3–4). The man carves a cane flute and gives it to the boy passing by the dead impaled on spikes along the road. Ash falls on the snow until it is all but black.

What would you live for, die for, abandon, salvage, save, or carry? the book asks the reader to ask. These are essential questions of dedication, survival, courage, and purpose in the face of horror and destruction—anti-heroic meditations on bearing nuclear winter. How it would feel, how the graying world might look, what the survivors could do to survive—ghostly, staggering, bedraggled pilgrims in limbo, tottering down the road of sorrow to nowhere, bound for hell, or hell-sent. The things they might carry: a boy's toy truck, an incomplete pack of cards, a butane lighter, canned food of ham and beans, beets, carrots, anything that might not go bad, a nickelplated pistol with two bullets, a plastic tarp and parka, decomposing shoes, binoculars, blanket rags, memories, hopes, courage, dreams, truth, a few words—all tumbled into a broken-wheeled shopping cart trundling down the road. There would be no jokes, no tears, no verbiage, no innocence, no looking back. No more "state" roads, no more states, no border-crossings, no stores, no cars or trucks or cycles of any kind, no governments, no laws or principles of shall not, just the fetid remnants of dying culture and murderous gangs and corpses and the stragglers sorting the picked over trash of the wrecks of civilization, the common sour smell of desiccated bodies.

Stay sharp to the signs, the story cautions, be alert and resourceful to stay alive among predators afoot. If there are tracks down the melted macadam roadway, beware.

>Who is it? said the boy.
>I don't know. Who is anybody?

There's nobody left besides them in this wasteland, anybody is nobody. What is left is only what fear means to them, usually a threat ruling out the company of others, an existential cul-de-sac at the end of time. A lightning-struck dying man collapses on the road. Papa says without emotion that there's nothing to be done for him. Burned-over walking corpses fall off the road, as the boy looks back crying, and Papa says they can't fix it. The boy broods on still another dying man, and Papa warns that they can't share what they have or they will die too. A hard patriarchal lesson, not well enough learned, nor early enough at the ending.

Moments of respite are few. Finding morel mushrooms to roast shows a simple good by contrast with all that goes bad. "This is a good place Papa, he said," and a reader recalls Nick Adams making a good camp in the Big Two-Hearted River aftermath of the first "great" war. Papa tells his son stories of courage and justice to put him to sleep, the old stories.

Looking back in his dreams, the man remembers that the clocks stopped at 1:17 during the night, the low concussions, no water in the bathtub, and his wife clutching her belly when the lights went out. They never heard migratory birds again. The golden-haired boy is born at the end of the world, and his mother can't go on. Moment by moment, bit by bit, observation by observation, the world stops being itself. How annihilation trickles in, the clock stops, time winds down is the story of *The Road*. There are momentary paragraphs of personal reckoning:

> No lists of things to be done. The day providential to itself. The hour. ·
> There is no later. This is later. All things of grace and beauty such that
> one holds them to one's heart have a common provenance in pain.
> Their birth in grief and ashes. So, he whispered to the sleeping boy. I
> have you.

The man's Sisyphean choice is to bear pain, to go on, to believe in the boy as humanity's narrowing future. There is no past to go back to. Hardly aware of time, the boy grieves a maternal absence and wishes he was with his mom, and the man says, "You mean you wish that you were dead." He musn't say it: the dead feminine cannot suffer this torment, the male principle struggles to bear up and on. Fate's coin toss: I will, or not? Nietzsche at the crossroads of life and death, tragic sanity versus annihilating bedlam.

The mother's backstory argues that no one survives. Fearing the worst and opting out, she says they are the walking dead in a horror film. "They are going to rape us and kill us and eat us and you wont face it." As distant cities burn, the woman has no stand to take, so she exits under her own curse, "faithless slut" to her new lover, death. Mom's heart was ripped out the night her son was born, and "eternal nothingness" frames her only hope, no sorrow, only acceptance of the end. She opts for the suicide's answer to endless despair, darkness at noon, sunset limited. "She was gone and the coldness of it was her final gift." Once again a persistent McCarthy chord laments a world without women, Orphic grief, the eternal loss of the feminine, the surviving male sorrow of endless blues, canticles of abandonment and widowed anguish.

The Oedipal triangle, nameless man and woman and boy, primal as before Eden or after Armageddon. The wife commits suicide with an atom-sharp obsidian flake, in the way her medical-savvy husband has taught her. No comment, only witness, acceptance. The boy knows before he's told. "She's gone isn't she? And he said: Yes, she is." As with aged, stoic cowboy Billy Parham in *Cities of the Plain,* friends and family are all dead, nothing left, only going south down the "long black road" which takes on a character all to itself. "The black shape of it running from dark to dark."

The book unfolds in a slow, brutally calculating, micro-sighted, desperate and blood-soaked narrative, one foot or event after another. No moon or stars in absolute dark of night, running through the woods, trying to escape "them." Field-dressed slain bodies are hauled away to be consumed. The rachitic hunter from the truck seizes the boy on his shoulders and defies the father's gun and takes a bullet in the head and they run on with the boy clutching his gore-covered forehead mute as a stone. The truck men boil and eat the knife-wielding man, leaving the gut remnants in the road. Papa washes the dead man's brains out of his child's golden hair in the icy river. The child pleads that his father not tell him how the story ends.

They eat their last tin of pork and beans, the good guys against all the rest, and the father pledges to his compassionate son that he will kill anyone who touches him. "Do you understand?" On the hopeful side, the boy knows they will persist because they're carrying the fire. Prometheus stole fire from the gods for human use, differentiating the raw from the cooked, and for that impudence he was chained to a rock where each day a vulture ate out his liver. Civilization followed, eventually God's holocaustal *fire next time.* Father and son bear the fire within as they trudge through a world of smoking, shrinking possibilities, the words of things diminishing as cindered things go away.

Red-scarved marchers in tennis shoes hunt for human food with pipe lanyards and truckspring lances. Armies of cannibals are trailed by slaves, yoked women, staggering food packs of dogcollared catamites. How long can we read on as they go on, the reader asks, what worse will happen to them? The single survival motive tests the reader's stomach for endurance, as our resilience is matched with that of the two travelers. "The snow fell nor did it cease to fall." Echoes of Anglo-Saxon Seafarer sojourn, dead trees falling in the dark night, a hibernating ursine den under a dead cedar.

Thinning boy, thinning prospects, pawing through the dregs. The man forages an outsized pinstriped suit coat from a deserted clothing store rack, but they have no food and little sleep for five days. They trudge on. In a large country house they find a pantry floor door locked with stacked steel plates, piles of clothing and mattresses before a fireplace. Everything left means something, or nothing, but don't mistake the evidence. Life depends on it. A forty-gallon cast-iron cauldron for rendering hogs and a smokehouse. Mute objects and silent details lead to a human meat cellar, a cache of emaciated bodies crying "Help us," and the two run for their lives again.

Can you do it? the man keeps asking himself. He has a small revolver and holds his son as he sleeps fitfully, waking to one more endless day on the road. "All through the long dusk and into the dark. Cold and starless. Blessed." The man begins to believe they have a chance. Theirs is humanity's devolutionary drama as our descendants watch and scavenge and hide from human carnivores and try to buck up no matter what. "The chary dawn, the cold illucid world." It's a Stephen King nightmare thriller with no cheap thrills, spot-on hyperrealistic, the next movie after *Dr. Strangelove* or *On the Beach* or *Resurrection,* back when Hollywood made true horror movies besides *Blade Runner* and *The Matrix* about this subject.

A scavenger hunt in an abandoned house dredges up a sugar-grape drink packet, a spoon, a boxcutter, a screwdriver. These things mean things, or will—the possibilities of tools, human ingenuity. Man the tool-using animal evolves beyond other primates to what end? Cows, birds, rats, fish, and dogs are extinct with all plants, a silent spring brought on by a deadly blast. Earthquakes and wild fires still rage. All seems lost until dry wild apples turn up underfoot in a dying orchard, the fallen Edenic fruit that saves their lives for a few days, and a cistern of fresh water. He can remember nothing anywhere of anything so good. Is their luck changing? "You did good Papa, he said." So they bear up and go on under a sad simile "like mendicant friars sent forth to find their keep."

The innocent boy has fears too, fears whether they would ever eat anybody. No, we're the "good guys," his father says, and we're "carrying the fire," he repeats, though he dropped their lighter in the human meat cellar. The story periodically recaps their lyric desolation with a Thomas Hardy despair of beauty and pitiless prospects. "The nights were blinding cold and casket black and the long reach of the morning had a terrible silence to it. Like a dawn before battle." With great staring eyes the boy has the look of an alien with candle-colored translucent skin. They have no way to think about beauty or goodness anymore, no comparatives, no good, only endless bad punctuated with momentary survival. And the man must see their existence through the tragic glare of what Pound called "a hard Sophoclean light."

> He walked out in the gray light and stood and he saw for a brief moment the absolute truth of the world. The cold relentless circling of the intestate earth. Darkness implacable. The blind dogs of the sun in their running. The crushing black vacuum of the universe. And somewhere two hunted animals trembling like ground-foxes in their cover. Borrowed time and borrowed world and borrowed eyes with which to sorrow it.

Joyce reduced this vision to "the cold of interstellar space, the apathy of the stars" in *Ulysses*. Without Poldy Bloom's tangible good humor, all is an Orphic tragedy looking back. We must be spare in remembering, the man thinks, so as not to alter collapsing memory.

Then he finds a bunker of survival goods, a vanished richness of the world. Papa tells his son that he's found everything. And the story takes another loop in the black road. "He'd been ready to die and now he wasn't going to and he had to think about that." The reader is thinking darkly in his shadowed peripheral existence, tagging raggedly along, sometimes unwillingly, picking through things with him. Ours is a surrogate traveler's journey with no spirit guide, no blind maestro, no hobo philosopher, no book of revelation. The first exclamation, an interjective touch of color in the story, comes exactly halfway or 122 pages down in the lucky bunker:

> What is that? he said.
> Coffee. Ham. Biscuits.
> Wow, the boy said.

It's not much left of the world, but a note of hope restored for the moment. The boy's prayer is infernally sweet. "Dear people, thank you for all this food and stuff....and we hope that you're safe in heaven with God."

Always the pursuers lurk behind the couple, anyone and everyone and no one. The constancy of survival paranoia keeps them alive, as it was in the beginnings of mankind, and in the endings. The man thinks that if trouble comes when you least expect, then maybe you should always expect it. Fear is functional, and there's always a death wish to end it, an alien dream. "Fear is what quickens me," the poet James Wright said, as he grieved the death of his Ohioan black swan and prostitute beloved in the oil-stained river.

The boy repeats his father's words without knowing really what he says and asks what are their long-term goals. The old rags man in the road expects the worst when offered a meal, "What do I have to do?" And the father says to tell us where the world went. A quiet, piercing, fatal irony settles around the pilgrims. The man calls himself Ely, the only name in the story, and a made-up one at that. He just keeps going down the road. Fictive Ely asks the questions to be asked at the end. "Even if you knew what to do you wouldn't know what to do." A man would not know if he wanted to do it or not, if he were the last one left.

Theirs is an existential crux, an unanswerable double bind. Nobody wants to be in the world and nobody wants to leave. As with surreal theater, a purgatorial, absurdist conversation goes nowhere, and in times like these the less said the better. But they do talk on to continue the story. Gods cannot fare where men can't live. You'll see, he says, it's best to be alone. Is there an existential riddle to quibble, or does the old rag man speak dead-on? Death's days are numbered when everyone's gone, he says. Candid, cryptic, hyperreal, the arachnoid geezer exits like a Japanese Noh character.

Things get worse. The incinerated dead line the road. Don't look at the horror, the man tells his son, what goes into your head stays there forever. Then a pregnant woman passes with some men, and the pair finds a charred headless infant gutted and blackening on a spit. Turn back to the campfire scene concluding *Outer Dark* or five hundred years to Bosch's *The Last Judgment* for Medieval Christian hellish corollary: monsters devouring naked bodies and farting blackbirds, dogs clutching naked women, skewered torsos of soldiers, headless corpses wrapped in snakes, poisonous toads defiling ladies, infant parts sautéed over a campfire or stolen away in baskets by beaked demons and simian devils.

They do make it to the gray beach and slow rolling combers of the leaden sea. The two are greeted by dead seabird bones and "the ribs of fishes in their millions stretching along the shore as far as eye could see like an isocline of death." Darwin gone rancid. The man discovers a capsized sloop of hope, *Pájaro de Esperanza,* and a useless brass sextant that stirs him, though he knows realistically that good luck might not be so. An ancient corpse rises and falls in the surf. The boy wonders if the dark is going to catch them. The man knows there is nothing and nowhere left to hide. The story begins to close with Papa coughing up more blood, growing weaker each moment. "Every day is a lie, he said. But you are dying. That is not a lie." Speak truth to death, show the courage to face fact, however terrible. Such is patriarchal honor in nuclear winter.

The man comes back from the sloop with a first-aid kit and a bronze flarepistol, and the boy responds interjectively for the second and last time in the book, "Wow, he said." The boy speaks guileless truth and still brushes his teeth in the morning. He knows there are not many people, if any good left, and the odds are against them, so he comes to the point for his father. "I don't know what we're doing, he said." And still they do what they're doing, leaving a thief naked in the road to die, the boy sobbing to help him. His father says that the boy is not the one who must worry about everything, and the boy mumbles something. "He looked up, his wet and grimy face. Yes I am, he said. I am the one." The boy too worries and plots and dreams and cares for his father and strangers. He may be the last child born on the earth. He's socially desperate for others in his life, a village drawn in the sand, the old man, the thief, the other boy double in the street who disappears early on. Did they kill the thief by stripping him? he ponders. The child faces death with Christ-like pity, the father with Old Testament *lex talionis*. But they did kill him, the boy says, by leaving the starving thief naked in the road. Papa is wearing down to his last dream words as cairns mark a dangerous bone-oracle crossing:

> No sound but the wind. What will you say? A living man spoke these lines? He sharpened a quill with his small pen knife to scribe these things in sloe or lampblack?

The man fears an ancient one comes to steal his eyes and seal his mouth with dirt.

Taking a crude arrow cut to his thigh, driving the killers away with his flarepistol, and stitching the wound himself, the bled man has no more stories, no life left to live or tell. The boy has come down to life being just "okay" now, but without purpose, storyless, asking his father what's the bravest thing he ever did. "He spat into the road a bloody phlegm. Getting up this morning, he said." No, don't listen to me, the father says, let's go on. Bravery, honesty, innocence, truth, words, stories.... Ponder what happens when men go mute and have only fading dreams of former lives, "softly colored worlds of human love, the songs of birds, the sun." They walk on in spondaic hexameters and trochaic pentameters through an interstate charnel of sunless hell:

> They *went on. Tread*ing the *dead world un*der like *rats* on a *wheel.* / The *nights dead still* and *deader black. So cold.* They *talk*ed / *hard*ly at *all.* He *cough*ed *all* the *time* and the *boy watch*ed him *spit*ting / *blood. Slump*ing *along. Fil*thy, *rag*ged, *hope*less. / He'd *stop* and *lean* on the *cart* and the *boy* would *go on* / and *then stop* and *look back* and *he* would *raise* his *weep*ing *eyes* / and *see him stand*ing *there* in the *road look*ing *back* at *him* / from *some* un*imag*inable *fut*ure, *glow*ing in that *waste* like a *tab*ernacle.

End-notes to end-times: it may be winter, he's lost track of seasons and the sun. The man knows he can't hold his son dead in his arms, and without hope he implores the boy not to give up. Looping back to the opening scene in his last words, the man says that goodness will find his little boy. "It always has. It will again." The father dies, "cold and stiff," silent as the morning, without drama or redemption.

One of the few "good guys" with a shotgun finds the boy in the road with his dead father and says "I'm sorry," his simple, nonthreatening compassion distinguishing him from all the others. You have two choices, he tells the boy, stay and die with your father, or come with us. "There's nothing else to be done." The boy sobs beside his dead father, then goes to a woman and siblings who will cobble his dreamed foundling family. She tells him that God's breath is his "yet though it pass from man to man through all time." What world will the orphan golden-haired boy grow up to?

The novel ends dreamily with brook trout wimpling in mountain streams, the vermiculate "maps and mazes" of the evolutionary world stippling their backs. *Deus ex machina* or hyperreal vision? The narrative drifts cryptic. "Of a thing which could not be put back. Not be made right again." It's a big two-hearted fable of brook trout swimming in regenerative stream currents. Are these end-time promises of renewal in a charred, war-blackened world where Adam remakes his own camp alone? To brook the truth, the trout under the waters of time—an old and renewed dream, or an illusion without rainbows. "In the deep glens where they lived all things were older than man and they hummed of mystery." Is this why the originating sea still holds promise of refuge and renewal?

Hyperreal dreams aside, the boy still has one bullet left in the nickelplated pistol.

No End

> My friend, you would not tell with such high zest
> To children ardent for some desperate glory,
> The old Lie: Dulce et decorum est
> Pro patria mori.
> —Wilfred Owen

What's to come?

After fifty years with ten novels, a screenplay, and two theater pieces, Cormac McCarthy stands among the master storytellers of contemporary American literature. He has written his way from old-growth Appalachian woods into riverfront postmodernism, across the Mexican border struggles and onto Southwest hardscrabble wars in our own time. The violence in his stories is legendary and unbearable to some, the integrity of historical witness faultless, the characters, settings, and details of his plots accurate and captivating.

McCarthy's steadily evolving output, broad range of diction, tone, and voice, his wide-looping narratives bespeak discipline, vision, guts, and passion for the daily work of writing. While detailing the Edenic diaspora, purgatorial outer dark, and orphan cast-offs of a Gothic god unknown, the artist drafted a screenplay about a milltown social tragedy in the postbellum South. He layered a five-act drama about a black stonemason family fractured by modern-day conflicts and the ravages of time itself, then three decades later crafted a one-act Manhattan dialogue between a white suicide and a black survivor of the freedom wars. From *The Border Trilogy* canticles to killing sprees in no desert country for any right-thinking man or woman, he has witnessed cowboys gone to war and back to trailer squalor with menial day labor, only to be blown away among catatonic bystanders by drug runners, corporate suits, and pitiless assassins. He has taken a father and son to the postholocaust end of the world, tendering acts of filial and fatherly love amid the barbarism of human slaughter and mass suffering.

The novelist's subjects range from Southern Gothic and backwoods rustic to urban abject and modernist baroque, from vigilante nihilism and callow courage to crossover western, bicultural coming-of-age, and cataclysmic end-times. All his works are edged with stoic tragedy, and his characters suffer their wounds honestly. His churls tend to be the small villagers of medieval carnival, his victims the witless innocents of biblical scourge, his faltering modernist protagonists up against dire probabilities, his villains the cohorts of Satan. In *The Border Trilogy* McCarthy's antiquated heroes are dying cowboys who cling to a vanishing code of hard work, animal caretaking, fraternal loyalty, and love of landscape as their failure to regenerate a frontier mythic life slips into blood meridian. The absence and mystery of women halo a working-man's cross. Industrialization and chicanery scar his heart's trial. Obsolescence shadows his soul's crucifixion.

The border wars of the past, frontier battles with indigenous tribes, the gun barrel justice of outlaw heritage surely doom western ranching struggles. Men who come after will never approach the cowboy's halcyon monasticism or romantic wanderlust or capacity to wonder at a New World falling away as he rides into an endless sunset. Military bases appropriate pastures, drug lords and human slavers suck at the marrow of civilization, vile corporations and hired guns blast down hapless citizens, antichrists and nihilists and psychopaths run hell-bent on sadistic self-gain and absolute terror.

McCarthy's readers cannot help but question groundless faith, goodwill sentiment, or blind optimism. If *The Sunset Limited* black victim of culture wars over life and liberty cannot save the white cerebral victor from suicide, will a pale-cheek humanity survive personal Armageddons with thieves, con men, villains, psychopaths, pimps, or corrupt politicians? Will the uninformed beat the odds of holocaustal war and nuclear winter, the meltdowns of global warming and metastases of viral pandemics? The key word is *uninformed*. Just before he was killed in the last days of the First "Great" War, entrenched Corporal Wilfred Owen began a Preface to his collected work, "All a poet can do today is warn. That is why the true Poets must be truthful." Candid to distraction, McCarthy's hyperreal fictions would wake a torpid reader to clear and present dangers, past and present, preemptive border wars to imperial deceptions. His canticles serve as elegiac praise-songs for the frontier heroic, lamentations for the tragic fallen, warnings for the witnessing survivors and hopefully generations to come.

Whatever the prospects, personal or public, McCarthy will go on writing, as Faulkner talked of a man still speaking against the fated ends of all things. The mentoring ghosts of his classical, biblical, populist, and epic masters will lead this writer through the wilderness again, over forbidding mountains, across sere wasteland, into troubled waters, and toward the promised land of the heart's last kingdom. Here he etches in stone the soul's final salvation through heroic sacrifice—the mind's courage to face the truth of things, no matter how terrible, however hyperreal.

The Cormac McCarthy Society tends a Web site *www.cormacmccarthy.com* where Diane C. Luce stocks an extensive bibliography, including 1400+ entries to date, arranged as Scholarly Studies, Dissertations, Theses, Interviews with McCarthy, Reviews, News Articles and Journalism from the 1960s through the present, and References in Interviews and Writing by Other Authors. The *Cormac McCarthy Journal* and *Southern Quarterly* have published brisk coverage of the author over the past couple decades.

Selected Criticism

Aldridge, John W. "Cormac McCarthy's Bizarre Genius." *Atlantic Monthly* (August 1994): 89–96.

Arnold, Edwin T., and Dianne C. Luce, eds. *A Cormac McCarthy Companion: The Border Trilogy.* Jackson: Univ. Press of Mississippi, 2001.

———, eds. *Perspectives on Cormac McCarthy.* Rev. ed. Jackson: Univ. Press of Mississippi, 1999.

Baldwin, James. *The Price of the Ticket. Collected Nonfiction 1948–1985.* New York: St. Martin's Press, 1985.

Baudrillard, Jean. *Simulacra and Simulation.* Ann Arbor: Univ. of Michigan Press, 1994.

Bell, Madison Smartt. "The Man Who Understood Horses." *New York Times Book Review* 97 (17 May 1992), sec. 7: 9, 11.

Bell, Vereen M. *The Achievement of Cormac McCarthy.* Shreveport LA: Louisiana State Univ. Press, 1988.

———. "Between the Wish and the Thing the World Lies Waiting." *Southern Review* 28:4 (1992): 920–27.

Berryman, John. *John Berryman. The Collected Poems, 1937–1971.* Charles Thornbury, ed. Noonday/Farrar, Straus and Giroux, 1971.

Birkirts, Sven. "The Lone Soul State." *New Republic* 211:2 (11 July 1994): 38–41.

Bloom, Harold. "Cormac McCarthy: *Blood Meridian.*" *How to Read and Why.* New York: Scribner, 2000.

———. *Modern Critical Views: Cormac McCarthy.* Philadelphia: Chelsea, 2002.

Borges, Jorge Luis. *Jorge Luis Borges. Selected Poems.* Alexander Coleman, ed. New York: Viking Penguin, 1999.

Broyard, Anatole. "Daddy Quit, She Said." *Aroused by Books.* New York: Random House, 1974.

———. "Where All Tales Are Tall." *New York Times* (20 January 1979): 19.

Charyn, Jerome. "Doomed Huck." Review of *Suttree. New York Times Book Review* (18 February 1979): 14.

Ciuba, Gary M. *Desire, Violence, & Divinity in Modern Southern Fiction: Katherine Anne Porter, Flannery O'Connor, Cormac McCarthy, Walker Percy.* Southern Literary Studies. Shreveport LA: Louisiana State Univ. Press, 2007.

Coles, Robert. "The Empty Road." Review of *Outer Dark*. *New Yorker* (22 March 1969): 133–39.

———. "The Stranger." *New Yorker* (26 August 1974): 87–90.

Cox, Dianne L. [Dianne C. Luce]. "Cormac McCarthy." *Dictionary of Literary Biography: American Novelists since World War II*. Second Series. James E. Kobler, Jr., ed. Detroit: Gale Research, 1980. 6: 224–32.

Davenport, Guy. "Appalachian Gothic." *New York Times Book Review* (29 September 1968), sec. 7: 4.

———. "Silurian Southern." *National Review* (16 March 1979): 368–69.

Delueze, Guilles. *The Logic of Sense*. New York: Columbia University Press, 1990.

Donoghue, Denis. "Dream Work." *New York Review of Books* 40 (24 June 1993): 5–10.

———. "Reading *Blood Meridian*." *Sewanee Review* 105:3 (July–September 1997): 401–18. Revised as "Teaching *Blood Meridian*." *The Practice of Reading*. New Haven: Yale Univ. Press, 1998: 258–77.

Ebert, Roger. rogerebert.com/movie reviews. "No Country for Old Men." *Chicago Sun-Times* (8 November 2007).

Eco, Umberto. *Travels in Hyperreality*. San Diego and New York: Harcourt Brace, 1983.

Ellis, Jay. *No Place for Home. Spatial Constraint and Character Flight in the Novels of Cormac McCarthy*. New York and London: Routledge, 2006.

Ellison, Ralph. *Invisible Man*. New York: Random House, 1952.

———. *Shadow and Act*. New York: Random House, 1964.

Foote, Shelby. Letter. *Memphis Press-Scimitar* (17 February 1979): 8. [Letter to book review editor responding to J. Z. Howard's review of *Suttree*.]

García Lorca, Federico. *In Search of the Duende*. Christopher Maurer, trans. and ed. New York: New Directions, 1998.

Guillemin, Georg. *The Pastoral Vision of Cormac McCarthy*. Tarleton State Univ. Southwestern Studies in the Humanities. College Station TX: Texas A & M Univ. Press, 2004.

Hall, Wade, and Rick Wallach, eds. *Sacred Violence: A Reader's Companion to Cormac McCarthy*. El Paso: Texas Western Press, 1995.

Hass, Robert. "Travels with a She-Wolf." *New York Times Book Review* (June 1994): 1, 38–40.

Heidegger, Martin. *Being and Time*. John Macquarrie and Edward Robinson, trans. New York: Harper & Row, 1962.

Hicks, Granville. "Six Firsts for Summer." *Saturday Review* 48 (12 June 1965): 35–36.

Holloway, David. *The Late Modernism of Cormac McCarthy*. Contributions to the Study of World Literature #115. Westport CT: Greenwood Press, 2002.

Jameson, Fredric. *Signatures of the Visible*. New York: Routledge, 1990.

Jarrett, Robert L. *Cormac McCarthy*. New York: Twayne, 1997.

Jordan, Richard. "'Just Write' Says Successful Author." *University of Tennessee Daily Beacon* (30 January 1969): 6.

Josyph, Peter. "Older professions: the fourth wall of *The Stonemason*." *Southern Quarterly* 36.1 (Fall 1997): 137–44. Revised in Wallach 119–40.

Kayser, Wolfgang. *The Grotesque in Art and Literature.* 1957. Ulrich Weisstein, trans. Bloomington: Indiana University Press, 1963.

Lilley, James D., ed. *Cormac McCarthy. New Directions.* Albuquerque: Univ. of New Mexico Press, 2007.

McCarthy, C. J. [Cormac]. "A Drowning Incident." *The Phoenix* [Univ. of Tennessee *Orange and White* Literary Supplement] (March 1960): 3–4.

McCarthy, C. J., Jr. [Cormac]. "Wake for Susan." *The Phoenix* [Univ. of Tennessee *Orange and White* Literary Supplement] (October 1959): 3–6.

McCarthy, Cormac. *All the Pretty Horses.* New York: Vintage, (1992) 1993.

———. *Blood Meridian, or the Evening Redness in the West.* New York: Vintage, (1985) 1992.

———. "Bounty." *Yale Review* 54 (March 1965): 77–85. Outtake from *The Orchard Keeper.*

———. "Burial." *Antaeus* 32 (Winter 1979): 87–100. Outtake from *Suttree.*

———. *Child of God.* New York: Vintage, (1973) 1993.

———. *Cities of the Plain.* New York : Knopf, 1998.

———. *The Crossing.* New York: Vintage, (1994) 1995.

———. "The Dark Waters." *Sewanee Review* 73 (1965): 210–16. Outtake from *The Orchard Keeper.*

———. *The Gardener's Son. A Screenplay.* Hopewell NJ: Ecco, (1977) 1996.

———. *No Country for Old Men.* New York: Knopf, 2005.

———. *The Orchard Keeper.* New York: Vintage, (1965) 1993.

———. *Outer Dark.* New York: Vintage, (1978) 1993.

———. *The Road.* New York: Knopf, 2006.

———. *The Stonemason. A Play in Five Acts.* Hopewell NJ: Ecco, 1994.

———. *The Sunset Limited. A Novel in Dramatic Form.* New York: Random House, 2006.

———. *Suttree.* New York: Vintage, (1979) 1992.

———. "Whales and Men." Unpublished transcript in Cormac McCarthy Papers. Southwestern Writers Collection. Albert B. Alkek Library. Southwest Texas State Univ., San Marcos.

———. "The Wolf Trapper." *Esquire* 120:1 (July 1993): 95–104.

McCarthy (Holleman), Lee. *Desire's Door.* Brownsville OR: Story Line Press, 1991.

McLuhan, Marshall. *Understanding Media.* Cambridge MA: MIT Press, 1994.

McGrath, Charles. "Lone Rider." *New Yorker* 70 (27 June–4 July 1994): 180–85.

McMurtry, Larry. *In a Narrow Grave: Essays on Texas.* New York: Simon & Schuster, 1968, 1996.

"Novelist Sells Archive." *New York Times* (16 January 2008): B2.

Owen, Wilfred. "Preface" in *The Poems of Wilfred Owen.* Jon Stallworthy, ed. New York: W. W. Norton, 1985.

Owens, Barclay. *Cormac McCarthy's Western Novels.* Tucson: Univ. of Arizona, 2000.

Pound, Ezra. *ABC of Reading.* 1934. New York: New Directions, 1960.

Preston, Richard, ed. *The 2007 Best American Science and Nature Writing.* Boston and New York: Houghton Mifflin, 2007.

Rothstein, Edward. "A Homologue of Hell on a River of Death." Review of *Suttree. Washington Post* (19 March 1979): B2.

Saussure, Ferdinand. *Course in General Linguistics.* New York: McGraw Hill, 1959.

Slotkin, Richard. *The Fatal Environment: The Myth of the Frontier in the Age of Industrialization, 1800–1890.* New York: Atheneum, 1985.

———. *Gunfighter Nation: The Myth of the Frontier in Twentieth-Century America.* New York: Harper Perennial, 1992.

———. *Regeneration through Violence: The Mythology of the American Frontier, 1600–1860.* Middletown: Wesleyan Univ. Press, 1973.

Sullivan, Walter. "About Any Kind of Meanness You Can Name." Review of *Blood Meridian. Sewanee Review* 93 (Fall 1985): 649–56.

Trachtenberg, Stanley. "Black Humor, Pale Fiction." *Yale Review* 55 (October 1965): 144–49.

Wallace, Garry. "Meeting McCarthy." *Southern Quarterly* 30:4 (Summer 1992): 134–39.

Wallach, Rick, ed. *Myth, Legend, Dust: Critical Responses to Cormac McCarthy.* Manchester: Manchester Univ. Press, 2000.

Wallis, R. Sanborn, III. *Animals in the Fiction of Cormac McCarthy.* Jefferson NC: McFarland, 2006.

Wegner, John, Edwin T. Arnold, William C. Spenser, and Dianne C. Luce, eds. *The Cormac McCarthy Journal.* Hattiesberg MS: Univ. of Southern Mississippi Press, 2001.

Williams, Don. "Annie DeLisle: Cormac McCarthy's Ex-wife Prefers to Recall the Romance." *Knoxville News-Sentinel* (10 June 1990): E1–2.

———. "Cormac McCarthy: Knoxville's Most Famous Contemporary Writer Prefers His Anonymity." *Knoxville News-Sentinel* (10 June 1990): E1–2.

Williams, William Carlos. *Notes in a Diary Form.* New York: New Directions, 1927.

Winfrey, Oprah, interviewer. *Oprah's Book Club.* Santa Fe NM: Santa Fe Institute, June 2007.

Wood, James. "Red Planet." *New Yorker* (25 July 2005): 88–93.

Woodward, Richard B. "Cormac McCarthy's Venemous Fiction." *New York Times Magazine* (19 April 1992) natl. ed., sec. 6: 28–31+.

————. "Cormac Country." *Vanity Fair* (August 2005): 98–104.

Yeats, William Butler. "Why the Blind Man in Ancient Times Was Made a Poet." [1906]. *W. B. Yeats: Selected Criticism.* A. Norman Jeffares, ed. London: Macmillan, 1964.

About the Author

Kenneth Lincoln grew up in northwest Nebraska south of Wounded Knee, where his great-grandparents homesteaded along the North Platte River and ranching sandhills. Graduating from public high school in Alliance, Nebraska, he went to Stanford University for a degree in American Literature, to Indiana University for a doctorate in Modern British Literature, and to UCLA where he has taught Contemporary and Native American Literatures for forty years. In spring 1969, Lincoln was adopted into the Oglala Sioux by the Mark Monroe family of Alliance and given the Lakota name Mato Yamni. Beginning with *Native American Renaissance*, *The Good Red Road*, and *Indi'n Humor*, he has published many books in American Indian Studies, chaired the country's first interdisciplinary master's program in the field, and written novels, poetry, and personal essays about Western Americana. His latest books are *White Boyz Blues: A Memoir* and *Speak Like Singing: Classics of Native American Literature*.

INDEX

Printed in the United States
152417LV00003B/12/P